THIRTY TO SIXTY DAYS

THIRTY TO SIXTY DAYS

ALIKAY WOOD

AMULET BOOKS • NEW YORK

PUBLISHER'S NOTE: This is a work of fiction. Names, characters, places, and incidents are either the product of the author's imagination or used fictitiously, and any resemblance to actual persons, living or dead, business establishments, events, or locales is entirely coincidental.

Cataloging-in-Publication Data has been applied for and may be obtained from the Library of Congress.

ISBN 978-1-4197-5230-8

Book design by Chelsea Hunter

Printed and bound in U.S.A.

10 9 8 7 6 5 4 3 2 1

Amulet Books are available at special discounts when purchased in quantity for premiums and promotions as well as fundraising or educational use. Special editions can also be created to specification. For details, contact specialsales@abramsbooks.com or the address below.

ABRAMS The Art of Books
195 Broadway, New York, NY 10007
abramsbooks.com

To my parents:

Dad, for giving me the gift of stories.

Mom, for giving me the gift of words.

And both of you, for encouraging me to write so that you could "retire in the manner in which you plan to become accustomed." You are truly an inspiration.

CHAPTER 1

"IS IT BECAUSE OF YOUR PARENTS?" SHE ASKED.

I widened my eyes until they welled up and a single tear streaked down my cheek. Mrs. Howard, the school counselor, watched it drip from my chin onto my hoodie. For a short white woman who looked like she'd barely ditched a training bra, she wasn't giving me much.

After a long silence I said, "I don't want to blame my parents."

She furrowed her brow and nodded, the face all adults make when trying to forecast that they're listening. She didn't say anything more, though.

I steepled my hands together and rested my elbows on her pristine white desk. A pink pad of excused absence notes rested on top of a stack of papers. A bouquet of wilting flowers tilted from a vase on the corner. Next to it was a framed picture of Mrs. Howard, a Chad-looking man, and a well-groomed dog crouched together on the beach. It was the kind of filtered perfection that I knew filled other people with a longing for the same white-minimalist background of a life. But it was the kind of thing that filled me with a desire to burn it all down—thinking that unsurprisingly got me pulled from class for a session with the school counselor.

I'd transferred to St. Croix High at the beginning of the school year, but this was my first time seeing Mrs. Howard. It was always difficult to deal with a new counselor. Lots of ground to cover.

Mrs. Howard leaned back in her chair and tapped her pen against her floral-printed notebook. There were two windows stamped on the wall behind her. Through them I could see the steaming parking lot and the beige strip mall across the street.

"It was a drug overdose," I said. "I found their bodies in the bathtub. And . . . I know I shouldn't say this, but it was sort of beautiful. They were holding hands, curled around each other with smiles on their faces. I'd never seen them look so happy."

Mrs. Howard's hand shook around her pen. "And then you lived on the streets for three months before being taken into foster care. That must have been very difficult."

I nodded. "Mean moms. Creepy dads. There was one week where all I had to eat was strawberry Pop-Tarts, which sounds amazing, except they weren't even the frosted kind and my poop got so messed up I had to go to the ER. I got a new placement after that."

Mrs. Howard's eyes were glossy with tears when she bent her head to make a note. Counselors aren't supposed to cry when they talk to patients, but my stories tended to inspire a lot of waterworks.

We sat in silence for another long moment, her looking at me with that furrowed-brow face, me looking over her shoulder, out the window. Asphalt, brick buildings sandwiched in between newer white buildings, empty sidewalks, antique-looking streetlamps. Looking at it made something clench in my chest. A creeping, itching sensation that made the idea of going back to class feel like a choke hold.

"Are you actually listening to me?" I asked. Mrs. Howard tapped her pen against her floral-printed notebook. "Adults don't usually listen to me."

She made eye contact for an uncomfortably long beat. "Of course I'm listening, Hattie."

She cleared her throat and reached for the little pink pad on her desk. *Finally*. But when she picked up the pad, her shaky hands sent a flutter of other papers to the ground. I bent forward and helped gather them up, choking back a gasp when I saw a flyer for Dream Fest.

Dream Fest was this huge music festival happening next weekend in Miami. Jordan Banner, a bops factory hitmaker who I was slightly obsessed with, was headlining, and I'd seen some Reddit theories that he was hosting an exclusive festival after-party at a tightly guarded location. I wondered if Mrs. Howard knew about the theory. Maybe she was one of the regulars on the r/ColorGuard subreddit. Maybe we'd been swapping memes for months without realizing it. The horror.

I let my hand tremble as I tore off a pink slip and slid it across the desk to her. I shuffled her other papers and put them back in her filing basket.

"I'm sorry to be such a burden. I just feel so triggered by Chemistry because, as I may have mentioned, I found my parents dead in their meth lab."

"Meth lab? I thought you mentioned the bathtub?" Mrs. Howard leaned back in her chair as if the very mention of the word *meth* might be contagious.

"I don't have the mental space to explain to you how meth labs work."

Mrs. Howard sighed and scribbled her pen across the pink slip of paper. "Normally, I wouldn't do this."

I nodded, eyeing dull signs on the strip mall stores across the street. I was so close to freedom.

"This is a one-time exception," Mrs. Howard said and slid the excused absence pass across the desk. "You have to go to class." But the glossy sheen of her eyes told me this would definitely be happening again.

I reached across the desk and snapped up the paper. She raised an eyebrow at how quickly I moved. Not a good sign.

"I know." I sniffled, laying it on a bit thicker. "It's just. Trauma."

"I understand." Mrs. Howard lifted her hands like she wanted to do something absurd like hug me.

I pushed the chair back from the desk and swung my backpack onto my shoulder.

Mrs. Howard dropped her arms. "We're here for you. I promise. Things *will* get better."

This wasn't the first time I'd heard those words, so it wasn't the first time I didn't believe them.

The whole afternoon stretched before me, free of fluorescent-lit classrooms and my peers in their carbon-copy outfits. All I had to do was grab my things from my locker, exit the school's property, and hold on until my eighteenth birthday in six months, when I could move to New York City and . . . well, likely still be miserable but at least be following in the long tradition of the miserable artists before me.

Mrs. Howard led me out of her office and into the open space of the Admin Office. Mr. Robins, the school's secretary, was babbling on about a reality show he'd seen over the weekend. A woman was leaning against his desk, filling out a neon visitor's badge. She was about my height with similar brown eyes and thin lips.

"Hattie," she said. No surprise in her voice.

Busted.

I unzipped my bag, pulled out a sour green lollipop, and popped it in my mouth. The sourness made seeing her a little easier.

"Hello, Mother."

Mrs. Howard, being the sweet, naïve cinnamon roll that she was, nearly collapsed from the shock. "*Mother?*"

Mom offered her a firm handshake. "Lauren Larken. I've been meaning to call you."

"But you're—" Mrs. Howard looked back and forth between the two of us. "And she's—"

Anyways, that's how the school counselor found out about my compulsive lying problem.

CHAPTER 2

"NOT AGAIN," MY MOM SIGHED. "WHAT DID SHE TELL YOU? WAS IT the one about the circus? I've told her that story's not funny. And why isn't she in class?"

Mrs. Howard pointed at her notes. "She has a learning disability—"

"No, she doesn't. Hattie tests off the charts," Mom said. "And she's not an orphan. I don't know why she tells people that."

Mrs. Howard's eyes were so big they were practically down in her cleavage. I worried she might never recover.

"I'm a compulsive liar," I said around the lollipop.

"No, you're not." My mom's shoulders slumped as she turned back to Mrs. Howard. "She's just having a difficult adjustment period. We moved from New Jersey this summer and starting at a new school as a junior has its challenges."

The only silver lining had been this new counselor, who I planned to regale with tales of woe for at least a year before she caught on to the fact that I was a middle-class kid with a functional mother and no interesting backstory whatsoever. But, as always, my mom was the one person I couldn't fool.

"Compulsive lying is a trait usually associated with sociopathy or narcissistic personality disorder," I told Mrs. Howard.

Mrs. Howard shuddered. "Oh my."

My mom's nostrils flared. "Hattie has not been diagnosed with either of those conditions. She also hasn't been diagnosed as a compulsive liar. There's nothing wrong with her."

Her eyes scanned my face while she talked. I crumpled the pink slip in my hand. I'd been so close to getting out. Sure, out on the streets of Marsh Rock, there was only humidity and strip malls populated by the terrifying kind of people who insisted on saying hi to strangers, but anything was better than the asylum-white walls of St. Crotch.

I should have just gone with my first instinct and sweet-talked the receptionist until he was distracted enough for me to grab a pink slip and forge my mom's signature. I thought performing for Mrs. Howard would be more entertaining. Amateur mistake.

"I can't believe it." Mrs. Howard's lip quivered.

"It's not your fault," I said quickly. Mrs. Howard was just trying to do her job; she shouldn't cry because of a screwup like me. "I'm usually able to get a pink slip in eight minutes flat. You lasted fifteen."

She sniffled. "Really?"

"Did you take the pad?" my mom asked.

"What pad?" I said automatically.

My mom held out her hand, and I reluctantly gave her my backpack. She opened the front pocket and produced the pad of pink slips I'd snatched from Mrs. Howard's desk when she knocked her papers over.

"Sorry about that," she said and handed Mrs. Howard the pad. "Hattie's a good kid. You'll see."

The thing about my mother was she refused to see anything but the best in everyone, which was annoying because I was a terrible person and doing my best to prove it to her.

"Maybe we should finish our session now?" I pleaded with Mrs. Howard. Anything would be better than staying in the same room with my mom and her steadfast belief in me. Mrs. Howard stared at me in shocked silence. "Even better: I really should go back to class. I think we're doing something really important and science-y today, so I wouldn't want to miss it."

Mom was still running her eyes up and down me. *What was her deal?*

"Actually, I need to talk to you," she said.

Mrs. Howard wiped away the last of her tears. "Stories matter, Hattie. Hopefully one day you'll understand that."

She spun on her heel and walked back to her office with the clenched fists of someone clinging to their dignity. I bit into my lollipop with enough force to split the hard outer shell open. The sour flavor coated the insides of my mouth, making it impossible to feel anything else.

"Would you give us a moment?" Mom asked Mr. Robins, who was lurking behind his desk pretending not to eavesdrop.

"Oh. I—" One look from my mom was enough to shut down his hopes of witnessing our mother-daughter showdown. "Sure."

Once Mr. Robins had scuttled into the teachers' lounge, Mom and I were alone.

"I should go to Chemistry," I said. Being in a walled space with her, even one as big as the Admin Office, made the itch in my chest burn.

"We need to talk; it's important," she said.

"Why are you being so weird?" I slouched in a chair against the wall and swished the crushed sucker pieces around my mouth.

She was wearing a black windbreaker with *DBD* stitched across the chest. The only remotely interesting thing Marsh Rock had going for it was that it was home to the Delworth Biological Defense company or DBD, and Mom working there made it infinitely less interesting.

Before selling out and going to work at DBD, Mom was a researcher at a small university in New Jersey. But when Dad died, she needed to make more money. OK, so he didn't die exactly, but the end result was the same. The bad news: With Dad out of the picture, Mom had to sell out to the one percent to make ends meet. The good news: Mom had to work nights and weekends because DBD was very intense about . . . whatever it was the company did. Something about science and biology and building the kind of weapons that always cause a lot of problems in sci-fi movies.

It wasn't that I didn't want to spend time with my mom. Actually, wait, that's exactly what it was.

Mom looked like me only with all the edges softened, and she fit in perfectly in a place like Marsh Rock where everyone smiled with all their teeth and didn't have any sharp corners. The bedrock of her kindness unlocked a sick kind of poison in me. And worst of all, she didn't blame me for any of this. Not even the money. I hated it. As soon as I was a legal adult, I planned on trading Florida's humid slog for New York's concrete glow. I'd be a filmmaker and performance artist, and I'd pay her back and be free.

"Hattie," Mom said. "This is serious."

"It won't happen again," I said.

"I'm not talking about Mrs. Howard," Mom said. She was the one person who could always tell when I was lying. "Hattie, I need to tell you—"

The double glass doors of the Admin Office swung open and a burly guy in a matching DBD windbreaker marched through, escorting a tall girl with perfect skin and the biggest backpack I'd ever seen.

Carmen Diaz. She would be cool if she didn't give off such teacher's pet vibes. She dressed in the kind of baggy clothes only skinny people with nothing to hide could get away with wearing and was the president or captain of almost every activity on campus. She also was one of only a handful of out LGBTQ+ kids at our school, which I had to admit was really cool. Too bad she was also a no fun know-it-all.

"Hi Carmen!" I squished my cheeks into a fake smile when she startled.

I'd been at St. Croix for only a few weeks, but I'd learned that as much as Carmen demanded the spotlight—with her stellar grades, absurdly hot girlfriend, and rocking body—she jumped a little anytime someone looked at her. I wondered what she was so afraid of people seeing.

Mom looked between us. "Are y'all friends?"

She'd started saying things like *y'all* since we moved to Florida.

"Yep!" I said.

"Not really," Carmen said as she walked past. Very honest, that one.

I made a pouty face. "Hurtful."

The DBD guy waved at my mom. "Kids, right?"

Mom nodded without taking her eyes off me. "Yup." He didn't move. "Thanks, Jeff."

He licked his teeth. "Welp. See you in there."

Ew. He was proving my theory that all Jeffs were inherently untrustworthy.

He marched Carmen out of the reception area and into the big conference room in the center of the office. I didn't know much about Carmen, but I knew enough to know she had never been in trouble a day in her life. So why did she have a DBD escort? (Also, why was that guy so excited to see my mom?)

More likely, Carmen wasn't in trouble at all. Mom was probably at the school to interview Carmen and other, smarter students for a DBD internship or some other opportunity for normal kids without a compulsive lying problem or poison in their gut.

I stood up and slung my backpack over my shoulder. "Well, I'll leave you to it."

Mom took a deep breath and when she spoke, it wasn't my soft-as-a-fresh-chocolate-chip-cookie mother talking. It was Dr. Larken. "Sit down. I need to ask you some questions."

I sunk back into the seat. "I didn't do it."

"I didn't accuse you of anything."

"Reflex."

I racked my brain, trying to think of anything bad I might have done lately. Shoplifting? Boring. Cheating? Took more intelligence than the schoolwork itself. Vandalism? Hadn't bothered in months. I did have a *slight* breaking-and-entering habit, but I doubted anyone would have found out about that.

Mom took the seat next to me. "Were you in the Cul du Lac on Sunday morning?"

So much for my breaking-and-entering habit staying under the radar.

"We live in a swamp," I said. "Why would I be at Cul du Suck when I could go swimming in our own backyard?"

"Hattie," Mom said in a warning tone.

She was sitting close enough for me to smell the lemon-scented lotion coating her hands. The room was too small. I needed space, fresh air, no walls, new skin.

"I need to go to class," I mumbled.

"I'm pulling you for the rest of the day," Mom said.

"I have constitutional rights, you know. It's called the fourth amendment. You can't keep me without probable cause," I said. Shout-out to all those true crime documentaries for teaching me about the Bill of Rights.

Mom twisted in her seat to look at me. "I need you to tell me if you were in Cul du Lac yesterday. It's important."

I knew it was futile. She could always tell when I was lying. Some freaky genetic connection. Still, the itching sensation rose up in my chest and I heard myself say, "I wasn't there."

Mom sighed, disappointment gleaming from her eyes. She fished a tablet out of her bag and tapped on the screen a few times before holding it up for me to inspect. "We have video from two different neighbors' security cameras. Of you swimming. In the lake."

"That's not me."

But when I looked at the video playing on the tablet screen, the figure emerging from the water with fading purple hair was, in fact, me.

OK, so I like to swim. Sue me. It's Florida. Isn't that kind of the whole point?

"Fifth amendment. I don't have to tell you anything."

My chest was doing that thing it sometimes did where it squeezed until it felt like my heart was so small and sick, I could scoop it out of my throat with my index finger and watch it flutter away like a baby bird. I'd made the appointment with Mrs. Howard to avoid this kind of thing. I was supposed to be spending a relaxing afternoon taking a nap in the marsh, filming the vacuum that was suburbia, and scaring window shoppers—not dealing with my overwhelming existential dread.

"A drone crashed into the lake on Saturday night," Mom continued, a slight tremor creeping into her voice. I'd only heard her sound that scared one other time in my life. "If you were in that water . . ."

My jaw fell open. "A drone crash? That's the best you can do? Is this some sort of expensive new therapy method where you try to scare me straight?"

Mom's eyes were glossy now. "I wish I could believe you."

Look, I know I'm a liar who occasionally stretches some rules and may or may not have been responsible for the incident involving detergent in the school fountain last week, but I was almost positive I hadn't crashed a drone.

Almost.

CHAPTER 3

A PERFECTIONIST, A SURVIVOR, AND A LIAR WALK INTO A CONFERence room. That's not a punch line to a bad joke—that's what happened when my mom gave up on asking me questions and escorted me into the conference room.

One wall of the room was spaced with windows capturing the parking lot in all its glory. A long, glassy table took up most of the space in the room. The four-wheeled office chairs tucked under it looked like spiders ready to strike. Carmen was sitting near the head of the table, across from a jittering boy.

Mom paused at the doorway. Her roots were tinged gray, and beneath her powdered makeup I could see the wrinkles carved around her eyes and mouth.

"Take a seat. We'll start when the other parents get here," she said. "Everything I've done—" She stopped, cleared her throat, and started again. "I'm so sorry, Hattie."

She was gone before I could ask her why she was apologizing to me when I was the one who hadn't been able to have an honest conversation with her since puberty and had high-key ruined her financial prospects.

Mom locked the window-paned double doors of the conference room from the outside. How had she gotten a copy of the Admin Office keys? I pressed my hand to the glass. She didn't look up before walking away.

I jiggled the handle, keeping my back to the other two kids in the room. I'd never made Mom mad enough to lock me in a room before. This must be really bad.

Carmen cleared her throat. "It's Hattie, right? You're new."

I grabbed another sour apple sucker from the pocket of my sweatshirt and unwrapped it, leaning against the door. "If you mean to planet Earth, then no. I've been here a while."

"I meant to St. Croix," Carmen huffed. She lowered her chin at the boy across the table. "This is Albie. Someone from DBD pulled him at lunch."

Albert Chang. Everyone knew who he was. He was the miracle, the survivor, the wonder kid who'd been diagnosed with leukemia in kindergarten, spent elementary school fighting it, and then emerged victorious into the bowels of middle school.

A part of me was jealous of him. I know that's a horrible thing to think, but I was a horrible person, and it's how I felt. He'd fought a tangible poison in his body and won. For the rest of his life, he'd have that badge of honor, the carcass of the physical enemy he'd defeated to prove his worth. My life was as beige and boring as the walls of St. Croix High. I was the enemy; there was no hero.

Albie's hair was raven-black and curling around his ears. His dark eyes darted back and forth between Carmen and me.

"We haven't met," I said. I knew who he was because Principal Patel had called him up during a General Assembly for Blood Cancer Awareness Month. Albie's brother had jumped on the stage and clapped him on the back. Everyone gave him a standing ovation. But Albie didn't say a word. There was also that incident at Cul du Lac the day before, but I was pretty sure he hadn't seen me, which meant it didn't count.

"Uh. Yeah." Albie drummed his fingers across the table. "I'm Albie. Carmen said that already. Hi."

Through the smudged glass windows boxing the conference room in, I saw my mom huddled over a tablet with Jeff. Jeff's body radiated nervous energy. Had Carmen or Albie crashed a drone? I wouldn't have pegged either of them as the type, but I'd been wrong before.

I spun away from the glass and took a seat next to Albie, swirling the disintegrating lollipop in my mouth. "So. What are you all in for?"

Carmen tapped the black notebook in front of her with her fancy-looking pen. "That's what Albie and I have been trying to figure out. There must be something the three of us have in common. Albie and I have been friends since kindergarten."

"Congratulations," I said.

"Thank you," Carmen said.

"She's being sarcastic," Albie said, a smirk tugging at the corners of his mouth.

Carmen wrote something down in her notebook. "Have you had acute lymphocytic leukemia?"

I popped the sucker out of my mouth. "Hmm. I'd have to check my day planner to be sure . . ."

"That, uh, can't be it," Albie said quietly. "Carmen, you haven't had ALL."

"Yes, but I was your best friend and spent a lot of time at the hospital while you were getting treatment. Maybe DBD is doing a study about childhood cancers and their long-term impacts on extended social circles."

Albie's drumming fingers stilled. "Long-term impacts?"

"It's a biological weapons company," I said.

"You're right." Carmen crossed something out. "That was a stretch anyway. Hattie, what extracurriculars are you involved with?"

I ticked them off on my fingers. "Heavy metal band, the European kind of football, the Committee to Ban Dances, disappointing my mother."

Carmen diligently wrote the first few down and then wrinkled her nose. "Albie and I were both in marching band in seventh grade for a brief period before he had to quit because of his decreased lung capacity, and I had to quit because I got too busy. Were you in middle school marching band?"

"That's it!" I said.

"Really?" Carmen asked.

"I think she's being sarcastic again," Albie said.

Carmen twiddled her pen between her fingers. "I'm in student government, model UN, track, debate, obviously."

"Obviously," I echoed, nodding seriously.

Albie snickered and Carmen shot him a look. He flattened his mouth.

"They asked me about the lake," he said.

Carmen's twiddling fingers stilled. "You were in the lake? I thought you couldn't swim."

"I can't," Albie said. "I was, uh, waiting for you on the dock and then I sort of fell in. It was a whole thing."

Carmen made a note. "It's perfectly legal to swim in the lake as a guest of a neighborhood resident. I looked it up."

The lock clicked, and our heads jerked toward the conference room door in unison. Principal Patel held the door open for Mom, Jeff, and four other adults and then shut it behind them without joining. Whatever we were in trouble for, the school didn't want to be involved.

Carmen's parents breezed through the room—you could tell they were her parents because her dad was wearing a shirt that said *My Daughter is the President of St. Croix High*. I wish I was joking.

"Carmie!" Her mother raced around the table and wrapped Carmen in a hug. "We were so worried. Is Jillian here, too? Your hair looks amazing! Do I need to call a lawyer?"

Her dad embraced her, too, sandwiching her between her two parents, and Carmen didn't flinch or shrug away. I wondered what that was like.

Albie's parents marched to the other side of the table and sat next to their son. His mom was wearing a sharp pencil skirt suit and his dad was wearing a track suit.

"You have your inhaler?" His mom asked. Albie held it up for her to see.

"Take some vitamin C," his dad said and handed Albie a fistful of vitamins that he dutifully swallowed.

You could tell they were Good Kid Parents. None of them asked what Carmen or Albie had done wrong or sighed and asked "What is it this time?" They didn't even look annoyed that the school had made them leave work.

Jeff from DBD hurried to the head of the table to pull out a chair for my mom. She took it without even acknowledging me. No hug. No knee squeeze. I rolled the lollipop so it was squarely on my tongue; the sourness made my face pucker.

"I'm sure you're all curious as to why you're here," Mom said.

"I'm missing an A.P. Bio quiz," Carmen said.

"I'm missing a hall pass," I muttered under my breath.

Mom gestured to Jeff, who was hovering over her right shoulder. He flipped up his tablet and propped it on a floppy keyboard, the fabric of his DBD windbreaker swish-swishing with every movement.

"I'm going to ask you some questions about your whereabouts on the morning of Sunday, September 18," he said.

He glanced back up at us. Carmen, Albie, and me. Somehow, we had become an *us*. Then the questions began:

"When were you in the lake?"

"For how long?"

"How far did you swim?"

"Did you notice anything strange about the water?"

Carmen laced her fingers together and rested her arms on the table. "I dove into the water at approximately eight a.m. and swam for exactly sixty minutes. I don't live in the neighborhood, but I swim in the lake every Sunday during the off-season for cross-training. Albie buzzes me in at the gate, and we have breakfast together afterwards."

"Is that true, Albert?" Jeff asked.

Albie looked up from his lap and nodded, and from that one look I understood everything about their relationship. They'd been friends since kindergarten. Carmen had visited him regularly while he was in the hospital. They'd joined marching band together. The reason why was clear. It was a tale as old as time, really: Albie was in love with Carmen, and Carmen was too nice to remind Albie that she was gay.

Jeff's fingers flew across the keyboard. "Thank you, Carmen, for those very . . . thorough answers. What about you, Albert? Why were you in the lake?"

"Me?" Albie asked. Circles of sweat stained his loose-fitting T-shirt. "I live there."

"But what were you doing in the water?" Jeff pressed.

"Albert doesn't go in the lake," Mrs. Chang said. "He can't swim."

"Albert?" My mom asked in a gentle tone, playing good cop as usual.

"I fell in," Albie mumbled.

"You *what*?" His dad asked. "You told me you were in the hot tub."

Mrs. Chang tapped furiously on her phone. "I'm emailing Dr. Wong. We should get you in for a test right away."

Under the table, Albie's fingers were drumming furiously against his leg. "Sorry," he said.

"Thank you, Albert." Then Jeff turned to me. "Hattie?" The disdain in his voice confirmed that he'd heard stories about me already.

I shrugged and gestured to the pile of faded purple hair piled on top of my head. "I can't get my hair wet. It would mess up the dye."

Carmen looked up from her notes and wrinkled her nose. "Then how do you shower?"

"Wouldn't you like to know," I said, the words sliding off my sour-stained tongue before I could catch them. Carmen's parents pulled her closer to them. I was just trying to get out of trouble, but Carmen probably got those kinds of insensitive, homophobic comments all the time. I'd said the wrong thing. Again.

"We have pictures of you in the lake," Jeff said.

"Circumstantial," I said.

Mr. Chang waved his phone in the air. "Does your throat feel like it's closing, Albert? That can be a symptom of drinking contaminated lake water."

Jeff pursed his lips. "That's not one of the symptoms on our list, but we've never dealt with an outbreak of this kind before."

"Wait. Outbreak?" I asked. I'd thought we were there because DBD suspected one of us of stealing their fancy drone.

"There's no need to panic." Jeff said. "We're just gathering information."

But you don't tell people there's no need to panic unless there is, in fact, a huge reason for them to panic.

My mom sat up straighter and swallowed back the planet-size tears glomming onto her eyeballs. My mom who I'd been in a nonstop fight with for four years. My mom who I'd let down at every turn. My mom who was a scientist with an expertise in mutating biological matter for new purposes.

"Albert has a compromised immune system," Mr. Chang said.

"And I have an A.P. U.S. History test on Friday," Carmen said.

Jeff plugged a cable into his tablet and the screen projected a hazy image onto the wall. A glowing orange-and-pink blob. It was exactly the kind of image a science teacher would show to explain cells or atoms or whatever it is that science teachers teach.

Jeff pointed at the image and said, "I think you've got bigger things to worry about than a test right now."

CHAPTER 4

YOU MIGHT BE WONDERING HOW A PERSON ENDS UP SWIMMING IN a gated neighborhood's mostly decorative lake—especially when they do not live in said neighborhood.

Going for a swim was never part of my Sunday morning plan. I hate Sundays. My mom usually had to go to the office for a few hours, and without someone to fight or a school to hate, the itch—to move, ignite, fracture—burned bright in my chest. So I'd started wandering around fancy neighborhoods, looking for houses to break into so I could film the most precious things inside. Not exactly legal, but it could be a lot worse, all right?

I didn't even take anything. I just liked to film the guts of a home: a scrapbook, a love letter, the dedication page of a family Bible. The kinds of things people store in a memory box under their bed and only look at when they're cleaning out the house. The kinds of things people could never bring themselves to throw away.

I'm sure Mrs. Howard would be *thrilled* to try to interpret what this hobby said about my mental state, but all I can say is this: I like collecting pieces of other people's lives. Not the expensive pieces; the true ones.

So this past Sunday, I rode my trash heap of a bike right through the thick iron gates circling the Cul du Suck after sweet-talking the guard. It's the kind of neighborhood where the streets are lined with freakishly tall bushes and trees, and each house is planted like a middle finger in the vast lawn.

For once, I found the heavy, humid air comforting. The sky was still threatening to dump rain into Cul du Lac at any minute, the same as anywhere else. As much as humans try to build and maintain perfection with big houses and iron gates, nature still finds ways to seep back through.

I turned my bike down the gap in between two mansions and popped out in an expansive backyard. There were no gates separating the yards—they were all big and manicured and backed up to the lake—so I rode straight around the perimeter of the water.

All the yards were eerie replicas of each other: hotel-size pool, bubbling hot tub, fake-looking grass, polished barbecue, repeat.

I kept riding until a pale pink house popped out around the curving drive. A row of palm trees in the backyard bent toward the roof, making it look like the house had on a toupee. There was a camera perched on the corner of the back porch. I would have rode on, waited to find a smaller house without an exterior camera or creepy palm trees, but as I watched, the red light on the camera flashed three times and then dimmed.

I veered my bike away from the lake and hopped off, then pressed my back against the gnarled trunk of a palm tree.

A boy with dark hair just long enough to tuck behind his ears emerged from the house and strode with great purpose to a dock stretching out from the grass into the lake. I recognized him from school. Albie Chang.

I peered out from behind the tree. I knew that Albie was a cancer survivor and had health complications from the treatment, so there was no way he could catch me on the bike—and also no way I was staying long enough to find out if I was wrong about that. I was a compulsive liar and a petty thief, not a fighter. Although I couldn't lie that it did cross my mind that if any trouble came up, I'd definitely be able to outrun him.

I've already admitted to being a horrible person. Let's move on.

Albie sat cross-legged on the edge of the dock, staring out into the murky water. He didn't turn back and notice the tire marks in the grass or the girl with purple hair trying to blend into a tree.

So you see, it wasn't breaking and entering when I squeezed through the back door of the Chang's house. Albie had clearly disabled the security system and left the door unlocked, so, technically speaking, it was just entering.

The house felt quiet compared to the chorus of lawnmowers and chirping birds outside. There was a neatly organized shoe rack just inside the back door. I slipped off my Vans and tiptoed through a short hallway into a massive kitchen.

Herb plants sprouted in vases and pots lining the window behind the sink. An intricately woven red charm dangled from the window.

A glance behind the kitchen revealed a large living area and spiral staircase. The walls were neutral-toned, the furniture oversized, the ceilings high. Clean, but slightly cluttered with papers and backpacks, sports equipment and poster boards.

The walls were lined with school photos of Albie and his older brother and sister. His brother's and sister's pictures progressed in the normal fashion: cute to awkward to almost adult. Albie had fewer school photos than his siblings. They started with him beaming in his childhood pictures, smiling so big I was surprised his teeth all fit in one mouth, and then there was a gap—from the time he spent in the hospital I guessed—and when they resumed, Albie looked tired and older, his smile tight, his teeth hidden.

I ventured farther into the kitchen. There was a color-coded calendar tacked to the fridge with everyone's schedule for the week. The only thing in Albie's color were doctors' appointments. A collage of pictures framed the calendar. The three siblings crammed into a photobooth, the whole family holding a big number-five balloon, and a photo of everyone surrounding little Albie in a hospital bed, tubes extending from his nose, his chest, his arm.

The corner of another photo poked out behind that one. I slid it out from beneath the magnet and saw that it was different from the others. In it, Albie was sitting on the ground between two bookshelves, maybe at a library or bookstore, surrounded by stacks and stacks of books. He was smiling as he looked down at the page. His eyes were big with the kind of wonder only a book can provide.

I'd just pulled out my phone to start recording when I heard a lock click. Someone was home. The door in front of the stairs creaked open.

"James? Albert?" a man's voice called. My stomach clenched at the memory of what it was like to have a dad who came home.

I slid the photo back under the magnet and tiptoed toward the back door. The key in these situations was to not panic. People didn't expect to find a stranger hanging out in their house when they come home, so if you happened to be a stranger creeping in someone's home, you had the advantage. By the time he got to the kitchen, I could've been out the door.

I ran to the back door and slipped on my shoes. Glanced back at the refrigerator. The gap-toothed smile. The books.

Clicking shoes echoed across the marble entryway.

I pressed record on my phone, sprinted back to the fridge, moved the magnet again, and zoomed in on the photo of Albie with all the books. When I'd captured him squarely in my frame I tiptoed back across the kitchen and then slipped out the back door.

"Who's home?" Albie's dad's deep voice echoed across the empty kitchen.

My breaths came out heavy. There was nowhere to hide. The back of the pink house was dotted with windows. There were no fences to hop over, and the closest tree was the one I'd ditched my bike behind next door, which was too exposed to risk the sprint across the open lawn.

That left the lake.

I ran toward it, slowing only when I got to the dock and saw Albie sitting on the end, leaning so far forward I thought he might be talking to a siren or something. I tiptoed onto the dock, crouched down, and swung myself underneath it, putting my phone in my mouth to keep it away from the water.

The underside of the dock was dusty and coated with spiderwebs. I bit back a squeal and locked my fingers around a supporting beam.

"Albert!" The voice was coming from a scary muscular dude. The man—Albie's dad, I assumed—had arms bigger than a tree trunk. "There's been a break-in!"

"Huh?" Albie replied.

My fingers were slipping, the phone in my mouth slick with drool. The Changs needed to take this family conversation inside before I lost my grip and fell into the water. Also, surely Mr. Chang was referring to a second break-in, right? There was no way he had actually noticed my presence when I'd barely been in the house for a minute, *right*?

"I'm calling the police. And what are you doing out here? You can't swim. I don't like you that close to the water."

"OK, Dad. I'm coming."

I've been an orphan, a refugee, and the bastard child of British royalty, but Albie spoke with more defeat in his voice than any of my invented personas had ever mustered.

A splinter dug into my palm, and I bit back a yelp.

Albie's dad's muttering quieted as he walked back to the house.

One of my hands slipped off the beam, splinters skidding into my palm as I pressed my fingernails into the wood to maintain leverage. My muscles screamed with the effort. I wasn't going to be able to hold on until Albie left. I counted to ten before letting go and plopping into the water.

It was cold and murky, the same deep, purply-blue as the Atlantic. My feet found the muddy bottom, and I kept my chin above the surface, phone dry.

"Who's there?" Albie asked, and then I heard another splash.

I poked my head out from under the dock and saw Albie floundering in the water.

I knew I should help him; he couldn't swim. Helping him was what a nice, normal girl would do.

I shook my head to clear the urge. I wasn't nice or normal, so I held my phone out and filmed the rippling water as I slipped out of the lake and ran back to my bike, catching the moment his head popped above the water.

After that, it was your standard getaway scheme. Tell the guard some sob story about how my overly competitive father made me train for triathlons soaking wet because it was better preparation for real-world conditions. Tell my mom I went to the beach to "think about my choices." Slice and edit the footage of Albie's house and the tidal pool in the water when he emerged from the surface, gasping for air.

It didn't fit with any of the other footage I'd collected from the stucco monstrosities populating Marsh Rock. It would have to be the start of a new series. Something about grief and fear and newness. I could already picture it projected on the stark white wall of a gallery or screening in an ornate, old-fashioned theater. I would write my mom a check and pride would glitter in her eyes and things would be different.

But none of that had anything to do with a drone crash or DBD, so I'd figured I was going to get off scot-free until my mom dragged me into a glaring white conference room and I saw Albie seated across the table looking like he was about to puke up all his feelings.

"Just because I'm at the top of my class doesn't mean I can miss a bunch of classes," Carmen said.

"I want a lawyer," I said.

Albie's parents each put a hand on one of his shoulders. They didn't know what I'd done, but they were smart enough to know they needed to protect their son from me.

"You're not under arrest. Why would you need a lawyer?" Carmen asked.

Actually, she had a point. My mom was a scientist, not a cop.

My mom's eyes were full of sorrow as she tapped the tablet. The image projected on the wall changed to an insect-like drone with four helicopter-looking limbs protruding from its stomach.

"Saturday evening at approximately 12:07 A.M., test drone D68 crashed into Cul du Lac," Mom said.

"Is this about the homeowner association's denial of DBD's request to drain the lake?" Albie's mom asked. Her fingers were flying across her phone screen, but her eyes were lasered on DBD Jeff. "Because my son should not be dragged into a legal dispute with the HOA."

"This isn't about the homeowner's association." My mom cleared her throat. "The drone belonged to DBD and was carrying samples of a new product for a routine test."

I leaned forward. Planted my feet to the ground. My mom was one of the top scientists at a super-shady company that made super-shady weapons that everyone thought were used for super-shady wars.

She couldn't. She wouldn't. But one look at her made it clear that she had.

"What did you do?" I asked. Every head in the room looked between us, wondering what we knew that they didn't.

My mom looked down at the table. "Neighborhood security cameras show only three people came in contact with the lake water before we secured the area."

"Secured the area?" Mrs. Chang said. "From what, exactly?"

"We must have been exposed to the product in the water," Carmen said. She took notes without looking away from the image projected on the wall. "What are the possible side effects? Should we be worried about radiation sickness?"

"We'll know more once we analyze the water and test the kids." My mom shuffled some papers in front of her. She still wouldn't look at me. "The product was a parasitic weapon, designed to infect a host's nervous system."

Her words threw the room into silence as everyone digested what she was saying. Then it was chaos.

"Albie has a compromised immune system—"

"How did it crash?"

"What are the symptoms?"

"This is unconscionable!"

I raised my voice and shouted over all of them. "How long?"

The room went quiet again. The projection of the drone cast swirling geometric white shadows over our faces.

"How long do we have?" I repeated.

My whole life, I'd felt wrong inside, and the only chance I'd had of feeling different was becoming an adult and going away to make art in a place as spiky and poisonous as me. Without the promise of that someday, I had nothing.

My mom stammered, "We need to run tests to confirm—"

Mrs. Chang held her phone up to her ear. "I'm calling Dr. Wong."

Carmen's mom clutched her daughter to her chest.

"How long?" I asked again.

My mom stopped shuffling papers and fiddling with her tablet. She finally looked me straight in the eye and said, "Thirty to sixty days."

CHAPTER 5

THIRTY TO SIXTY DAYS. ONE MONTH AGO, I'D BEEN STARTING AT this new school. Two months ago, Mom and I had rolled into town in a moving truck full of dented cardboard boxes and a few pieces of worn-down furniture. In one month, I'd likely be dead. In two months, I'd definitely be dead.

I'd always known there was something unnatural in me, a poison that infected and destroyed everything good. But I hadn't guessed its existence would become quite so literal.

Once the initial barrage of shouting from the parents quieted, Jeff clicked to the next slide. It showed a purple blob swirling in a test cylinder. Carmen's hand was white-knuckled around her pen. Albie hung his head and didn't say a word.

"The drone in question was carrying test vials of a mutated Toxoplasma gondii parasite, or MTP," Jeff said.

Carmen's parents had all four of their arms around her. Albie's dad had placed a single, shaking hand on his shoulder, and his mom was typing furiously on her phone. My mom squeezed out of her seat and walked around the table to kneel beside me. She reached out her hand; I shook my head. If she touched me, I knew I would shatter.

Jeff continued his science lesson. "Toxoplasma are an incredibly common intracellular protozoan. About forty million people are infected by the parasite in the U.S. alone. Almost none of those infected exhibit any symptoms . . ."

The sounds: Jeff's voice, Mrs. Diaz's gasping sobs, the buzz of the projector. The sights: a middle-aged man who needed to surrender to his receding hairline, air particles hazing through the projector's light beam. The feeling: a black hole yawning open in my gut.

"Where are your parents, sweetheart?" Mr. Diaz whispered to me. "You shouldn't be here alone."

"That's her mom," Carmen replied, jerking her chin in my mom's direction.

The eyes of the four parents in the room widened in judgment. Carmen's mom took out a rosary and thumbed through it.

Jeff clicked to a new slide featuring speckled purple blobs.

"A rare strain of the parasite, called Toxoplasma gondii, has the unique effect of weakening an animal's control over their own nervous system, specifically the frontal cortex. It's quite fascinating, really—"

Mom jerked her head at him. "*Jeff.*"

He cleared his throat. "Right. Not fascinating. Sorry."

Her hand was hovering close to mine. A magnet buzzing above my skin.

Parasite. Parasite. Parasite.

Finally. A name for what I was.

"Essentially, the parasite disguises itself in the nervous system until it's taken complete control," Jeff continued. "The drone flight yesterday was testing how the MTPs reacted to high altitude.

"Once they've attached to a host, the MTPs spend several days acclimating to their environment before targeting the nervous system. Some of the symptoms for the host body include delusions, increased impulsivity, and a lack of fear."

Jeff explained everything calmly, in the language of someone who was used to breaking down complicated science to people who didn't understand it.

Carmen jabbed her pen at her notebook. "To summarize: You invented a mind control parasite as a weapon, presumably for the use of creating soldiers or zombie civilians, and accidentally set it loose in a lake, and now the three of us are infected?"

"Albert. Is. *Immunocompromised*." Albie's dad slapped his palm against the table after each word.

"Dad," Albie started then sank back into his chair, the fight sucked out of him with one pained look from his father.

Mom stood up. "I understand that, Mr. Chang. A grave error has been made, and I am personally going to do everything I can to make it right."

Mrs. Diaz looked at her with disgust. "You infected your own *daughter*."

"I did," Mom said. The weight of the words slumped her shoulders. "That's why you can trust me when I say, I'm going to find a cure and make sure our children survive. But to do that, I'm going to need your cooperation. DBD's set up an isolation ward at Marsh Rock Memorial—"

Albie's head snapped up. "The hospital?"

Carmen's hand stuttered over her notes, but she didn't set the pen down even for a second. "An isolation ward?"

Jeff snapped through projected images of sterile hospital rooms with windows looking out over the swampy bay. Images of the parasite tumbled in front of my vision. I took only the bare facts of Jeff's speech.

DBD had a floor set up at the local hospital. They were flying in their top doctors, scientists, and researchers. They wanted the three of us to move there for testing and treatment full-time. They'd have everything we could need there: a cafeteria, an exercise room, an on-site tutor . . .

A parasite.

Mrs. Chang laughed when Jeff finished. "You want us to put our kids into the care of the people who put their lives at risk? That's ridiculous."

Mrs. Diaz clutched Carmen closer to her. "Carmen needs to be home with her abuela and her sister and Jillian. We're not leaving her with strangers."

Albie had his hands clasped in his lap, lips pressed together. His jittering legs rattled the floor.

"Our son's not going anywhere with you," Mr. Chang said. "You should be in jail."

Mom didn't even flinch, which meant it wasn't the first time the thought had occurred to her.

"Albert was treated at Marsh Rock Memorial, wasn't he?" my mom asked quietly. "I read about you in the paper. Your prognosis was serious. Childhood leukemia always is. But your family knew you had a good chance of survival if you followed a treatment plan. They said Albert—" She stopped and looked at Albie. "Do you prefer Albert or Albie?"

Albie's jittering paused. "Uh, Albie."

His mom raised an eyebrow.

Mom nodded. "Everyone interviewed in the article said Albie was a diligent patient. You changed his diet, his clothes. Pulled him out of school and moved him into the hospital. And it worked. He fought and won. Albie's almost ten years in remission."

She smiled at Albie. He winced back. I could tell this wasn't a story he wanted told.

"You trusted the doctors before," she continued. "You trusted the science and the treatment plan and it saved your son. What I'm telling you now is that putting your child in an isolation unit run by DBD may not sound ideal, but it is the best treatment plan."

Mrs. Chang shook her head and let out a low chuckle.

Mom slapped her hands down on the table. "Sue DBD. Take me to court. Get a second opinion. I don't care about any of that. All I care about is the survival of our children. An isolated unit with twenty-four seven monitoring and an ICU on the floor below is the best way to keep them alive. I made this parasite. I built it and mutated it. It's possible the kids aren't infected and they'll be out of the hospital in a week. It's possible I made a faulty product. It's possible I'm wrong. But I'm not willing to gamble my child's life on that chance. Are you?"

It was silent for a moment. I'd never heard Mom talk like that.

Mr. and Mrs. Chang looked at each other. Finally, Mrs. Chang said, "We'll consult with Albie's doctors."

Mom nodded. That was as good as she would get out of them.

"Carmen has a pediatrician," Mr. Diaz said. "Maybe she knows someone . . ."

Carmen raised her hand. "It's possible we're not infected?"

Mom tilted her head. "I wouldn't bet on that probability."

"But it's possible." Carmen snapped her notebook shut. "I'm going."

"We'll discuss this as a family—" Mrs. Diaz started.

"If the experts recommend an isolation ward, that's what I should do."

"They did this to you," Mr. Diaz said.

"And they're also my best chance," Carmen said.

My mom exhaled, the weight of Carmen's future clearly settling heavy over her. "I understand."

Carmen finally put her pen down. "When do we leave?"

CHAPTER 6

WHAT SHOULD YOU DO WHEN YOU FIND OUT A PARASITE'S CRAWLED into your veins? When you find out your body is occupied territory and the insurgents will surely win? When the someday you dreamed about fizzles away? When your mom is the one who started the war?

I didn't know the right answer, but what Mom and I did was go to Taco Bell.

Mom leaned out the window of our clunker car to order. "We need two cheesy gordita crunches and two burritos, one with no onions and one with extra sauce."

Parasite. Parasite. Parasite.

"We also need six mild and six Diablo hot sauce packets," Mom continued.

She glanced over at me hopefully. Taco Bell used to be our special place. Mom would take me there for mother-daughter dates back when that was still a thing we had to carve out special time for rather than the default arrangement of our family.

I turned to face the window. School was letting out for the day. A group of kids from my Algebra class streamed into the restaurant, laughing and talking over each other. The world hadn't stopped spinning when my life imploded. The sun had the nerve to keep shining, and the moist air refused to give me any personal space.

The innards of my locker were scattered across the back seat of the car. It hadn't been much. A black wire shelf. A crumpled picture of Joan Didion. Textbooks. A few empty folders. A bag of useless coins from a game my dad and I used to play. Dozens of lollipop wrappers.

I'd emptied out my few possessions while, down the hall, Carmen dismantled a collage of pictures and medals. Her girlfriend, Jillian, a vanilla girl with freckles speckled across her white skin, hovered over Carmen's shoulder, clearly confused. Carmen remained focused on the task at hand while her parents and Jillian stood by, helpless spectators of her life.

Albie and two boys I always saw him eating lunch with were huddled around his locker. Tears trickled down Albie's cheeks, but he didn't wipe them away or hide his face. His parents were the ones who stripped his locker bare while he said goodbye to his friends. His older brother, James, had stopped dead in the middle of the hall when he saw his parents and Albie, his muscles tightening into a taut bow string.

Mom had asked me if I had anyone I wanted to say goodbye to as she hefted a pile of books into the trunk. There were kids everywhere, more than a few stopping to ask Albie and Carmen what was going on. Had they been expelled? When would they be back? Did they want to go to Sonic after school?

But I didn't have anyone, which made Mom feel bad enough that she drove to Taco Bell even though we were supposed to go straight to the isolation ward.

Mom flashed me a small smile as she pulled forward. "I asked for extra hot sauce. Your favorite."

All I could think about was that *thing* inside me. I stared down at my gurgling stomach. *Was that it? Or were my stomach noises a normal Pavlovian response to the Bell? Where was the parasite in my body now?*

Mom cleared her throat. "I know it's a lot. I know . . . How are you feeling?"

How was I feeling? Whoever said there was no such thing as a stupid question clearly had never dealt with a worried parent.

I felt relieved that I could surrender, stop lying, rest. I felt angry and horrified that I would never get to move away and become someone else—that feeling was so gnawing and intense that I wanted to burn DBD to the ground and make my mom watch. I felt a sadness so big that I knew if I looked it in the eye, it would take over my brain and cause me to self-destruct before the parasite even got the chance.

But that's not what people want to hear when they ask how you're feeling. People pretend like they don't like that I lie. They act like it's a problem, but really, it's what I've been trained to do.

"Hattie?"

I stared at my gurgling stomach. "I think it might be in my stomach. It's making weird noises."

Mom squeezed the steering wheel. Her Parent Training had prepared her to see the best in me and in every situation. To stay bubbly and tear-free and positive. It hadn't prepared her for my imminent doom.

"You might start experiencing symptoms soon," she said. "Seeing things that aren't there, lowered inhibitions, increased impulsivity."

I patted my stomach to see if I could feel the outline of the monster in me.

"Hattie," my mom pleaded. "Talk to me."

"I don't know what to say."

That wasn't true, of course. It wasn't that I didn't know what to say; there was just too much to say. All the words caught in my throat, made it impossible to swallow, to breathe, to feel anything other than the existential panic that was always lurking in my gut, waiting for an opening. And if I said one thing, I would say everything.

How could you?

Fix this.

I'm scared, Mom.

I rested my head against the smudged window, felt the heat of the glass simmer against my skin. Pain on the outside always felt better than pain on the inside.

Mom pulled up to the payment window, handed the employee her card, and took a warm paper bag in exchange. She passed it to me and focused her eyes on the road, driving slowly through the smoothly paved roads of Marsh Rock.

"DBD's biological experts will be here by Friday. I've got everyone at central lab working overtime to find a solution. I'll be back tonight with your clothes, and I'll visit every day. And when I'm not with you, I'll be running tests on the drone and the MTP to figure out the strength of the parasite and how we can counteract it. Jeff is working off prototype data already." She kept talking, going faster and faster as we neared the massive hospital complex, hands gesturing around the steering wheel. "We don't yet know how the MTPs will interact with subjects in the real world, and we won't have confirmation that you're even infected until we get the lab results back. Once we know the depth of the infection, we'll formulate an aggressive treatment plan. It kills me that you'll be in the hospital instead of at home, but a sterile environment with doctors nearby is the best option. And as soon as I find a solution, you'll be back at home."

There were seagulls cawing overhead and a raging beat pounding from the car behind us. All I wanted in this moment was not to be trapped in this car. The same one we had in New Jersey, the one my dad used to drive me to school in.

"I'm not coming home," I said.

Mom flexed her hands around the steering wheel. "Don't be silly. Of course you are."

I twisted in my seat to face her. "You made this MTP thing. I know you think I haven't been paying attention to your work all these years—which is mainly true—but I know that you're good at what you do, and when you make things, they work. So we can cut the bullshit."

"I'm going to fix this. I promise."

"I begged you not to take this job," I said.

"You know I didn't have a choice. After what happened with your father—"

"Now I'll never be able to pay you back."

Mom reached her hand out to me but dropped it when I flinched. Pink stucco buildings and a never-ending swamp scrolled by like movie credits outside the window.

The car was covered in a heavy blanket of silence. I heard her sniffle and cough, trying to swallow her tears, but I couldn't look at her.

This was why I didn't bother with the truth. It turned the cold numbness in my chest into a burn.

"You don't owe me anything," my mom finally said.

Mom turned into the maze of parking lots sprawling out from the hospital. I could feel hot, heavy tears boiling behind my eyes. The desire to bury my head in her neck and cry out the disease was eating up my insides. I used to curl up on her lap and tell her every hurt, externalize my broken heart for her, back when I believed she could put it back together.

She tentatively brushed a tear from my cheek. "Do you believe me?"

"Do you want me to lie?"

She dropped her hand. "No. Never."

The car was so small. We were breathing the same recycled air. The same genes were chained together inside our skin. Seeing her cry broke something open inside of me. My warm, kind mother.

The car was still moving. I couldn't take it anymore, the tears, the air, the truth of who my mother and I were and the things we were capable of doing to each other. I hooked my arm through my backpack and hugged the bag of food to my chest.

"You deserve better than me," I said.

Then I threw open the car door and ran.

CHAPTER 7

THE AFTERMATH OF JUMPING OUT OF A MOVING CAR AND RUNNING away was kind of a letdown. Mostly because I ran straight into the hospital, which was where we were heading anyway. I had nowhere else to go. And also because I was so winded that I had to take a walking break before making it into the lobby, which was embarrassing.

The lobby was a hushed hive of activity. People in scrubs and white jackets hurried back and forth. Nurses juggled plastic clipboards and concerned family members. It was a place where time moved both fast and slow all at once.

"Where have you been?" I turned to see Jeff—still sporting the DBD windbreaker; that man was nothing if not committed—marching toward me with Albie and Carmen in tow. Carmen had her notebook out. Albie's eyes were on the floor.

Jeff didn't stop moving as he peppered me with questions. "Why are you late? Where have you been? Where's your mom?"

I jerked a thumb toward Carmen and Albie. "Where are their moms?"

"Their parents dropped them off with me personally *and* filled out the appropriate paperwork before going home to retrieve their belongings," Jeff said.

Carmen looked up from the notes she was scribbling on honest-to-god paper like she lived in the honest-to-god medieval times. "Did you stop at Taco Bell?"

I pulled out a burrito, took a bite, and said, "No. Why do you ask?"

Carmen raised her eyebrows. Albie and Carmen didn't know why I'd been in the lake or about the compulsive lying. This could be fun.

"Hey, Hattie"—Jeff leaned forward and lowered his voice—"your mom didn't leave a message for me, did she?"

"Oh, yeah, she told me to tell you she's madly in love with you," I said flatly.

He smoothed back his thinning tufts of hair. "That's not very nice."

Guilt panged in my chest. Jeff was into my mom in a non-joking way.

"Well, I'm not a nice person," I said.

Jeff herded us into a steel-paneled elevator, talking endlessly about the history of DBD's partnership with the hospital, how it was exciting that the DBD ward would finally be put to use, and all the cutting-edge technology we were going to be "lucky" to put to the test. Carmen's pen raced across her page as she took nonstop notes.

A doctor stepped onto the elevator on the third floor. His face lit up when he saw Albie, then quickly crinkled in concern. "Albert? I wasn't expecting to see you until the party next month."

Albie stood up a little straighter. "Hi, Dr. Wong. I'm, uh, not going to oncology . . . I'm here because of something else."

"Something else?" Dr. Wong looked between us.

Jeff stuck out his hand. "Jeff. Lead researcher at DBD. We've been trying to get hold of you."

When Dr. Wong took his hand, Jeff shook it, and then pulled him closer and whispered harshly in his ear.

Albie chewed on his lip and looked down at nothing. I couldn't bear to see him cry again, so I reached into the crinkled bag and handed him the second burrito.

"No onions," I said. My mom hated onions.

"Albie's gluten intolerant and dairy free," Carmen said without looking up from her notes.

Albie took the burrito anyway. "Thanks."

The elevator doors dinged open on the fifth floor.

Dr. Wong buried his hands in his lab coat pockets and turned to Albie. "I'm so sorry. If there's anything I can do to help . . ."

His voice trailed off. We all knew there wasn't anything he could do.

Albie's mouth pulled up into something that I think was supposed to be a smile but came across as more of a wince. "Sure."

Dr. Wong stepped out but stood unmoving in front of the elevator doors until they were completely closed.

Jeff started his pep talk again as the elevator slid upward until the doors dinged open on the seventh floor.

"Home sweet home!" he said and made a big show of pretend-holding the elevator doors open while the three of us stepped into the hall. Rows of green-cushioned chairs lining the wall, hallways jutting off in every direction, and although the floor was quiet, it felt like something might erupt at any moment. A sign announced the area as the DBD PAVILION.

Jeff led us to the left where instead of another hallway, there was a walled-off, closet-size box labeled "Anteroom."

"DBD is one of the biggest funders of the hospital," Carmen said, turning to Albie and me. "They're one of the only private companies in the country to have their own wing in a hospital."

"Why do you know that? Did you pick up a side hustle as their intern?" I asked.

"No," Carmen said. The girl really didn't get sarcasm. "I did some light research on the drive over."

"The wing is specially designed for DBD to do testing and research," Jeff said.

The door made an unsealing sound when Jeff opened it. He gestured for us to step inside. The three of us shared a skeptical look.

Jeff chuckled and stepped through. "It's just the anteroom. This space is designed to decontaminate anyone entering or exiting the floor. Its primary use is for airborne, infectious diseases. But we don't need to run the full decontamination system because the MTP is neither contagious nor airborne."

"Except when it's in a drone," Albie said. He was still clutching the wrapped burrito in his hand.

An exhaled wheeze escaped me. Miracle Boy had made a joke. "Good one," I said.

Jeff led us through the cold, whooshing anteroom and into the isolation ward. I chewed through the last of my burrito and both gordita crunches while Jeff took us on a "tour of our new digs," as if our quarantine was an exciting vacation.

The floors were cheap-looking, gleaming tile; the overhead lighting a haunting, pale orange. The nurse's station was the nerve center. Patient rooms, a rec room, and conference room veined off from it. Everything was clean and white and soulless.

"Wait until you see the view!" Jeff pranced across the rec room and threw open the curtains to reveal a stretch of marshy wetlands.

The Taco Bell filled me up enough to take the edge off how I'd felt in the car with Mom, but not enough to insulate me from the asininity of Jeff's entire being. I pulled up an image of the toxoplasma parasite on my phone. It didn't look like something that would kill me. It was just a purple blob.

I don't know how long I stared at the image before Jeff called me out for not listening.

"You should pay attention," Jeff snapped. "I don't want to sound dramatic, but your life may depend on it."

I rolled my eyes and slid my phone back in my pocket. "My life depended on a company not using me as a test subject for a weapon that will kill me, but here we are."

Jeff's demeanor faltered. "DBD is the most equipped company in the world to handle this sort of disaster, and your mother is one of our most brilliant scientists. This is the safest place for you."

Ah, to have the naivete of a man who has never been betrayed by the system.

Jeff's little DBD pep talk did nothing to lift any of our spirits, but he looked like he felt much better at least. He guided us back around the nurse's station to a row of identical bedrooms. Each room had speckled tile floors and furniture and paintings of sunflowers on the wall. The windows peered out on the bay, thankfully, and not just another marsh. In the distance, I could see boats bobbing near the dock. A neatly folded pile of DBD swag rested on each bed.

The itch of my claustrophobia sprouted like a shadow in me. I was out of lies or hope for the future; there was no exit.

"You have twenty minutes of free time before the doctors will start the tests," Jeff said, checking his wristwatch because he was the kind of man who still found it necessary to wear a wristwatch. "All I need is your phones, and you're good to go."

"Our phones?" Albie asked.

"Smartphones aren't allowed in the facility. I have to turn mine over, too!" He patted his chest as if that would make us feel better.

"You don't have any legal grounds to confiscate our property—" Carmen began.

"Smartphones have unknown radioactive consequences," Jeff retorted. "To create a clean environment, we need to remove as many toxins as possible."

"My parents won't accept that," Albie said. It was the first time he'd really sounded sure of himself.

"I'm student body president. I'm in charge of homecoming!" Carmen said as if that explained everything.

"Of course. That's why DBD is generously supplying you with these." Jeff pulled three devices out of his jacket.

"I don't understand how a calculator will help with homecoming," Carmen huffed. "We're already significantly under budget."

"It's a phone," I said.

Carmen gasped. Albie grabbed one of the phones and shook it by his ear. I rolled one over in my hands. It was slim, black, and ridiculous. No internet access, no apps. Just an old-fashioned dumb phone with a fuzzy screen and actual buttons.

"You will definitely be hearing from Albie's mom about this," Carmen said. "Right, Albs?"

Albie let out a defeated sigh. "Yeah. If I can't FaceTime her, she'll be furious."

But I handed my phone over without a fight. Both because I was going to be dead in two months anyway and because I had a second smartphone hidden in my backpack for . . . reasons.

"That was fast," Albie said.

"The three of us should rendezvous in the conference room," Carmen said. "We can discuss the phone issue and finish the real-time map of Cul du Lac I'm diagramming for DBD. We need to create timelines and pinpoint our exact location—"

"Have fun with that," I said. "I'm going to take a nap." There was no point anymore, no future, nothing I could do to pay back my mom. I was ready to surrender. I backed up into the closest bedroom.

"Just don't be late for the testing," Jeff said. "And then your parents will be here in an hour for the orientation."

"I don't want to see my mom."

Jeff rolled his eyes. "Don't be silly."

"I read the intake forms," I lied. "You can't force me to accept visitors."

Carmen turned on Jeff. "I don't remember that stipulation."

Jeff blustered, "But your mom—"

"Will be better off without me."

With that, I slammed the door of my room and settled into the muffled stillness for a few seconds. Once it sounded like the others had splintered off, I whipped my second smartphone out of my backpack to numb myself out with some scrolling.

I swept the pile of DBD clothes Jeff had left in our rooms as "welcome presents" off the bed and curled up on my side as I scrolled through pictures of girls in yoga pants and boys with their "boyz" until I got to a post from Jordan Banner. I knew he was a pop robot, but I loved him. Or maybe I didn't and it was all just an ironic joke. It was anybody's guess, really.

The photo showed Jordan Banner wearing a full face of glittery makeup, holding a hand over his heart.

You're only alone if you don't reach out, the caption read.

I wished there was a dislike button so I could express how nauseous that sentiment made me feel, fan or not. I scrolled to the comments, internally wincing in preparation of the snark I assumed would be found there.

Truth.

This is why you're my inspiration.

I scrolled through supportive comment after supportive comment. I hadn't realized how earnestly people would respond to the slightest hint of vulnerability.

I hadn't posted on social media much since the thing with my dad. I hadn't had anything that felt important enough to share. But I was dying now, so what did it matter if I wasn't sharing life-altering revelations? Maybe there was something in just posting to leave something behind. I still had a burner account I used to look at memes and viral videos. The avatar was a picture of a spinning coin. The screen name was @BadRoll13.

I opened my camera and started filming. Seeing the world through a lens had always soothed the burning inside me. I captured the sterile room, sealed windows, stiff bed.

I'd never shared my videos with anyone before, but wasting away in a hospital seemed like a good time to start. I went to upload the edited video of Albie's house, splicing it with intercuts of the hospital room, and added the caption **Freedom is a cage with strange bars**.

I'd lied about everything else, but the last thing was true. My mom had been dragging around the deadweight of my existence for too long. It was time I set her free.

CHAPTER 8

AFTER LETTING A COLD-FACED DOCTOR WITH ROUGH HANDS POKE a needle in my arm and draw blood until my veins felt dry, I'd locked myself back in my room for the rest of the night and finally fallen asleep around three A.M. after chewing through half a dozen suckers and scrolling mindlessly on social media as absolutely no one liked or commented on my artsy video post. I would have slept until noon or—better yet, until the MTP had done its thing—but the overhead lights flicked on right at eight.

I was as surprised as anyone when my refusal to see my mom actually worked. Fun fact: Apparently in the state of Florida, doctors didn't need parental consent to provide hospital care to minors in "emergency situations." Say, for instance, if a minor was infected with a rare and deadly parasite that was going to take over their nervous system any day now, the doctors could complete patient intake without a parent present.

Jeff pleaded, but I didn't relent. Finally, he told me they'd have my blood results within a week and asked if I wanted to pass a message along to my mom, since "she was worried about me." I'd just swung my legs off the examining table and asked if I could leave.

After I retreated back to my room, it sounded like the other parents got an orientation and ate dinner together as a group. But I wasn't going to be tricked. I may have been stuck there, but that didn't mean I had to become besties with everyone and their mom.

I'd been planning to try to hide most of today, too, but there was no way I could stay here with those overly bright fluorescent lights, which I apparently had no control over.

When I opened the door, I found a lumpy black suitcase outside my room. My favorite hoodie and band tees were inside, along with a jumbo-size bag of sour green suckers, a bag of coins from that stupid game, a copy of *Slouching Toward Bethlehem*, and a note that said *I love you big* in my mom's loopy handwriting.

I filmed myself crumpling the note and throwing it away and posted it on my page. My mom had given up on saying those words to me when I was fourteen. Why pretend now?

Jeff knocked on the door a few minutes later.

"The first group therapy session starts in fifteen minutes! Failure to attend will result in a parent-doctor conference."

Well, we couldn't have that.

I threw on a cutoff shirt and oversize sweatpants and stumbled out toward the rec room.

DOORWAY TO ACCEPTANCE.

I nearly gagged at the sign taped to the door. That hadn't been there yesterday, so clearly Jeff or one of the nurses had put it up to try to make us feel accepted or some bullshit.

Two nurses clacked at keyboards at the circular desk. Jeff waited outside the conference room door with his clipboard. Another man in a DBD windbreaker sat by the door to the anteroom playing a game on his phone. There was no getting out of here.

"Did you sleep OK, Hattie?" Jeff asked as I walked through the door.

"My mom will never love you," I shot back.

Jeff pinched his lips together. "Not nice."

I shrugged. "As advertised."

The floors of the room were the same dull tile as my own. A green couch and two cushioned chairs were angled around a coffee table with a fanned spread of magazines on top. Albie was slumped on the couch, Carmen sat in one chair, and the person I assumed was our therapist was in the other.

She looked to be about my mom's age. She was Black, her hair pulled back in twists, and her face was kind. My gut sank at the sight of her. She had the professionally trained look of someone who wouldn't be easy to fool.

"Hattie, thank you for joining us," she said. "My name is Dr. Ryan. It's nice to meet you."

"I thought Jeff said we were starting at 8:15. I wasn't trying to be late or anything."

She smiled. "You're not. Take a seat."

I curled myself into the opposite corner of the couch from Albie. I could feel his eyes hovering over the side of my head. There was a photo of the marsh hanging on the opposite wall—because the view of the actual marsh outside our windows wasn't enough apparently.

A layer of lily pads and grass floated across the dark water toward a glowing sunset. I locked my eyes on the picture and ignored Albie's burning gaze.

"Alright, now that we have everyone, we can get started," Dr. Ryan said as she settled back into her chair. "A little background about me: I'm a trauma-informed specialist. I grew up in Alabama but have been practicing in Florida for the last ten years."

Carmen flipped her notebook open and made a note.

Dr. Ryan crossed one leg over the other. "I'll start by stating the obvious: No one knows exactly what they're doing here." She let that sink in for a moment before continuing. "This is an unprecedented situation. So I'm not here to tell you how to feel or pretend I can solve your problems. I'm here to hold space for whatever you're feeling and walk with you through this difficult time. We'll start by filling out an evaluation form."

I'd ripped off my fair share of school counselors in my time, but I'd never regularly attended *therapy* therapy. It was expensive and Mom didn't have good health insurance until she got the job at DBD (LOL, joke's on me). We'd gone a few times together when we first moved to Marsh Rock, and then the therapist said I might have a compulsive lying problem and Mom said that was ridiculous and I said maybe not and we never went back again.

The form reminded me why therapy had always given me an itch. I wanted to numb out. I wanted an emotional anesthetic. I wanted the guilt for the debt I owed my mom not to be a physical weight on my chest. The last thing I wanted to do was fill out a form that asked questions like: *In the past two weeks, how often have you felt hopeless? Anxious? Desired to hurt someone else? Yourself?*

Carmen finished the form in seconds, checking each box as aggressively as a punch. Albie moved less aggressively but just as quickly. I wondered if he'd had practice when he was in the hospital for treatment.

How often do I feel down, depressed, or hopeless?

I couldn't remember a time where I'd felt anything else. The form was trying to boil my mind down into a number on a scale, to grade my wellness. I quickly weighed the pros and cons of answering honestly or lying to try to appear normal, and decided the safest bet was to say as little as possible. I wrote *I FEEL NOTHING* across the top and handed it to Dr. Ryan.

Dr. Ryan flipped casually through the papers and smiled when she saw my headline. Not a good sign. After a moment, she slid them into her folder.

"These assessments will help me gauge how you're feeling and guide our time in these sessions, both individually and as a group. You'll fill them out at the start of each of our meetings each day."

Each day. For twenty-nine to fifty-nine days. I'd have to fill out twenty-nine to fifty-nine forms. A lot of opportunities to feel nothing.

Dr. Ryan poised her pen over her legal pad. "Does anyone want to share first?"

Carmen's hand shot into the air.

"You know your participation grade doesn't depend on this, right?" I asked.

"Hattie, I'm counting on you to help make this a safe place," Dr. Ryan said. "Go ahead, Carmen."

Carmen tapped her pen against a notebook page that was filled with indecipherable scribbling. "I've spoken with Jeff and the doctors and statistically, there's only a fifty-three percent chance that we were infected with a large enough sample size of the MTP to create a risk to our nervous system, and that's only if the test vials in the drone were carrying a viable product. I'm in excellent physical condition and have no underlying health problems. Sorry, Albie."

"S'OK," he said, shoulders caving as he hunched forward.

"What I'm trying to say is I don't have time for this quarantine," Carmen continued. "I'm here because it was the recommendation of medical authorities, but I'm not convinced it's totally necessary."

Dr. Ryan nodded. "That's all good to know. Can you tell me how you're feeling about that?"

Carmen ran her tongue along her teeth. "I'm angry."

Neither she nor Albie appeared shocked at how bluntly Carmen stated how she felt.

"Can you say more about that?" Dr. Ryan asked.

"This is a preventable situation. Why is DBD testing biological weapons in civilian spaces? Why weren't there fail-safes in case the test went wrong? Why didn't they shut down Cul du Lac as soon as the drone went down?"

She stopped herself and smoothed her hands down her thighs.

"I'm angry because my grandparents immigrated here from Mexico, and my parents are the first people in their families to go to college," she continued, her voice strained. "I'm one of two openly lesbian students at my school. I work ten hours a week at the yacht club. I'm the fastest runner on the track team, have the top GPA in our class, and am class president. And anyone who thinks I would let a parasite ruin the future my family sacrificed so much to give me is kidding themselves."

Carmen planted her feet wide and leaned forward.

"Thank you for sharing, Carmen," Dr. Ryan said after a moment, when it was clear she was done. "It's an important skill to be able to connect our feelings to our reality. Anger, stress, sadness—every emotion is acceptable, and none are more or less valuable than the others. We're here to acknowledge our feelings, not judge them."

I glanced back to the photo on the wall and started counting the lily pads layered on top of each other like icing in the picture. Thirteen. When I finished, I counted the number of leaves on the trees.

"I have one more thing to say," Carmen said. Dr. Ryan nodded at her to go ahead, and Carmen twisted in her seat and leveled the full intensity of her gaze on me. I was too much of a coward to stare back. "It's your mom's fault we're here. You look just like her. Seeing you makes me the angriest of all."

CHAPTER 9

Dr. Ryan held up a hand. "All feelings are accepted in this space, Carmen, but in group sessions, we've got to retain respectful boundaries of our peers."

"She didn't want this job," I mumbled. Carmen's words sliced into me and the guilt I'd kept so tightly contained spilled into my consciousness. "She had to take it because of me."

Numbers and ideas swirled in my head. *How high was the debt the last time I'd seen it? Was there a way to make money while stuck in the hospital?*

"What was that, Hattie?" Dr. Ryan asked.

I didn't think I could repeat myself without everything else in my head tumbling out, so I just shook my head.

I could feel her eyes on me, but I refused to meet her gaze.

"Alright. Albie? Would you like to go next?" Dr. Ryan asked.

Albie sat up straighter on the couch. "Uh, OK. I'm not really mad about being in the hospital. I've spent a lot of time here, so it feels pretty comfortable."

Dr. Ryan tilted her head. "Why have you spent a lot of time here, Albie?"

Albie exhaled his answer in one long breath. "I was diagnosed with leukemia when I was five. Spent a few years in and out of the hospital doing chemotherapy. I had to drop out of school, and when I came back, they held me back a year and kids made fun of me for being bald—" He stopped himself. "Sorry. That's not what you asked."

I thought of the picture of the boy on the fridge and how happy he looked simply to be surrounded by books, and how small he'd looked in the picture of him in the hospital bed.

"You don't need to be sorry. Feel free to share anything on your mind," Dr. Ryan said.

"Well, I survived. Obviously." That made me chuckle. "My ten-year remission celebration is coming up next month, but to me it's never felt like the cancer went away. It changed everything. My siblings went to China every summer to visit our extended family, and I never got to go because my mom thought I wouldn't be able to handle flying. I had to drop out of marching band because I developed asthma. And by the time I came back to school, my friends had moved on."

"Assholes," Carmen said.

"Except for Carmen," Albie said, glancing over at her. He was so clearly in love with her it made me sick. "So yeah. I guess, I feel like I never stopped being sick, and this isn't that different."

"That's denial, Albie," Carmen interjected. "According to the Kübler-Ross model, there are five stages of grief, right, Dr. Ryan?

Denial, anger, bargaining, depression, and acceptance. You're clearly in denial about being sick."

Albie deflated. "Oh."

Dr. Ryan angled herself toward the two of them. "Carmen, thank you for your thoughts, but in order to make this a safe place for sharing, let's not interrupt Albie when he's speaking."

Carmen raised her eyebrows and leaned back. I unwrapped a lollipop and popped it in my mouth. The artificial sourness blurred the memory of the pictures of Albie I'd filmed at his house.

"Maybe I am in denial," Albie said. His voice was thick and wavery in a way it hadn't been before. "I don't feel any different. My lungs are still weak, and I still have chemo brain sometimes and I thought I'd gone through the worst part of my life already, but I guess I was wrong."

He looked down at his lap, not hiding his tears as they started to fall.

I handed him the box of tissues on the table next to me. "That's so unfair."

He cradled the box on his lap. "I shouldn't have even been down there. I turned off the security cameras in my parent's backyard so I could go down to the lake. My dad told me to get away from the water, and I lied when I came back in and said I was wet from the hot tub."

"It's not your fault," I mumbled.

"Hattie's right," Dr. Ryan said. "None of you are to blame for what's happening to you."

The video on my phone suggested otherwise. It wasn't Albie's fault he'd fallen in; it was mine.

"I'm grateful for your openness, and I hope we can continue to process your experience together," Dr. Ryan said. "Is there anything you'd like to share with the group, Hattie?"

The three of them turned to look at me expectantly. I squeezed the sucker into one corner of my mouth and lasered my line of vision back onto the picture of the marsh, tried to push all the thoughts of credit card bills and debt aside. Time for a show.

"My dad was an acrobat. He was one of those people who know exactly what they want and don't care about anything else except getting it. He decided he wanted to be in the circus when he was ten, and that was that."

Carmen and Albie leaned slightly toward me. I had them.

"He traveled with the Cirque de la Vie. Juggling and tightrope-walking, delighting audiences every night. When I was little, my mom and I traveled with him. I spent every night in the circus tent watching my dad do these impossible things. When you grow up in the tent, a place where everyone flies and knows how to do magic, you start to think you can do impossible things, too. So one night I snuck into the tent after the show and climbed up the tower to walk across the tightrope. There was no net. No one to catch me. I got scared halfway across and froze, had to call for my dad. He came running, but it was too late. I fell. Broke my leg. It was a whole *thing*."

Dr. Ryan didn't take any notes or react to my story at all. Nerves took root in my stomach, and I coughed to try to shake them loose.

"When we were sitting in the hospital, I asked my dad how he did it, how he was unafraid of falling, and he said, 'I don't look down. I don't look up. I don't look to see who's watching or who's following behind. I only look at the step in front of me. I only need the courage for a single step.'" I wiped my eyes for good measure. "Anyways, he died in a motorcycle accident when I was eleven, and we stopped traveling with the circus after that. I've never been able to find that one-step courage, and now I'm thinking maybe his advice was worthless because there's only one step left and I'm still terrified."

It was silent for a moment and then Carmen said, "Wow."

Albie handed the box of tissues back to me. "That was beautiful."

I fiddled with the sucker in my mouth. Dr. Ryan stared at me until I had no choice but to look back. "I appreciate you sharing, Hattie. Truly. But I've seen your files. Your mother gave me permission to access them. Was any of what you just shared true?"

Carmen's and Albie's eyes darted between the two of us.

I took the lollipop out of my mouth with a pop. "I broke my leg when I was a kid."

Dr. Ryan kept staring. Her eyes were so big and kind, I would have said anything to get away from them.

"OK, fine. I've never been to the circus, and I'm bitter about it. You caught me."

Albie and Carmen shared a look.

Dr. Ryan clasped her hands together calmly, as if she had all the time in the world. "Jeff told me you've refused to see your mom. Why is that?"

Because I only make everything worse.

Dr. Ryan had said it with that air of permanency—you've refused to see your mom—and I realized I might never see my mom again. I took one shallow breath, then another. My vision blurred until I couldn't make out the lily pads.

Carmen tentatively raised her hand. "I have a question. What's with the lollipops?"

"I like bubble gum wrapped in sugar."

Dr. Ryan sighed. I was disappointing her like I'd disappointed everyone since entering puberty. At least I was consistent! "Do you want to say something real, Hattie?"

"I don't have anything to say."

"I doubt that's true."

I bit into the sucker hard enough to make it crack. When I spoke, my voice was cold. "It doesn't matter if I have something *real* to say or if I lie or how we deal with this situation. It doesn't matter because we're *dying*. Nothing matters. Nothing counts. It's over."

Dr. Ryan's expression didn't change. "It seems like you did have something to say, after all."

Gross. Was this how therapy worked? You felt terrible and then you shared and felt more terrible but also lighter? Like you'd just kicked up a dusty tornado in the attic of your own mind?

Dr. Ryan didn't push me to say more, though. "OK, before we finish for the day, I want you to think about what you want the most out of your time here."

She handed us another form. It was filled with even worse questions than the first one. *What do you hope to achieve through therapy? What do you want to accomplish by the end of our next session?*

Albie and Carmen put their forms on the table after just a few minutes. Albie's was nearly blank—only a few words scribbled across the empty space. Carmen's was covered in a neat bulleted list. I saw something about a boat, a break, water. I wished I could film the papers, make the tragedy into art.

"Time's up for today, Hattie. You're welcome to take the sheet back to your room if you need more time," Dr. Ryan said.

I couldn't think of a good lie, so I wrote down the truth that had been crawling around the basement of my mind since I'd stepped through the anteroom doors, a truth I had been too scared to admit to myself:

I want to get out of here.

CHAPTER 10

Once the session was over, I went back to my room and threw myself down on the bed.

I took a video of the pile of worksheets Dr. Ryan had handed out as "supplementary" work before our next session and posted it on social. I captioned the post **Therapy is more work than actual high school**. Then I tried to doomscroll my way out of the black hole spinning open in my chest. It didn't work.

I'd meant what I said about nothing mattering. It didn't. But the therapy had made me realize something: I wouldn't be able to rest until I'd handled Mom's debt.

I'd gone through her mail the month before (shout-out to me for casually committing a federal crime!) and tallied up the total. It was close to $23,000 and the interest grew daily. The kind of money I could never repay under normal circumstances.

And I wasn't even living in normal circumstances anymore.

What to say about the debt . . .

Let's just say the toxoplasma wasn't my first encounter with a parasite. I'm talking about my father, obviously, who was neither a circus performer nor dead. Just your classic story of a deadbeat dad and a naïve daughter who now owed her mom $23,000.

I didn't want to die owing anyone anything, much less my mom.

Old plan: Netflix and chill until the parasite ate me alive.

New plan: Figure out a way to make $23,000. How hard could it be? Old white guys made money every day. *Then* I could Netflix and chill until the parasite ate me alive.

When one is a teenager locked away in hospital quarantine with no practical life skills, the key to making money is the same as when one is a teenager living at home with no life skills: the internet. I'd been called a bad influence by most adults who'd interacted with me since I turned thirteen. I might as well lean into the label and become an actual influencer.

Slight problem: I had no followers and the artistically exquisite videos I'd posted so far had gotten me nowhere. Which meant it was time to sell out and make whatever videos it took to appeal to the masses.

After five minutes of sweet-talking Jeff into the idea that I absolutely *had* to visit the hospital gift store so I could buy a present for my mom, he'd agreed that I could go as long as Andres, the DBD guy who'd been stationed at the door to the wing as a "guard," came with. The moral of the story is: Never underestimate the power of someone having a crush on your mom.

I thumbed the smartphone in my hoodie pocket on the elevator ride down to the first floor. All I needed to do was find something magical to film, gain a bunch of followers, and then monetize that following. In thirty to sixty days. How hard could it be?

The hospital gift shop was on the ground floor tucked across the hall from the cafeteria.

"Fifteen minutes," Andres said, barely looking up from his phone. The other moral of the story is: Never underestimate a man's commitment to Wordle.

I walked backward into the store, keeping an eye on Andres as he wandered over to a coffee cart nestled just inside the cafeteria. I turned to examine a shelf heaped with books and baubles and collided with something warm and solid.

"Ow!" The body attached to the boyish voice smelled like tea-tree mint and dryer sheets.

"Albie?" He was pressed against the shelf with his arms clutched around a book and his eyes closed. "What are you doing?"

This close up, I could see that his lashes were long and thick, and he had sharp cheekbones that Tim Burton would have admired. I twisted to face him, my hip bumping his.

"Why are you power napping in the gift shop?"

He opened his eyes. "Hattie?"

I leaned closer, refusing to be the one who backed down first. "How did you get down here?"

"Uh, are we not allowed? I had a break before my doctor's appointment, and I wanted to get down here before my parents visit."

"Seriously? They just let you go? I had to sweet-talk Jeff to get down here."

"Well, there wasn't anyone at the door, and people don't usually notice me." He was still pressed against the shelf, my hips angled against his. He finally got his bearings enough to wriggle away. I stepped back, not wanting to make him uncomfortable.

"Good to know," I said, trying to sound like the Very Cool Girl I absolutely was not.

He smelled good, and he was right in front of me. I took out my phone and held it up like a shield between us as I started filming the store.

Albie looked at my smartphone. "Where did you get that?"

"The phone store."

"They took our phones. How do you still have that?"

"Don't ask so many questions."

Albie's brow furrowed. "Are you recording?"

"That's a question. But yes."

"Why?"

I framed Albie in the shot. "I'm making a documentary," I lied.

"About what?"

"The human experience." That's what all art was about at the end of the day anyway, so it was kind of the truth. I pointed at the book in his hand. "What'd you get?"

"Oh, uh, nothing. It's stupid."

I wrapped my fingers around his wrist and lifted his hand up so I could read the cover. "*You Have the Right to Remain Afraid.*" I dropped his wrist. "Very emo title."

"It's just a poetry book. By Elliot Why?"

I shook my head. I didn't read poetry unless forced to for class, and even then, most teachers didn't notice if I skipped the reading. The open, expansive emotions of poetry gave me that itching, burning sensation in my gut.

"He's this kind of reclusive social media influencer," Albie said. "And, I don't know . . . It's silly, but I just think his poems are really beautiful."

"That's not silly," I said. "The world is ugly. When we see something beautiful, we have to hold on to it to remind ourselves that ugly isn't all that exists."

I wanted to swallow the words as soon as they left my mouth. Albie's eyes widened in surprise.

"Wow. Yeah, I hadn't thought about it like that, but you're right." Albie tucked a lock of thick black hair behind his ear. "Feelings. Do you have them? I mean. How . . . are . . . they?"

"About the parasite?" I framed my shot to capture the aisle lined with spinning racks of cards, buckets of refrigerated flowers, stuffed animals, candy, smiling balloons. That was the best humans could do in terms of feelings.

"Honestly?" I asked.

"Why not?"

Why not? Because I'd always assumed I'd die young, but not like *this*. It was supposed to be in a bank heist or tragic accident on the set of my groundbreaking indie film at some point in the future when I'd managed to transform myself into someone interesting and paid my mother back. Not from sneaking into other people's houses. Not in *Florida*. Why not? Because there's not much difference between a truth and a lie; they're both stories we tell ourselves to make life more bearable.

I lowered my phone and told Albie the story I could bear right now. "It's everything at once." I got a close-up shot of a sad-looking teddy bear. "How about you?"

He flipped through the pages of the thin book in his hand. "Yesterday, I thought I was OK, but today I'm devastated," he said simply. "I hate being back here. Everyone was always so kind to me but the lights, the smell, the food. I hate it. That's why I wanted to come down here. When I came to Memorial before, I never got to go anywhere but the third floor."

What could I say to that? I was a troubled teen with cliché daddy issues and a bad attitude. Albie was a cancer survivor. He'd already fought for his life. It was so unfair of the universe to make him fight for it again. I doubted that's what he wanted to hear, though.

"I'm sorry."

Albie shrugged. "It's not your fault." Albie reached into one pocket, then the other. "Shoot. I forgot my wallet." He looked down at the poetry book. "I'll just have my parents bring it to me later."

I snatched the book out of his hand before he could put it back. I wasn't good at words or feelings or sports or any kind of extracurricular activity, but this was one problem I knew exactly how to solve.

CHAPTER 11

I GRABBED ALBIE'S HAND AND PULLED HIM TO A DUSTY BACK CORner of the gift shop where they'd shelved out-of-season holiday goods. Sad Santas, dingy Easter baskets, and scratched New Year's glasses. It was far enough from the register that no one could see what we were doing. I started recording again as we were walking. With a little direction, Albie might be the perfect subject.

Albie stopped in front of a perverted-looking Santa Claus doll. I reached for his belt.

"Ah!" He shrieked and slapped my hand away like a Renaissance maiden trying to fight off a virtue-stealing knight.

"Relax." I handed him the poetry book, holding my phone steady in my other hand. "We'll tuck this in your waistband and walk out like normal."

"*What*? But that's . . ."

"Stealing."

"And stealing is illegal!"

"Definitely."

"And you're recording!"

"Sure am."

"And we're in a hospital, which is basically church."

"False." I stepped closer and curled a finger through his belt loop. "Besides, the rules no longer apply to us. Did you know when people climb Mount Everest, they step over the people who have fallen on the trail and are dying because if they slow down, they'll die, too. It's called Exit Ethics. Look it up."

I hoped he didn't. The Everest thing was kind of true, but I'd made up the term on the spot.

I watched him on the phone screen. His eyes darted to the checkout counter and then to the frosted glass windows to the cafeteria full of nurses and doctors and worried families.

"Why can't you do it? You seem, uh, familiar with this activity?"

Shoplifting had never really been my thing, but I didn't bother correcting him. Other people's assumptions about me—slut, thief, waste of space—were the strongest kind of armor.

"I don't have anywhere to hide it."

Albie's eyes trailed from my crop top down to my stomach for a moment before he jerked his chin back up to my face.

I raised an eyebrow. "Do you really want to go back to the isolation ward without the words of Elliot Why to guide you?"

"You're really good at rationalizing," he said.

"It's one of my top five skills."

He leaned his head back against the shelf and said, "I can't believe I'm doing this."

I couldn't either, but I wasn't about to let him know that.

"May I?"

When he nodded, I put my phone down on the shelf for a moment as I lifted up his shirt and slid the book into his pants so it was wedged into his waistband, resting against his stomach. Albie looked pointedly away while I pulled his shirt down and smoothed it over his skin. I could feel a surprising amount of muscle through the soft fabric.

"Now what?" he asked.

I grabbed my phone and started recording again, relieved to put something between us. "Now we leave."

I'd planned on leading the way, but Albie shouldered past me, walking with a slight waddle directly across the store and in front of the register. I shadowed behind him. He paused in front of the cashier.

"You need anything?" she asked, barely looking up from the magazine she was reading.

"If I die young," Albie said seriously, "I'm donating my savings to this gift shop."

She turned the page. "Good for you."

Albie stared at her, his stomach poking out slightly above his pants.

"Don't ruin it," I said, grabbing his arm and propelling him out the door and around the corner.

"I can't believe I did that," Albie said, dazed.

"Me either."

"You told me to!"

"Yeah, but I didn't think you would."

"That's fair." He looked lost in the hustling hive of people moving through the hallway. "I should get back."

"See you up there."

He ambled off, placing his hand protectively on his stomach until he'd gotten to the elevators. I missed him when the elevator doors closed, which didn't make any sense because I didn't know him.

I checked my phone and saw I still had five minutes before babysitter Andres would return. I shot some B-roll of the entrance to the gift store, the deflating balloons in the window, and the feet of people walking by. Everything moving at hospital speed: fast and slow, fast and slow. My fingers buzzed as I flipped through the shots, settling on one of Albie tilting his head at the camera. There was something there.

I found Andres two minutes early and rushed us toward the elevator bank. Once on the DBD wing, I power walked through the common area and straight to my room to stitch together the video of Albie. I intercut between the B-roll of gift store aisles and location-establishing shots and his swooping hair, the mole on his right jaw, the flash of his teeth when he gave me a small smile. Added some sound effects and overly dramatic background music.

I captioned the video **Baby's first shoplifting** then posted it before I could overthink it. In the comments I left a bunch of hashtags, like I'd seen other influencers do to help get attention. I put the phone under my pillow to distract myself from it but pulled it back out immediately. I refreshed the page. No comments or views. Refreshed again. Still nothing. I searched Elliot Why's page and found a video of a poem that was just the word *pain* flashing across the screen in different fonts. No thank you. I went back to my video and watched it over and over. The only views were my own.

But I knew this video was special. *Albie* was special. That had to count for something.

••••

I woke up with my phone still clutched in my hand. Through blurry eyes, I opened the page with the video and refreshed.

I blinked. Rubbed my eyes. Refreshed again.

I had 2,000 followers and the video had been viewed 8,000 times. I wasn't the only one who found Albie impossible to look away from.

CHAPTER 12

I CURLED FORWARD, HUNCHING MY BODY INTO A PRETZEL. WHOEVER invented yoga had a sick, twisted mind.

"Breathe into the pose."

It was Wednesday afternoon and Jeff had commandeered the rec room for a mandatory yoga class. He'd finally ditched the DBD windbreaker, but he'd replaced it with a DBD T-shirt and extremely short shorts.

"*Don't know if your mom mentioned, but I'm a bit of a yogi,*" he'd said as I wandered in.

"*My mom never mentioned you at all,*" I'd replied and Jeff's normally blooming red face had faded to a pale pink color. Sometimes the truth was just as bad as a lie.

The couch and chairs where we'd had therapy had been pushed back against the wall to make room for our thin yoga mats. The air in the room was cold and dry, the walls pulsing and sagging from the threat of a hundred hurricanes. Carmen set up her mat directly in front of Jeff and followed him through the poses with the jerky force of an MMA fighter.

Albie and I rolled around next to each other a bit farther back. I wouldn't have come to the stupid class at all if it weren't for Albie. I needed more videos of him in action to know if the first one was a fluke. It shouldn't have been possible for anyone to be worse at yoga than me, but somehow Albie had managed.

"Psst! Albie!" I could see him upside down between my legs. I peeked my smartphone out of my bra and recorded him transitioning into Warrior II. He wobbled back and forth on one foot, his face purpling with exertion until Jeff transitioned us into Tree Pose.

I crammed the phone back into my sports bra before Jeff saw it. I was still a compulsive liar with a parasite crawling through my veins and $23,000 hanging over my head, but with Albie I saw a glimmer of hope.

The video of him shoplifting the book had rocketed to more than 30,000 views overnight. People in the comments had started calling Albie the Snack Attack—which I didn't totally understand; something about him being attractive and also safe during daylight hours. Look, I didn't make the rules.

There had to be money in that somehow. The only problem was figuring out how to make videos of Albie a) without him knowing what they were for, b) while we were stuck in a hospital with nothing to do, and c) when I wasn't supposed to have a smartphone.

Carmen picked a fight with Jeff about his transition instructions while Albie and I cat-cowed. The picture of the lily pads chasing the still water toward the sunset greeted me every time I lifted my head.

Albie glanced between me and the front of the room and then shuffled his mat closer so we were cat-cowing shoulder to shoulder.

I bit back a smile and arched my back.

"I, uh, need to talk to you about something," Albie whispered.

"OK." I kept my eyes straight ahead, curving my back around the lightness in my stomach.

Albie closed his eyes, leaned into the pose, and said in one sharp exhale, "I think we should escape."

I fell out of the Cow Pose. He couldn't have surprised me more if he told me Carmen had once gotten a B on a pop quiz.

"Why aren't you saying anything?" Albie asked as we transitioned to Downward-Facing Dog.

"I'm trying to think of a way to tell you how stupid that idea is without being mean."

Albie twisted his head over his shoulder. "You don't want to stay here."

I pressed my heels toward the floor. I wished I had a lollipop. "We can't leave."

"Why not?"

All the blood was rushing to my head and making it difficult to argue. "Because."

"Exit Ethics, Hattie." The way he said my name was so tender it drew my eyes to his. "We only have twenty-eight to fifty-eight days left. I don't want to waste them in a hospital."

We slid to the floor and crossed our legs.

"Place your hand over your heart," Jeff said. Sweat was dripping from his face. "Breathe into this moment."

"*If* we were to leave, which I'm not saying I want to do—" I started.

Albie's eyes lit up with excitement. "You definitely do."

"How would we get out? You're good at being invisible, but I'm not." Albie chewed his lip. I'd thought it was an obvious observation. "That was mean, wasn't it?"

"Uh. Kind of."

"Sorry."

Albie clasped his hands over his heart and breathed deep enough to lift his shoulders to his ears. "We'll figure it out."

Figuring it out consisted of Albie pulling me aside after yoga and having me spend the rest of the afternoon casing the ward. I didn't actually want to escape, OK? I just needed to get videos of him being his Snack Attack self that I could somehow monetize.

The windows in our room were sealed shut. The air vents were accessible, but we didn't have a map to know where they led. (And escaping through air vents was way too cliché to tempt me. Also, gross.) The only exit was through the anteroom at the front or a locked door at the back.

So Albie and I grabbed candy and coffee from the vending machine and settled into the tables in front of the nurse's station to observe. Two nurses worked the desk during the day, one at night. Their desks were positioned so their backs were to our rooms. The doctors only came in during the day. And then there was Jeff and Andres, who were here to keep us in, not keep other people out.

"Could you fake a medical emergency?" I took a sip of the bitter hospital coffee.

Albie made a face. "That would only get me sent to the ICU. It wouldn't help you and Carmen."

"Carmen?"

"Exit Ethics means you don't leave a teammate behind," Albie said.

"That's actually exactly what it means."

Albie spun a plastic stirrer through his coffee, creating a mini hurricane. "She didn't leave me when I was in the hospital. I'm not going to leave her."

I gulped down some more coffee. Making Albie a social media sensation without him knowing would be difficult. Making him a sensation without Carmen knowing would be near impossible.

The anteroom door swooshed open, and Mr. and Mrs. Chang and Albie's brother, James, stepped out.

"Later," I said.

"Rec room?" Albie whispered. "After dinner?"

I retreated to my bedroom, but I heard Carmen's parents shuffle in a few minutes later. I knew it was them because of the squeak of her dad's sneakers, the way her mom burst into tears the minute she saw Carmen, and because they both yelled "SURPRISE!"

"It's Jilly," her dad said after a heavy silence. They must have surprised Carmen by bringing her girlfriend for a visit.

"Hey, you," Carmen said.

Outside my door was a symphony of family chatter and clattering silverware. I ignored my growling stomach and stayed in my room, too ashamed to eat alone or succumb to the pity of either of their parents and eat with Carmen or Albie. Instead, I sliced together the videos of Albie doing yoga. He was wearing loose sweats and a tank that showed off his lean, sculpted arms.

I captioned the video **It was the downward dog for me**.

A short eternity later, Carmen's and Albie's families paraded out of the ward. A few minutes after that, I heard a quick knock on my door. Albie poked his head in a moment later.

"What are you doing in here?" he asked.

"Making a gratitude list. Number one is that I'm an only child and people don't just randomly burst into my room," I deadpanned.

"Do you ever give a straight answer?" he asked.

"I'm a compulsive liar. A doctor said it and everything," I blurted out. There. That should get him to leave me alone.

Albie tilted his head. "Wouldn't a compulsive liar lie about being a compulsive liar?"

"Probably."

He considered this for a moment before marching up to my bed and wrestling my phone free of my hand. "C'mon. Carmen's waiting for us."

"Hey!" I rolled out of the creaky hospital bed and padded after him. He waved to the nurses at the station before ducking into the rec room. The lights were off, and Carmen was curled up in one of the chairs with her notebook open and pen poised.

Albie gestured for me to sit on the couch. He handed me a plate with tidy portions of salad, broccoli, and congealing macaroni and cheese. "I saved you some dinner."

"I'm not—" My stomach interrupted the lie with a gurgle. "Thanks."

Albie stood, the lights from the hallway casting a silhouetted shadow from his toes across the floor. "So," he said. "When are we escaping?"

Carmen didn't react.

"*We* are not doing anything," I said.

"We can't stay here," Albie said.

I scoffed. "Carmen won't leave unless student council is in danger of a mutiny."

Carmen looked up from her notebook. "You're rude."

I picked up the fork on my plate.

Albie stepped between us. "What Carmen means to say, Hattie, is that your dark humor and fuck-you vibe don't scare us."

I froze with the fork halfway to my mouth. "I can't believe you said the word *fuck*."

"I can't believe you made me cry about your nonexistent acrobat dad. The world is full of surprises," Albie said. The boy was quick. "So how are we going to escape?"

I looked over to Carmen. "Why are you going along with this?"

She gave off unmistakable teacher's pet, suck-up-to-adults, never-broken-a-rule-in-my-life vibes. The only reason I could imagine for her even entertaining this conversation was so that she could report it back to Jeff.

"I'd do anything for Albie," she said, as if it was the simplest thing in the world.

He had that effect on people, I guess. I thought of the numbers climbing on my phone. My burner account already had 5,000 followers. The commenters were engaging in vigorous debates about Snack Attack's best and most attractive character traits. I'd done some research while I listened to Albie and Carmen spend time with people who loved them. If I got 10,000 followers, I could connect my account to Catch a Dream, a social media platform that would allow me to raise money as an influencer.

"I won't be a burden—" Albie said.

"OK, I'm in."

"I think I can be a big help for the—oh. Really?"

"On one condition," I said.

"Anything."

"You have to let me record you for the documentary." I didn't know how Albie would feel about me splashing his awkward adorableness on the internet, so I left that part out. If I didn't ask, he couldn't say no. "And Carmen has to be nice to me."

"That's two conditions," Albie said.

Carmen made a face. "I don't like you."

"Do you want to help Albie or not?" I asked.

She threw her head back. "Ugh. Fine. But only until we break the two of you out. Then I'm coming back so I can prep for treatment and go back to disliking you."

"Fair enough," I said.

Carmen set her notebook down on the table, revealing a cramped scattering of diagrams and lists.

"Good," she said. "Because I have a plan."

OPERATION CONSTITUTIONAL RIGHTS (CARMEN SAID OPERATION Escape was too obvious) began the next evening after the parents went home after dinner and there was only one nurse on duty.

Phase 1: Putting the good in goodbye

I packed a bag with the essentials: suckers, headphones, phone charger, a change of clothes, the bag of coins I'd been holding on to since middle school, more suckers.

While Carmen and Albie said goodbye to their parents, I said goodbye to mine.

Dear Mom.

Mother.

Dr.

I scribbled out a dozen options before settling on:

I'm going to make it up to you. I'm sorry. Love, H

Phase 2: Slumber party montage

Carmen clasped her fingers together the way politicians do at stump rallies and stared Jeff down. "Dr. Ryan and I agree that it would be beneficial for the three of us to spend quality time together in a non-medical setting. We're experiencing the stages of grief together, and we need to deeply bond in order to move efficiently through those stages and respond positively to treatment."

Albie and I stood behind her at either shoulder.

"I don't understand anything she's saying," Albie whispered. He was close enough that I could feel his breath on my neck.

"She's good," I said begrudgingly. It figured that Perfect Carmen, the girl who was good at everything, would also be better at lying than me.

Jeff hugged his clipboard to his heart. "I'm not sure that's a good idea."

"It's the doctor's recommendation," Carmen insisted. "Call her and check if you want."

This was what we in the business like to call a Bold-Faced Lie. Aka: If Jeff called Carmen's bluff and contacted Dr. Ryan, he'd quickly learn we were making this whole thing up. Jeff cleared his throat and looked between the three of us. "I don't know . . ."

"It's what my mom would want," I said. Carmen glared at me over her shoulder. I ignored her and looked pleadingly at Jeff. "*Please*."

Jeff fingered the DBD logo stitched across the chest of his polo. "Fine. I'll just have to let headquarters know. But I'm on overnight duty, so no funny business or whatever you kids call it these days."

"We're not going to have sex if that's what—" I started.

"We really appreciate your respect of our treatment program," Carmen interrupted. "We promise to be on our best behavior."

Carmen turned on her heel and we followed her. She was an authoritarian control freak, but she got what she wanted.

The three of us set up shop in Carmen's room because it was closest to the exit. The nurse helped wheel the hospital beds out of mine and Albie's rooms and sandwiched them around Carmen's.

Then we got to work. I pulled out the dumb phone Jeff had given me. I'd never bothered turning it on. When I did, a string of texts poured in from my mom. The last message started: *Nothing you could do—*

I didn't read any further.

"You're sure about this?" I asked Albie. "We don't know what DBD will do when they find out we've gone."

"I don't want to die in a hospital," Albie said.

"And you?" I asked Carmen.

"I'm in if Albie's still in. Besides, I need to run an errand," she said. "Then I'll be back. What about you? You're sure?"

I crossed my arms over my chest. "I've never been sure of anything."

Albie produced a multi-pronged connecting cord and plugged in the dumb phone to a portable speaker his parents had brought with them. We placed the setup in the middle of the room and tested it a few times.

Once we confirmed the technological piece, Carmen put on loud rock music on her laptop and shot me a look as if I would be impressed with her edginess. Sad but true.

The three of us changed into the DBD gear Jeff had left in our rooms on the first day. Albie looked pointedly away while I pulled on a navy sweatshirt with *DBD* emblazoned in big, sticky letters across the chest. I took a video of him staring out the window, then slapping a hand over his eyes when he realized he could see Carmen changing in the reflection. Getting footage of Albie in the outside world was going to be very good for business.

Phase 3: Waiting

Albie perched on the edge of Carmen's bed. His eyes glazed over as he took in her things. The sports bra strewn casually on the chair, the box of tampons poking out from her suitcase. For a person giving off strong control-y Virgo vibes, Carmen's room was a mess.

Carmen stuffed her notebook, a toothbrush, and some clothes into a backpack.

I watched her from the chair by the window. "You're packing a lot for someone who's coming back tonight."

"Do I strike you as someone who underprepares?" she asked. "Did you get everything, Albie?"

Albie robotically ticked through the items in his backpack. "Inhaler. Refills. First aid kit. Hydration pills."

Nerves took root in my stomach. Should we be doing this? Albie was—as his dad liked to remind us every few minutes—immunocompromised. The MTP wasn't supposed to start affecting us for a few more days, but once it did, who would take care of him?

Albie must have sensed my concern. "I'll be fine," he said.

Carmen zipped her bag shut and crossed the room to look out the window set in the door. We'd positioned the beds so they were only visible if you stepped right up to the door.

"We need to make our move early enough that your mom could feasibly need something from the lab and late enough that they won't discover you're missing until morning," Carmen said.

Albie and I had come up with the idea to escape. OK, mostly Albie, but still. It was *our* thing. I didn't buy that Carmen was helping because of her deep, platonic love for Albie. The only thing that brought Carmen joy was adult approval. There must be something on the outside that really needed doing.

"What are you staring at?" Carmen asked.

"The complex inner workings of the teenage mind," I said.

Phase 4: More waiting. But at least we got snacks.

Albie and I held a bag of chips open between us and ate them while watching Carmen watch the door. Occasionally Carmen would look back, and she and Albie would do that thing friends do where they have a conversation without saying a word.

"You two are close, huh?" I asked.

He crunched a chip into his mouth. "Most of my friends forgot about me when I started chemo. It's not their fault. Second graders aren't supposed to understand what death means. But Carmen stayed. She visited me three times a week, and when I got held back after returning to school, she kept sitting with me at lunch even though the other kids made fun of her for it."

"She's a good friend," I said.

"She's here," he said.

Phase 5: The call

At 10:15, Carmen gave the signal to initiate phase 5. The signal was her making a hand gesture at me that I didn't understand, followed by her saying, "Just do it already!"

I stepped into Carmen's bathroom. Albie followed and shut the door to muffle the sound of the music playing. I dialed Jeff's number on my secret smartphone. Carmen had already gotten his phone number because she was the kind of person who had a lot of adults' phone numbers "just in case."

We hushed when we heard his phone ringing just outside.

"Hello?" his voice asked through the phone.

"Jeff? Is that you?" I put on my best flirtatious voice and twirled a lock of purple hair. "Your voice sounds so much deeper over the phone."

"Sorry, who is this?"

"It's Lauren. Don't you recognize my voice?" Albie fake-gagged. I waved him away. "Listen, the reason I'm calling is, I'm having trouble with my ID badge. I can never handle these pesky tech problems when you're not here. Do you think you could run down to the lab and let me in? I'm sorry to ask; I just didn't know who else to call."

"I'll be right over," Jeff said. I heard him shuffling on the phone as he hurried to leave.

"I'll see you soon," I said.

I'd done a lot of terrible things to my mother, but opening the door to Jeff's advances was probably the worst. It would be worth it, though, to pay off the debt. It had to be.

Albie and I tiptoed out of the bathroom and watched Carmen slowly creak the bedroom door open and look both ways. The nurse at the station was facing the other way. The doctors were off for the night. It was just us.

"We're clear," she said.

Phase 6: The escape

Carmen said it was fine to call phase 6 "The escape" as long as we didn't discuss it in front of any non-team members, aka adults. This led to a long discussion about just how dumb she thought I was, which ended with Albie forbidding us from speaking to each other for five minutes even though Carmen was the only one who had made promises to be nice, and I owed her nothing.

We grabbed our bags. Carmen held the door open and kept her eyes on the nurse's station while waving Albie and I out of the room. This was the riskiest part of the plan. If the nurse heard the swooshing sound of the anteroom door opening, we were doomed. Hence, the loud music blasting from Carmen's room.

Albie looked back at me. We weren't good enough friends for me to speak to him with my eyes, so I put both middle fingers up and mouthed *Exit Ethics*. He twisted the handle on the anteroom door and pulled it open. The three of us dashed into the small chamber and pulled the door shut behind us.

We froze for a moment before Carmen regained her composure and opened the door on the opposite side. "We need to keep moving."

We shuffled into the hall and waited for the elevator. Doctors in mint scrubs wheeled a man past in a gurney. I pulled out my phone and started recording the conflicting emotions warring across Albie's face.

Albie stepped back. "This was a terrible idea."

Carmen pushed him through the elevator doors when they opened. "No, it wasn't. My plan's foolproof. Hattie, aren't you supposed to be calling the room?"

I rolled my eyes, pulled out my phone, and made the call. My job was to dial the dumb phone we'd left in our room with my smartphone and try to hear if the nurse was coming. Carmen's job was to be lookout. Albie's job was not to have an asthma attack.

My mind spiraled as the elevator descended. Once we got out of the lobby, we wouldn't be the MTP kids anymore. There would be no therapy or prepared meals or external evidence that something was happening in our bodies.

The doors dinged and slid open to the lobby. Carmen stepped out first, standing up straight and puffing up the DBD on her chest. I couldn't let her look more badass than me, so I followed, grabbing the strap of Albie's backpack to make sure he stayed with us.

We marched through the quiet tangle of adults in the lobby. None of the nurses or security guards gave us a second look.

Past the parking payment machines and the check-in desks. Past the army of waiting chairs and pacing people. Past the first set of sliding doors and into a silent glass box. To the very edge of the hospital.

"I don't think I can," Albie said.

I recorded him with one hand and used the other to yank him outside into freedom.

CHAPTER 14

Phase 7: There was no phase 7.

The air was thick and heavy with the smell of rain, the sky streaked with the damp purple colors of night.

The three of us stood outside the front doors, relishing the feeling of freedom for about five seconds before a large family rushed for the entrance, babbling something about Aunt Susan's kidneys and jostling us out of the way.

Albie surveyed the parking lot like a battlefield. "I can't believe that worked."

"Of course it worked. I made the plan." Carmen fidgeted with her phone. She looked around like she was expecting to see somebody besides Albie and me waiting for her. "What's next?"

Albie and I had never talked about what would happen once we got past the sliding hospital doors, but I couldn't say that to Carmen. She looked more scared in that parking lot than she had when Jeff showed us the picture of the MTP and said it was eating us alive. If I didn't act fast, she'd head straight back to the isolation ward, and Albie would follow her because he wouldn't know what else to do.

I couldn't let that happen. Albie had a megawatt smile and killer hair and was kind to everyone. The video of him in the gift shop had almost 100,000 views already.

"This way," I said and marched away so confidently I hoped they would assume it was a well-thought-out strategy. I skirted the edge of the main hospital building, heading toward the mud-drenched stench of the marsh.

Albie jogged to catch up. "Where are we going?"

I couldn't hide the smile that flashed across my face. He'd followed me. "You'll see."

"She doesn't have a plan, Albie," Carmen said, catching up to me in just a few long strides. "You should just go home. Your parents will be so worried."

"We literally just stepped outside. Chill," I said.

Carmen fell into step beside me. I had to take two huge steps for every one of her graceful strides. She stayed Velcroed to me as we crossed through the parking lot and across the thin paved path that separated the hospital from the bog that gave Marsh Rock its name.

I turned left and followed the path toward the row of docks floating in front of the kitschy downtown area. I didn't know what to do or where to go, but I knew several things to be true:

- I needed to pay off the $23,000 my mom owed because I'd been weak enough to be conned by my father.

- I needed videos of Albie to raise said $23,000 on Catch a Dream.

- And the hardest fact to face: I needed to convince Carmen to come along for the ride because Albie wouldn't leave her behind.

I knew only a few things about Carmen. She had a hot girlfriend. She ran very fast. She thought she was always right (which was especially annoying because she usually was). She'd mentioned working at the local yacht club, and I'd seen her write something about a boat on the dream worksheet Dr. Ryan made us fill out.

A sleeping army of boats rocked back and forth gently against the docks, their shining white exteriors glowing orange in the street-lights. I stepped onto the swaying dock and surveyed the boats. Which one looked like it had an owner dumb enough to leave a set of keys inside?

Carmen shouldered in front of me. "What are you doing?"

"Finding our ride," I said.

"Uh . . ." Albie started, staring out at the boats in wonder.

"That's *stealing*," Carmen hissed.

Stealing was exactly what I planned on doing, but I took offense that she would assume it was the only option available to me.

I nudged past her. "My family has a boat out here somewhere. It belongs to my grandparents. You shouldn't make assumptions."

"Sorry. I didn't know." She glanced back at the hospital. It looked like a perfectly symmetrical jack-o'-lantern, each boxed window glowing with artificial light. Was she already thinking about leaving?

I ticked down the boats tethered to the dock. Sailboat. Sailboat. Bigger sailboat. Ugly sailboat. There had to be a drivable option.

I stopped in front of a sleek boat with wood paneling and an engine almost as tall as me. *Seas the Day* was painted on the side in bold curling letters. I was willing to look past the punny name only because I could see a set of keys dangling from the ignition.

"Here she is," I said, caressing the side of the boat in a way I hoped projected intergenerational wealth. "Grandpa's pride and joy."

Albie shoved his hands into the pocket of his DBD hoodie. "Uh. I haven't been on a boat before."

"It's like learning to drive. You get your learner's permit, get into two non-fatal accidents, and then everything's fine," I said. I hoisted myself over the side of the boat, stumbling a bit when the waves rocked me to the side.

"I'm pretty sure that's not how driving works," Albie said.

"You're going to love it." I offered him a hand, hoping that would be enough.

"I don't know how to swim," he said.

"Don't worry, I'm a strong enough swimmer for the both of us. I won't let anything happen to you."

Albie turned away. "Carmen? Are you coming?"

Carmen dragged her hand along the side of *Seas the Day*, examining the bulking boat. "I just came to help you get out."

She was organized and responsible and knew something about everything. All very annoying qualities, but as I listed them, I had to admit, they'd be very useful for a water escape.

"Bullshit," I said.

"Excuse me?" Carmen asked.

"You didn't leave because of Albie. There's something you said you needed to do, but instead of gutting up and just doing it, you're using him as a crutch."

Carmen's nose twitched. "You don't know me."

I planted my feet and rested my hands on the side of the boat. Mom had told me that power posing helped project confidence. "Listen, I know you don't want to go back to that ward. I know there's something you need to do before the MTP gets to your head. And I know you work at the yacht club."

"I wait tables there," Carmen said.

"Exactly," I said, forging ahead even though I'd been picturing her doing something more useful for sailing purposes. "But you had a dream about sailing, right?"

Carmen scoffed. But she didn't walk away. "I dream about traveling on a yacht. I'm sick of watching them from the windows without ever having been on a real boat myself."

"Well, my grandparents call this boat the yacht of their heart," I said.

"This may be our only chance," Albie said before he clambered onto the boat. "We've never done anything, Carmen, and now—" His voice wobbled. "We may never get the chance after this. So we have to make it count. It's called Exit Ethics."

"That's not a thing." Carmen looked back at the hospital, her phone, the boat. We almost had her. "But Dr. Ryan did say I should honor my desires for experience."

I stretched out my hand again and asked, "Are you coming?"

CHAPTER 15

Carmen didn't hesitate long before taking my hand and stepping aboard *Seas the Day*. She must have decided that it would be easier to use us as an excuse to run than to face whatever she needed to do in Marsh Rock.

Whatever she was avoiding doing must have been pretty bad.

Carmen and Albie untied the thick twisted rope tethering the boat to the dock. Carmen cleared her throat when she came back and saw me sitting in the driver's seat.

"This is my family's boat," I said, hating the way my voice trailed upward into a question mark in her presence.

"But do you know how to drive it?" she asked.

The only thing I knew how to drive was people nuts. The brightly lit windows of the hospital looked down on me like a pack of eyes. The most important thing was leaving—we could figure out the rest as we went.

I moved out of the way and stretched out in the padded curved seat lining the bow while Carmen checked the lights and pulled out a map to use for navigation.

I pressed my smartphone to my ear so it would look like I, too, knew what I was doing. It was still on a call with the dumb phone in Carmen's hospital room.

Carmen eased away from the dock and maneuvered us so our backs were to the antique streetlamps and whitewashed buildings of Marsh Rock. She slowly eased the gas forward and we slipped through the glassy water, past the lines and lines of boats and out into the empty bay.

We were rounding the corner of the bay, nothing but rippling black water to occupy our eyes, when I heard Jeff's voice through the phone.

"You kids OK in there?"

I could barely hear him, so I waved at Carmen and Albie to be quiet.

"We're alive," I said into the phone. Albie had connected the dumb phone to his speaker, thinking it would be loud enough to fool Jeff. Hopefully he was right.

I held the phone up to Carmen's cheek so she could say something. "Dr. Ryan was right about the importance of communal trauma processing."

"Hmm," Jeff said. "Hattie, your mom called asking me to let her into the lab because it was an emergency but when I went over, she wasn't there. Have you heard from her?"

"Nope! Maybe the hot guy from the Chem lab let her in," I said.

"What? Chem lab, I'm not familiar . . ."

"Well, I wouldn't worry about it too much," I projected a loud yawn into the phone. "Wow. It's getting late."

There was a shuffling on the other side of the phone, followed by a long silence. Carmen and I shared a nervous look. If Jeff took the time to check Carmen's room, he would find it empty.

Finally, I heard a sigh. "I'll check in on you in the morning."

"Good night!" Carmen chirped.

We listened to the staticky silence on the other end of the phone for a few seconds before I hung up.

Carmen looked back over her shoulder at the layers of lights cascading from Marsh Rock, a warm beacon in the darkness. We hadn't discussed where we were going or what we would tell DBD when we came back. None of us knew what would happen when DBD found our empty beds the next morning. I was pretty sure we hadn't done anything illegal (besides the shoplifting and boat stealing), but if we started showing symptoms, our parents might have the right to hospitalize us against our will.

Carmen turned back around and fixed her gaze on the horizon, following a sliver of moonlight into the velvet darkness. I didn't ask her where we were going or if she knew how to get there. She looked into the darkness with such certainty.

When we were far enough away that the shore looked like a blurred shadow, Carmen cut the engine and let the boat rock in the waves.

"I can't believe how close the stars look," Albie said.

We stared at the stars spattering the sky.

Well. Carmen and Albie stared up at the sky. I recorded a video of the awe on their faces as their eyes swallowed the sight.

Albie stretched his hand up and his fingers looked almost close enough to the sky to wrap around a fistful of stars and drag them down to earth. "I thought stars were only this bright in movies. I didn't know the sky had so much light."

Carmen stood next to him with her head craned back and hands braced on the steering wheel like she would drive straight into the galaxy if she could. "When I was a kid, I used to think stars were glitter God had rolled across the sky and, if we could see them, God must be throwing a party for something."

"I wish that were true," Albie said. He hooked his thumbs through the straps of his life jacket and angled his head as far back as it would go.

"Me too."

I crouched on the deck, angling the camera upward and using the moon as a spotlight. Albie traced the constellations with his fingertips.

When the wind became cold enough that my teeth started chattering, Carmen directed the boat to a gas station bobbing at the edge of the docks of Fleverton, the next town over. Carmen and Albie fell asleep in their chairs, blanketed by starlight. I curled up in the bow, using the shaky signal from the dock to intercut the video of the two of them looking up at the stars with the still footage I had of Albie's house. The subtext of the videos of Albie's hospital appointments on the calendar and the photo of the boy beaming surrounded by his books, contrasted with the awe in his voice when he talked about the night sky, was bound to get the Snack Attackers' hearts racing.

Carmen and Albie looked so happy with their heads craned back and their mouths hanging open, like their dreams were hungry enough to gobble up the sky. I added the caption **Match made in the heavens?**

••••

When I woke up the next morning, the first thing I did (after making sure I hadn't drowned) was to check my video views and likes. The video of Albie and Carmen looking up at the stars already had 110,000 views. The comments section was full of people theorizing about why he had been hospitalized and suggesting what he should do next. I checked my profile page.

The account had grown from 7,000 to 12,000 followers overnight. I rubbed my eyes to make sure I'd seen the number right. Twelve thousand was enough to connect my account to Catch a Dream and start raising money.

The radio crackled, jerking me back to the cool morning air. Carmen sat up and rubbed her eyes.

"Sailing vessel *Seas the Day* MMSI 6327 is missing, presumed stolen, from Marsh Rock Marina. *Seas the Day* is a Starcraft 20. Copy."

"Stolen!" Carmen spun in the driver's seat to face me. "You said this was your family's boat."

Well, this wasn't good. "Did I? That doesn't sound like me."

Albie opened his eyes and said, "Would now be a bad time to mention that Hattie's a compulsive liar?"

Carmen spun her chair to face him. "*What?*"

I reached into the backpack I'd been using as a pillow and pulled out a sucker.

"It's true. A doctor diagnosed me and everything."

One doctor. After talking to me for half an hour. That was all it took.

"You mean to tell me that we"—Carmen dropped her voice to a whisper—"stole a boat."

The only response was the slushing of the water and the creaking of the dock.

Carmen jumped away from the steering wheel. "Ohmygodwestoleaboat!"

"Technically, there's no 'we' seeing as how you were the one to untie the boat and drive it away," I said.

"*Technically*, I'm going to murder you if you don't stop talking."

I pressed my lips closed around the sucker. My stomach growled, hungry for something richer than the sour sugar. But I was in as much shock as Carmen. I was a good liar and not great person, but I'd never stolen anything bigger than a tampon before. What a rush.

Carmen sprinted into action, unfolding her map and running back and forth between the two ropes anchoring us to the gas station.

I checked the numbers on my phone again. 12,702 followers. The two videos featuring Carmen had the highest views.

Carmen's hands were shaking around the rope. "I don't know what I was thinking. The MTP is clearly affecting your judgment. I never should have let you leave the isolation ward."

She dropped her head into her hands. I didn't know if I should say something or give her a hug or jump into the ocean, so I bit into the sucker and let the sourness punish my tongue.

Albie and Carmen were my ticket to $23,000. I needed to keep this adventure going, because I needed them. Also, I felt a little bad for being the reason Albie had fallen in the lake and been exposed to the MTP in the first place. The least I could do was help him Seas the Day while we still had the time. Just kidding, that boat name is still terrible. But I still needed them to stay.

Albie wrestled his seat belt off and knelt by Carmen's side, the life jacket puffing up around his shoulders. "I'm sorry, Carmen. All of this is my fault. I just got so angry about this thing"—he rubbed his chest—"inside of us. All those years of chemo and my hair coming out in my hands and puking up everything that wasn't white bread and never experiencing my first kiss or first anything . . ." He shook his head. "I just can't fight like that again. I don't want to."

Carmen straightened. Whatever storm was brewing inside her, her face was as placid and beautiful as ever. Which is frankly just unfair.

"You're in the anger stage of grief, Albie," she said slowly. "That's good. It means you're progressing closer to acceptance. Hattie's still in denial. Obviously."

I clenched my phone. "I'm not in denial. I know I'm going to die. I know that no matter what I do, dying will be excruciating. That's acceptance."

Carmen looked at Albie and mouthed the word *denial*.

"I can see you!" I sat up and took the sucker out of my mouth. I needed them to understand I was serious. "There's this saying: You have to play the dice as they roll, and a good game lies not in rolling the right numbers but in playing a poor roll well."

"Are you actually high?" Carmen asked.

"Isn't that from that weird *Land of Invaders* game?" Albie asked. "My friends are always telling me I should play."

"My point is I'm playing the roll," I said. I didn't want to talk about *Land of Invaders*.

"How are we supposed to trust that anything you say is true? You literally said you were a compulsive liar," Carmen said. They were a *we*. I was alone.

I put the sucker back in my mouth. "You can't."

Carmen considered that for a moment. "We can't steal a boat."

"We already did," I said.

Albie stepped between Carmen and the driver's seat. "Hattie's right. This"—he gestured at the ocean, the sky, me—"is how we'll move through the, uh, staircase of grief."

"Stages, not staircase." Carmen slid her fingers along the gunwale. "What about the test results?"

"The doctor said even with a rush order it will take the lab like a week to process the results," Albie said. "So we can do our cathartic grief thing, move through all the, uh stages or whatever, and then come back before the test results are even in. Right, Hattie?"

I thought of the views ticking up on my videos. "Right. We'll be back before Jeff even has time to prepare a slideshow about the test results."

Carmen stared lovingly at the helm. "I did really like being the captain."

"You were a great captain." OK, now Albie was just babying her.

"Five days," Carmen said. "Off the record, Jeff told me the earliest the results would come in would be today. Given all the bureaucracy and red tape surrounding the situation, that means we won't get them until Monday at the earliest. We should be back by then so that on the off chance there are any traces of MTP in our system, we can begin treatment ASAP."

"Back by Monday," Albie said. "Three days. Easy."

Three days to make a Catch a Dream account and enough videos to pay off Mom's debt. It would have to be enough.

"Hattie?" Albie asked.

I nodded. I never made promises I intended on keeping, but I knew this was one Carmen would hold me to. "Three days, and I get to film all of it."

"Fine," Carmen said. "But I'm not going to believe a word you say."

"Promise?" I bit back.

Albie stepped aside so Carmen could take the driver's seat again. The radio was still crackling with calls. Every boat in the area would be looking for us soon.

"Where are we going?" Albie asked.

Carmen spun the chair around and flexed her hands around the wheel. "Albie, if you could go anywhere in the world, where would it be?"

France. Kenya. South Africa. Yosemite. Places with mountains and rivers and wonder.

We could fill the boat up with gas and sail to the Bahamas or Mexico.

There was a whole world of possibility, but instead Albie said, "Miami!"

CHAPTER 16

While Carmen and Albie dreamed about all the "amazing cultural experiences" we would have in Miami on the boat ride over, I used the weak internet signal to create a Catch a Dream account. I used the same username as my burner account and uploaded a still of Carmen and Albie looking out to sea as the profile picture.

Carmen threaded *Seas the Day* through the tangle of land and water surrounding Miami, and Albie hung his head between his knees because now that it was light out and he could see the water all around us he was even more terrified of drowning. I angled my body away from them and wrote an "About Our Dream" section for the profile.

I couldn't tell the world my real dream about becoming an artist so good and so rich I could make up for my personality to my mother. And I couldn't tell the world about Mom's debt, so I wrote some nonsense about Carmen and Albie and friendship. I submitted the page for review as Carmen and Albie tied up the boat. Now all I needed was a content opportunity.

When the boat was docked, Carmen took a break to call her family. Albie and I sat on the warm wooden dock, me dangling my toes over the water and him picking at a bag of cherries his mom had brought to the hospital for him.

"No mamá—escúchame, estoy a salvo. Regresaré en tres días." Carmen paced back and forth as she tried to explain to her parents why she'd broken out of the hospital and couldn't tell them where we were. "¿Qué pasa con Jillian?"

Carmen continued pacing up and down the dock, speaking in hushed tones and switching effortlessly from Spanish to English and back again. *Seas the Day* was bobbing in the water nearby. A web of islands, highways, and curving marinas spread out around us.

"Cherries were my chemo snack," Albie said. He was still wearing a life jacket over his DBD sweatshirt. "My mom saw some study about how eating them could kill cancer cells."

Sometimes the things Albie said were so sad, I couldn't let my heart really comprehend them or it would crack right open.

There weren't any other people on the dock—a small blessing considering we didn't own the boat or know anything about how to pay for parking. Videos of Carmen and Albie together were going to be my real moneymakers, but Carmen was busy. So I'd need to find another angle.

I jerked my chin at his red backpack. "What else is in there?"

"Uh, an inhaler, EpiPen, allergy meds, first aid kit. Just the basics."

"What about a toothbrush or a change of clothes?"

His face fell "That would've been smart. I haven't traveled much. So I wasn't really sure what to bring."

He looked over my shoulder at the stack of glittering skyscrapers that formed the walled backdrop of Miami. I imagined Albie going from school to his house to the hospital over and over again for seventeen years. There was nothing about that I wanted to capture on video.

"Want to see a trick?" I asked.

He twisted toward me. "Uh. OK."

I took a cherry from the bag and bit off the stem with my front teeth. Albie's eyes widened. I twirled the stem in my fingers and placed it on my tongue, scrunching up my nose in concentration. I swished the stem around my cheeks and flicked it across my tongue before swallowing it and opening my mouth wide.

"Ta da!" I coughed.

"I don't get it," Albie said. "Is that a party trick?"

I could feel my cheeks reddening. "I swallowed it. Instead of tying it in a knot with my tongue. Get it?"

Albie looked at me blankly. That's what I got for trying to be socially competent.

"It's how I impress all my dates."

The last part was a lie. I'd never been on a date in my life. Shocker, I know.

"It's probably just me," Albie said quickly. "You're way too cool for me."

My stomach flip-flopped. I looked out at the ocean, flat and calm from a distance, turbulent and choppy up close. "I'm not cool. Just a good liar."

Albie looked down the dock to where Carmen was now marching back toward us. "I wish I could be like that," he said under his breath to me, then scrambled to his feet to greet Carmen. "Did you talk to Jillian?"

"Not yet," Carmen said. "My parents are pissed though. They think the MTP is influencing my decision-making."

I bit my tongue to keep from pointing out that they were definitely right.

"What'd your parents say, Albie?" Carmen asked.

"I, uh, didn't call them," Albie said. "They're probably so worried, and if I talk to them, they'll guilt me into coming back."

"Same." I didn't mention the weight of my phone in my pocket. The single text I'd sent my mom from my phone when we landed in Miami.

I'm sorry.

Or the flood of texts that had poured in in response.

Hattie? Is that you?

Where are you?

I'm terrified.

Come home. Please.

"Do we have anything else to eat? I'm starving," Albie said.

"Nice to meet you, I'm Hattie." I don't know why I said it. It was the type of bad joke my parents used to giggle at together. Major cringe.

Albie offered a hand to help me up. "Oh, I get it. Because I said I was starving. Like a name! Good one."

"It's not a good one, Albs," Carmen said, looping her arm through his. "It's a Dad Joke and it is, by definition, not funny."

I walked behind them, refreshing the views on my latest video. The comments section of the star video was filling up with internet sleuths.

Does anybody know what school they go to?

What are the letters on their jackets?

My phone buzzed with an incoming email. My Catch a Dream account had been approved. I could link to it in the next video I posted and ask people to donate money.

As we walked toward the city, Miami burst to life around us. It was so colorful and sparked with energy, I could only digest our surroundings as simple facts:

- The sun was halfway up the sky, the humidity settling like a blanket over the city.
- The hotels and condos lining the beach were emptying people onto the sand.
- Bright pink and turquoise lifeguard stands checkered the beach.
- Muscular guys walked past us dragging coolers and smelling like thousand-year-old weed.
- Boat shoes, short shorts, and stringy bikinis were everywhere.

My stomach growled. I wondered who was hungrier: the parasite or me? Trick question. We were the same.

We peeled off onto a swirling pink and white path that paralleled the beach.

"What do you want to do first, Albie?" Carmen asked in the sweet tone of voice she reserved only for him.

"Why are there so many people?" Albie asked, shadowing closer to Carmen's side.

I didn't answer, too focused on scouting potential video ideas. Albie learning to swim in the warm waters of the Atlantic? Carmen and Albie playing beach volleyball against some of those meatheads? It had to be something that would simultaneously tug on people's heartstrings and make them want to donate.

The walking trail was lined with trees and bushes and humping couples and food stands. We stopped at a run-down-looking stand that smelled like coconut and sunscreen. Carmen and I got hot dogs and Albie got an acai bowl.

"I haven't had processed food since before the diagnosis," he said. "I don't want to give the MTP anything to feed on."

"Besides your brain?" I joked.

"That's not funny," Carmen said, which was proof that she was also a liar because zombie jokes are always funny.

We stood in silence, our energy dipping at the mention of the MTP. There was something trying to kill us. We'd escaped from a hospital and stolen a boat and made it to Miami (the self-proclaimed Magic City), but the parasite was still there.

A metallic shriek jerked us from our thoughts. Albie ducked and covered his ears with his hands. I spun around in search of the sound.

Carmen pointed to a black speck much farther up the beach. "Is that?"

"Dream Fest," I sighed. The biggest music festival of the year. I forgot it was this weekend.

I squinted and saw a massive stage farther up on the beach. The tower of speakers looked as tall as some of the skyscrapers across the walking path. A grassy area had been cleared around it and a clump of people was already dancing under an arch of screens the size of the Lincoln Tunnel.

Albie unfurled from his defensive position. "Who's playing?"

"Jordan Banner," I breathed, then caught myself. "Gross."

"I love him," Carmen said, easily and without defense. "He's an icon."

"Yeah," I said, noncommittally.

"I wonder if Elliot Why will be here," Albie said.

"It's a music festival, not slam poetry night," I said, regretting my tone immediately when I saw the way his face fell.

"It doesn't matter anyways," Carmen said. "Tickets have been sold out for months."

Carmen and Albie chucked their trash into a can and continued down the path. I trailed behind as they stopped to watch street performers and admire homemade jewelry that artisans were selling on the side of the path. The two of them were so engrossed in whatever conversations BFFs have that they didn't notice the stares we were getting.

A group of giggling girls in neon bikinis stopped mid-step when they saw us walking toward them.

"Is that—"

"Ohmigod he's so cute. I'm literally obsessed with him."

You and a brain-eating parasite, I thought. See? Zombies = always funny.

Carmen and Albie strolled past them unaware. I glanced back a few seconds later to see the group of girls hunched together, following us.

A few minutes of giggling and hushed whispers later, Carmen noticed, too.

"Are those girls laughing at us?" Carmen asked, pressing closer to Albie's side.

"Maybe because you're wearing business casual clothes on Miami Beach," I said, scanning Carmen's wrinkled DBD polo. Albie had unfastened the life jacket but refused to take it off completely.

I stopped at a water fountain to take a drink and buy us some time. The girls caught up to us, just like I'd hoped. I didn't know what was about to happen, but I knew it could be just the thing to kick off the fundraiser. I pulled out my phone and started recording.

A girl with light brown skin and box braids approached me, eyes on Carmen and Albie over my shoulder. They'd purchased a foldout map of Miami, plotting which tourist traps we should visit next.

"Is that the boy from @BadRoll13?" She asked. I couldn't believe she knew the name of the account.

"Snack Attack? Sure is," I said with more confidence than I felt. This could all come crashing down if she told Albie what I'd been doing with the videos of him.

"Wow." She whipped a phone out of her bikini top and took a picture of him. That wasn't enough for a video, though.

I stepped in front of her, blocking her view of Albie. "You know, he's really shy, but I'm sure he'd be flattered if you asked for a photo with him."

"I *couldn't*," the girl said, but her tone of voice made it clear she very much *could*.

"Seriously, he's *so* nice," I said, imitating her bubbly voice. "You should just do it. He'll be like, *so* excited."

I pulled out a lollipop as Neon Bikini Girl skipped up to Albie. The sour taste hit my tongue as she leaned over and, loudly enough for everyone on the pathway to hear, whispered, "I'm a big fan."

I framed them in my shot and waited for the girl to snap a selfie. It would be good B-roll for my next video.

"Uh." Albie glanced nervously at me, eyes widening when he saw that I was recording. I gave him a thumbs-up. "Of what?"

She laughed. "Of you, silly."

Albie looked at me. "I don't get it."

"You're so funny," the girl said and then threw her arms around his neck and kissed him.

CHAPTER 17

The girl was like an octopus. Limbs everywhere. Sucking on everything.

My mouth dropped so wide open that the lollipop toppled out and fell to the ground. Watching a strange hot girl make out with Albie wasn't part of the plan.

But it would be great on film.

I got down on one knee and tilted the camera up to get a better angle. I watched on the screen as Albie pawed at her waist and back like a drowning man and she rolled her tongue around his mouth and tugged him closer to her by the straps of his life jacket. For some reason, the sight of them sent a pang through my chest. Probably the amount of saliva they were swapping.

Carmen rushed toward me. "Who is that? Why is she kissing Albie?"

"Because he's cute? Or something. I mean, how should I know?"

"But... the germs," Carmen sputtered.

"Don't ruin this for him," I said, keeping my camera trained on them. If Albie had been trying to push the girl away, I would have been the first to pry her off him and give her a lecture about the importance of a little thing called consent. But Albie's mouth was open, his hands roaming, his tongue (gross) moving.

"He could get sick!" Carmen charged forward and pried their limbs and lips apart.

Note to self: Carmen would not make a good wing woman.

She turned on the girl. "Don't you have a spring to break?"

The girl tilted her head in confusion. "It's September."

"It's never going to happen," Carmen said, stepping in front of Albie.

"I'm Natasha." Natasha reached into the triangle of her bikini (Seriously? How much stuff could she fit in there?) and pulled out a small piece of paper. "Call me."

Had she just handed him a business card? God, the girl was cool. I zoomed in on the paper, then out to catch Natasha and her friends sauntering away.

Albie's eyes were glazed over. "Yes. Call you. I, uh, have a phone!" He dug his dumb phone out of his pocket and waved it in the air triumphantly.

Carmen shook him by the shoulders. "Snap out of it! What were you thinking? She could get you sick."

Albie shrugged her off. "With what? I'm already infected. And you scared her away!"

I stopped recording. Albie looked both elated and on the edge of tears.

"How was it?" It killed me to ask, but Albie deserved to share.

"She kissed me," he said, dumbfounded. "Her tongue was in my mouth. She didn't know about the cancer or the parasite or anything. She was just kissing *me*."

I swallowed my guilt. Natasha had known exactly who he was. "Good for you."

"No! Bad for you. Very bad for you!" Carmen said. "Hattie, stop being a bad influence. Albie, stop being dumb. Just because I'm allowing the two of you to explore your grief in an unstructured setting doesn't mean you can kiss anyone you want."

"You're not allowing us to do anything," I said.

"She *kissed* me," Albie said, his voice full of wonder. Then, with more confidence, "She kissed *me*."

A stream of beachgoers wound around us on the path, everyone and everything moving while we stood still. A pack of frat boys staggered down the path. One of them, a beer-bellied, baby-faced bro, stumbled as he walked past and elbowed me in the stomach.

"I'm underage, pervert," I said. What a creep.

He pointed. "Is that Snack Attack? From the videos?"

My stomach clenched. How many people in Miami were following my account? "Yup."

"Sick." The boy's eyes were bloodshot as he swaggered over to one of the other guys and wrestled a box out of his arm. He carried the torso-size cardboard box to us and thrust it into Albie's arms.

"Bro. My name is Brad. You're an inspiration," the boy said. "This is for you, bro. Use it wisely." He seemed unsure how to end his speech so he just said "Bro" again and walked away.

Albie nodded seriously. "I'll make you proud. Wait. What?"

"Seriously?" Carmen reached for the box. Albie spun so it was out of her grasp. "That could be a"—she looked around before whispering—"bomb."

Albie pressed his ear to the box. "I didn't get that vibe from Brad."

"If you knew anything about the outside world, you would know you can never trust a Brad," Carmen said.

I stepped aside while the two of them bickered about whether it was discriminatory to condemn all Brads. My fingers flew across the phone, slicing the video of Albie and Natasha kissing and adding sound. I captioned it **Baby's first kiss** and added a link to my Catch a Dream account.

"What are you doing?" Carmen tried to take the phone from my hand. I hid it behind my back.

"Watching the video of Albie making out with that hot girl," I said, which was partially true. Shout-out to me. "It's great raw footage for the documentary."

"She was hot, right?" Albie hugged the box to his chest.

"That's irrelevant." Carmen planted both hands on her hips. "Delete the video. Now."

"Uh." Albie held the box away from his torso. "I think this thing is *moving*."

"You're not the boss of me! And yes, I know that's a lame comeback. I blame the toxoplasma."

Carmen stared me down. "I don't know how, but I know this is your fault."

As usual, it definitely was.

"Uh. You gals might want to see this," Albie said, desperation creeping into his voice.

"Why can't you just be happy that something good happened to Albie for once?" I deflected. "You're his friend. You should be rooting for him."

"I'm rooting for him to stay alive!" she shot back.

"You have the same exposure risk we do," I said. "Stop pretending like we're the only ones who are infected."

"Gals!" Albie shouted.

"What?" We yelled in unison, still glaring at each other.

"Look." He set the box down on a bench and folded back the flaps. The box rattled back and forth.

Carmen gawked. "Is that?"

"A Kemp's ridley," Albie said. "They're critically endangered."

I leaned over them and peered down into the box to see a thick shell, scaly skin, and sad eyes.

The frat dude had given Albie a rare sea turtle.

Carmen yelped and jumped behind me, peering over my shoulder as Albie gently removed the turtle from the box.

Albie lifted the turtle up to his face, looked deeply into its eyes and proclaimed, "Fully grown ridleys can weigh up to a hundred pounds. He must be a baby. Also, his name is Scooter."

"That's it." Carmen pulled out her dumb phone. "I'm calling animal control."

"No!" Albie shrieked and set Scooter on the ground. "Run! Be free, my friend! Be free!"

"Do you have animal control's number memorized or something?" I tried to grab Carmen's phone and accidentally knocked it from her hand. The dinosaur device clattered across the walkway.

"Why are you like this?" she yelled as she dove through the crowds of people streaming past to grab the phone.

Albie was on his hands and knees crawling after Scooter. The crowd broke around them. Albie probably thought Scooter was making his grand escape back to the ocean, but he was *definitely* heading to an overflowing trash can. Sadly, dear sweet Albie didn't realize that until Scooter started chewing on a crumpled cigarette.

"No, Scooter, no!" Albie pulled the cigarette out of his mouth and picked the turtle up again. "The world is too dangerous for such a soft-shelled creature."

I pulled out my phone and looked up some pictures of turtles. "Kemp's ridleys are really endangered. It pains me to say this, and I mean that literally, but maybe Carmen is right."

"Give me that," Albie said and swiped my phone out of my hand.

Carmen clenched her hand around her phone. She stared at the broken screen in disbelief. Her voice was thick and cracked when she spoke. "I need to go home. I thought I could help, be a good friend to Albie, that this would—I don't even know. This is hopeless. Hopeless."

I had a feeling she wasn't talking about me anymore.

Before I could stumble through a response, Carmen put her phone in her pocket, marched through the crowd crisscrossing the path, and plunged into the bushes on the other side.

I turned to Albie, but he was too engrossed in the turtle to even realize anything was wrong.

"Albie! Your girl is leaving."

"My girl?" He looked at me.

"Carmen!"

"Carmen?" He spun around. "Where'd she go?"

"She's freaking out and ran that way," I said.

"Carmen can't freak out," Albie said. "That's my thing!"

"Well, if she goes back to the hospital, she'll lead DBD right to us. So let's move it."

Albie tossed me my phone. "He's definitely a Kemp's ridley. We can't give him to animal control. They're basically poachers!"

"Focus!" I said.

I put my hands on his shoulders and steered Albie and Scooter through the crowd and into the bushes. Albie held Scooter above his head while we waded through the scratchy mop of brush separating the beach path from the main road.

"Carmen, wait!" I said.

"Come back! I need you!" Albie called.

Carmen was standing on the edge of the sidewalk next to a busy road, phone against her ear, arm raised in the air.

We jogged over and sandwiched her.

"What are you doing?" Albie asked, shouting to be heard over the whizzing traffic.

"Hailing a taxi."

"Carmen, I hate to be the one to tell you this, but uh, taxis aren't really a thing anymore," I said.

"I don't have my phone or running track or student government or anything!" Carmen's breathing shortened, and each word came out like a gasp.

"You have me," Albie said.

"You're ignoring everything I say!"

"Only when what you say keeps me away from hot girls and rare sea turtles."

"My family needs me. I have things to do at home," Carmen said.

"Like whatever thing it is you're avoiding by running away to Miami?" I asked.

She dropped her arm. "What?"

"I don't care, alright? Avoid doing whatever you want. But that thing inside you telling you to quit and go home? That's not Carmen Diaz. That's the parasite. It wants to control you, and you can't let it."

She gritted her teeth. It was time to go in for the kill.

I hadn't been planning on telling them unless the situation became desperate. There was only one thing big enough to guarantee they'd both stay for the whole weekend.

"There's a reason we came to Miami," I said.

"Because I've never been allowed to go anywhere, and Miami is the closest metropolitan area?" Albie asked.

"So I could protect Albie from your psychopathic ways?" Carmen asked.

"Those were just added bonuses," I said. I let the suspense build for a moment. "We're not here because a parasite is eating away at our brains or because DBD fucked up. We're not here to grieve or mourn. We're here because when you only have thirty to sixty days left, you have to play a poor roll well."

I turned and looked over my shoulder at the mountain of speakers and scattering of stages in the distance.

Albie perked up.

Carmen eyed me warily. "Are you saying—"

"I got us passes to Dream Fest."

CHAPTER 18

I FEEL LIKE THIS SHOULD GO WITHOUT SAYING, BUT OBVIOUSLY I hadn't gotten tickets to Dream Fest.

Carmen was suspicious at first. "How did you manage to get tickets? I've been trying every day for months."

"Well, my grandmother left me a bunch of money when she died. I was saving it for college, but I guess that doesn't matter anymore," I lied then pointed to the sky. "Thanks, Nana."

"The same grandmother who owned the boat we stole?" Carmen asked.

For someone who didn't like me, she paid way too much attention to what I said.

"No. The other one. That was Grandma, this is Nana," I covered.

Albie thrust Scooter into the sky and jogged around in circles. "Go, Nana! We're going to the greatest music festival in the history of teenage wastelands! The MTP, DBD, and probably some other letters tried to keep us down, and we emerged victorious with a girl's business card and a rare sea turtle!"

"I'll show you the tickets once I have better service," I said. The biggest trick to selling a lie is to really commit to it.

"It's Jordan Banner," Carmen said, all the anger from the previous moment gone and replaced with a cool seriousness. "You wouldn't lie to me about seeing my favorite artist, would you?"

"Jordan Banner is sacred," I said, the first time I'd ever dared breathe aloud even one word about what Jordan Banner meant to me. I wanted to tell her I had every Jordan Banner album on vinyl, about the fan forums I was a part of, and that I, too, considered myself one of Banner's biggest fans—a member of the Color Guard. But the truth got stuck in my throat.

Carmen's eyes fluttered. "Come on. You're way too pretentious to be a fan of someone as basic as Jordan Banner."

It's an awful feeling, to sell a lie about yourself. It's even worse when someone buys it. "Guilty," I said. "But I got us tickets, just the same."

•••••

We spent the rest of the morning on the smooth, white sands of Miami Beach. Albie found enough change in his pockets to buy Carmen and me more hotdogs and himself a salad. I found a screenshot of three Dream Fest tickets online and showed it to Carmen.

"It's not VIP or anything," I said, trying to sound bashful.

"It's Dream Fest," Albie said. He had finally taken off his life jacket and was using it as a makeshift bed for Scooter.

"I can't believe I'm going to see Jordan Banner live," Carmen said.

"What's your girlfriend's name again? Jillian?" I asked in what I hoped was a casual tone. I knew exactly who Jillian Jones was. Her family was loaded. Maybe she could get us tickets . . .

"Um. Yeah." It was the first time I heard Carmen sound anything less than completely self-assured. "Don't worry, though. I didn't tell her where we were or anything."

Huh. From what I'd heard, Carmen and Jillian had been dating since middle school. Whenever I saw them eating lunch together or waiting at each other's lockers, they were staring into each other's eyes like that was their only source of oxygen. Why hadn't Carmen gone straight from the isolation ward to her girlfriend's arms?

"I didn't tell her anything," Carmen repeated.

"Cool," I said. Maybe I could use the Carmen and Jillian angle in a future video. After what should have been an illegal amount of small talk, Carmen fell asleep using her backpack as a pillow and her DBD windbreaker as a blanket.

"What if it's the MTP?" Albie shot Carmen a worried look. I'd been hoping to leave talk of the parasite at the hospital, but no one else seemed as committed to avoidance as I was.

"Exhaustion isn't one of the symptoms," I said automatically. I'd memorized the list my mom gave me: *Seeing things that aren't there. Lowered inhibitions. Increased impulsivity.*

The kind of symptoms that would make three sick teenagers think it was a good idea to break out of a hospital and steal a boat.

"Just a few more days," Albie said. "MTP or not, I'm going to miss this."

He went back to playing with Scooter. I dug my fingers into the sand and hoped the searing heat of it would hide how his words melted me a little bit. When that didn't work, I pulled out my phone and scoured the internet for Dream Fest tickets, flicking past the onslaught of messages coming in from my mom.

I'm not angry. Please come home.

Not for me—got new info on MTP to share.

Please, Hattie. I'm begging.

I put my phone on Do Not Disturb mode. Whatever they'd learned about the MTP—probably something useless like how much parasite (How did you measure a parasite? Pounds? Inches?) had contaminated the lake—it was too late to go back now.

My heart was racing, palms sticky with sweat. Jordan Banner was headlining in five hours. I needed the tickets *now.* My Catch a Dream account had received only $1,000 in pledges from the video of Albie and Natasha macking. A few comments on the video gave a hint as to why: Followers couldn't believe the Snack Attack would so quickly ditch the girl from the hospital.

My heart lit up at the words before I remembered the commenters couldn't be referring to me because I'd never shown my face on camera. Carmen was the girl whose face they'd seen and loved. I was going to have to up their fake romance in future videos.

One thousand dollars was more money than I'd ever had, but it was nowhere close to enough to buy three Dream Fest passes—the few tickets I *could* find online were going for at least $800 a pop.

I dug my fingers into the hot sand. Claiming to have Dream Fest tickets broke the cardinal rule of lying: Never tell a lie you can't talk your way out of. Maybe the MTP was already affecting my decision-making.

Carmen jolted awake from her nap around four. The beach was scattered with couples on walks, children hunting for seashells, and college kids engaging in the ancient flirting rites of seeing who could drink the most beer. The sun was beginning its long descent across the horizon.

Carmen shook the sleep from her eyes and stayed quiet for approximately one second before bursting into motion. "We should get in line. I want to make sure we get a good spot."

Albie looked up from the lettuce leaf he was dangling over Scooter's mouth. I wish it was an exaggeration when I say that they'd spent the past few hours staring lovingly into each other's eyes. "Yes! Scooter's so pumped."

I jumped to my feet, casting a long shadow that cut through the sand around us. "We can't!"

Carmen eyed me suspiciously, and I knew that she knew something was up. That's one of the benefits of being a liar though: There's never a hole I can't dig deeper.

"We can't go," I continued, floundering to come up with something, "looking like this."

I gestured to our wrinkled DBD ensembles.

Carmen sniffed her polo and made a face. "You have a point."

Albie hugged Scooter to his chest and said, "Scooter could use a sweater. I don't want him getting cold."

"I'm sure there's something nearby," I said, frantically searching on my phone for the farthest store I could find.

Thirty minutes later, we were standing outside the doors of Ethel's First Class Secondhand Shop. It was a squat, single-floor building, the lone holdout on a block of mirrored skyscrapers.

The outside of the store looked, and I don't say this lightly, like Alfred Hitchcock's most vivid dreams come to life. The window displays featured mannequins dressed up as witches and priests, surrounded by stuffed birds and foxes.

"This looks . . ." Albie's voice trailed off.

"Like a good place to get murdered," Carmen said. "I don't care what we wear. Jordan Banner's going on in four hours and it's more important that we get a good place to stand."

"Vibe check," Albie said. He and Scooter leaned closer to the door. "Scooter and I agree that this place is, uh, creepy."

"These are just scenes from *Land of Invaders*," I realized as my eyes landed on a display case full of the board game's signature colorful dice. "The shop owner's into tabletop games, that's all."

"Those are carcasses," Carmen said. "*Carcasses.*"

"Maybe their avatar is the Hunter," I said. "Seriously, it's fine. And I don't want to look cringe at Dream Fest."

I threw open the door to the store, setting off an ominous ding-dong bell.

For once, Carmen and Albie weren't overreacting. The store was a bad vibe, and I didn't want to go inside any more than they did.

But I also wasn't going to give up now.

I turned back to Albie and Carmen. "OK, where should we start?"

CHAPTER 19

"I LOOK LIKE A BAD MODERN ART PIECE."

Carmen flung back the curtain of the dressing room and emerged wearing a red tube skirt and a pink top covered in puffy balls. I filmed her as she made a gagging face in the mirror.

"OK, so not your vibe," I said.

I stopped recording and refreshed the search on my phone yet again, hoping that someone had decided Jordan Banner *wasn't* the greatest artist of our generation and wanted to sell three Dream Fest tickets for cheap. No luck.

Albie was sifting through a pile of dusty baby carriers in the corner. I'd decided not to contemplate why the store had so many baby carriers and no baby clothes. It was too horror movie to consider.

I angled the phone closer to my chest and sliced together clips of Albie and Carmen stepping hesitantly past the threshold of Ethel's First Class Secondhand Shop and screeching when they looked up and saw a stuffed fox peering down at them. My explanation that the fox was one of the most common creatures in *Land of Invaders* didn't seem to comfort them.

"Hattie?"

I jerked my head up to see Albie holding up a black strapped concoction for my inspection.

"Very sexy," I said.

"It's for Scooter."

"Even better."

"Are you OK?"

"Always." I grabbed a handful of clothes off the nearest rack and hurried to the dressing room.

I spliced together a few more shots of Carmen trying on outfits and posted the video, asking followers to donate to the Catch a Dream account to help make the Snack Attack and his Mystery Girl's dreams come true.

And if that didn't work and the views plummeted, I could ditch Albie and Carmen without saying goodbye. I could . . .

I buried my face in the clothes and inhaled their stale scent until I coughed, but it wasn't enough to choke the thought into silence. *I'm dying. All of this smoke and mirrors won't fool me, and it won't fool the parasite.* The world wasn't round. It was a cliff, and I was hurtling toward the edge. *I want my mom.*

"Hey, Carmen." I saw Albie's Converse-clad feet shuffling closer to Carmen's dressing room curtain. "Can I? Uh. I need to talk. To you?"

Ugh. Just my luck. Albie was finally getting up the nerve to confess his feelings to Carmen, and I was going to have a front-row seat to it.

"I need to talk to you, too," Carmen said. *Parasite take me now.*

I heard the curtain of her room swish open. "Do you think this outfit is too much?"

"Uh . . ."

"Hattie?" Carmen shook the curtain of the dressing room I was hiding in. "I need you to look at this outfit and tell me if it's too much."

So much for keeping my cover. I flung the curtain back and saw Albie rushing away to another part of the store. A gauzy, rainbow-colored skirt fluttered to Carmen's ankles. Underneath, neon pink biker shorts glowed against her legs. She'd also selected a bedazzled crop top so shiny it reflected a sea of diamonds onto the ceiling. She looked like a gem in the midst of all this junk.

I hadn't had a friend since middle school. I didn't know the rules for how to talk about clothes like this. "You don't look like yourself," I finally said.

"Good." Carmen nodded curtly and headed back into the dressing room.

Across the store, Albie dinged the bell on the front counter. It was all glass, cluttered with brooches and clip-on earrings and dusty game pieces. A woman with snow-white hair and wrinkled white skin shuffled out from a door behind the counter.

"Oh," she said, seeming surprised to see Albie. "I didn't hear anyone come in."

"You must be Ethel," Albie said. He held up a stained baby carrier. "Exactly how much weight will this hold? For example, would it hold an extremely wide baby with a tough exterior who weighs approximately fifteen pounds?"

Ethel adjusted the collar of her fur coat. "You look too young to have a baby, much less a wide one."

Albie bent over and picked up Scooter. "That's ageist and body shame-ist and still doesn't answer my question."

Ethel's eyes blazed when she saw Scooter. "And who's this now?"

Carmen emerged from the dressing room, rainbow outfit folded over her arm, and planted herself in front of me, blocking my view of Albie. "Jordan Banner takes the stage in less than four hours, so we're already late, but I cannot let you get away with whatever this is." She gestured to my baggy pants and DBD top. "Are you a middle child?"

"Uh. No."

"Then stop dressing like one. Come on."

Carmen looped her hand through my elbow and dragged me around the store, flinging items off the rack and into my arms and then circling us back toward the dressing room. Albie was still bickering with Ethel about Scooter. The only item I managed to grab was a pair of buttery-soft cowboy boots.

Carmen shoved me into a dressing room, pulled two pieces out of my arms, and hung them on a hook for me to try. "You have three minutes. Don't make me start a timer."

She stepped back and swooshed the curtain shut, leaving me alone with the clothes and the mirror and lack of Dream Fest tickets. I needed to stall.

"Being on our own is really helping Albie come into himself," I said through the curtain, picking up the first option to try on.

Carmen's sneakers paced back and forth. "Albie has decided that if that turtle doesn't get enough skin-to-skin contact with him, it'll die. He's delusional."

"This one's a no." I took off an itchy, sparkling sweater and threw it over the curtain rod. "What phase is he in now?"

"Bargaining," Carmen said. I wondered how Carmen had developed the confidence to spit her thoughts out without a trace of doubt. "He's making a deal with the universe that if he gets to have this one magical weekend, he'll go back to the hospital and fight to get better. It's not logical."

"And what stage are you in?"

"I told you already. Acceptance. Did you read the presentation Jeff put together? Because I did. Slide 17 said the toxoplasma dies in water, and Slide 53 went into all the problems they were having with the experiment—including with getting it to latch onto nervous systems. The odds of me getting the MTP are low, and I'm in great physical condition, so even if I do have a small trace of it, my immune system will fight it off easily."

Carmen was smart. She had to hear the denial laced through every word of that sentence. I knew how much concentration it took to lie to yourself though, the vacuum it created around every other idea.

"And me?" I asked, barely listening anymore. My phone lit up. It was my mom's number. Buzz. Buzz buzz. I hit ignore.

"I don't think you've started going through the phases yet," Carmen said. "It's like you're somewhere else entirely."

I hmmed in response. The video of Albie and Carmen in the store already had 7,000 views. My connected fundraiser on Catch a Dream only had $1,700 in pledges though. Albie's fans couldn't get over him making out with someone besides Carmen.

A text flashed across the top of my screen. I got to *Hattie I love you please* before swiping it away.

Carmen cleared her throat. "Are you smoking in there or something? Just because the MTP is impacting your nervous system doesn't mean you should give up on your lungs. Also—and I'm not saying this is as important; it just happens to be relevant information—Jordan Banner is going on soon and I know you think he's a sellout pop factory, but I love him."

"I don't think that." I pinched my eyes closed even though she couldn't see me through the curtain. "Don't tell anyone, but I'm kind of a Bannerhead. And I don't smoke."

"Oh. I just assumed," Carmen said. "Because of the black clothing and nihilistic worldview."

"Fair enough. Smoking would be very on brand for me," I said. I used to love the armor other people's assumptions provided me with, but the problem with armor was it could be placed right over an old wound. Carmen had no way of knowing that I couldn't smoke because the smell reminded me too much of my dad, but the wound was now reopened just the same.

I examined the pile of clothing and picked out shredded jean shorts that would reveal a long stretch of my thighs and an off-the-shoulder vintage Joy Division T-shirt. Good enough.

I ripped open the dressing room curtain, leaving a pile of faded clothes behind me. "This is it." I held up the outfit. "I'm not trying on anything else."

"It's not terrible." Carmen flipped over the price tag. "Yikes. $80?"

I hadn't pegged Ethel as the type to sell things for a high price just because they looked tastefully destroyed, but good for her.

I batted Carmen's hand away. "It's fine. Everything's on Nana, remember?" I held out my hand for the outfit she'd picked out.

Carmen held the gauzy rainbow ensemble out of my reach. Tall people should be illegal. "I can't let you do that."

"I have to spend this money somehow. You'd be doing me a favor, OK?" Might as well go all-in with this lie.

Carmen's big brown eyes drilled into mine for a moment. She slowly lowered her arm, and I snatched the clothes. "Thanks."

Oh no. Carmen was being nice to me. It lit something up inside me that I needed to demolish.

Carmen checked the time on her dumb phone. "I know moving through life in slow motion is kind of your thing, but could you maybe hurry up? We're going to miss the opener."

There was the disappointed Carmen I knew.

"Sure thing," I said, with my biggest, most annoying smile.

I bundled the pile of clothes to my chest and poked my head down every aisle until I found Albie digging through a bin piled high with hats.

"Where's Scooter?" I asked.

"He needed quiet time," Albie said.

I held out my hand for the clothes he'd picked out. "I'm buying."

I'd seen his house in Cul du Lac. He lived the kind of life where you didn't have to worry about covering your friend's tab.

Albie handed me a pair of acid-washed jeans, a bright pink muscle tee, a faded black bandanna, and an enormous pair of mirrored sunglasses. Everything had a noticeable odor.

"I'm going for an Elliot Why look," he explained.

"You don't look anything like him," I said. They had a similar shaggy haircut, but so did half the pubescent boys in America.

"The point of Elliot Why is that he could be *anyone,*" Albie huffed. "That's why he wears the bandanna to cover his face and does the whole sunglasses thing."

From what I'd seen online, Elliot Why gave off the vibes of a waspy white kid who thought he'd had a tough childhood because he had to wear braces and wasn't invited to a friend's birthday party one time. Albie was a Chinese boy who grew up in a white-dominated town and spent his childhood fighting cancer.

I wanted to be the kind of person who could explain to Albie why he didn't need to dress up as someone else. Why he was perfect just the way he was. But I wasn't, so I said, "Get the bucket hat, too."

He grinned. "Thanks, Hattie."

Albie added the hat and then left me standing in the aisle alone.

A Dimensional Door, one of the most important game pieces in *Land of Invaders*, spun in the corner, watching me as I opened my backpack and started stuffing the things in.

I didn't have tickets. I didn't have the money or the connections to get tickets. Carmen and Albie were going to find out. They'd be mad, but who cared? I'd been disappointing people my whole life. Why stop now?

I finished cramming everything into my bag and crept toward the front door, sticking to the outer aisles. Carmen and Albie were bickering near the entrance.

She pinched one of his cheeks. "Why is your face so red? Are you feeling OK?"

Albie caught my eyes as I approached, but quickly looked back to Carmen. Carmen followed his former sight line and furrowed her brows at me. Did she realize I hadn't paid for anything?

I sped up, fingers clenching around my backpack straps. "We're good. Let's go."

I reached for the door handle and pulled. But the door didn't budge. I rattled the handle.

Carmen nudged me out of the way and pulled on it herself. "What's the problem?"

"It's locked," I said.

"Scooter?" Albie called. "Where'd you go, buddy? Scooter—"

He fell silent when we heard a clicking noise behind us. Goose bumps crawled across my body.

"Don't move," a rattly voice said. "Turn around."

"Those are contradictory instructions," Carmen said.

"Don't try to confuse me," Ethel said. "I know all about you kids and your witchcraft and twitching and stealing."

We all slowly turned around. Ethel stood a few feet back, her snow-white hair glowing against the colorful backdrop of the store. She was aiming a weapon straight at us.

"Is that . . . a crossbow?" Carmen whispered.

"I can hear you!" Ethel said.

Carmen cleared her throat. "You have no legal right to keep us here against our will."

"Where's Scooter?" Albie looked around frantically. "Please! We didn't do anything."

"Didn't you?" With a chuckle, Ethel stalked forward. She grabbed my backpack and yanked me around.

"Hey!" Carmen said. "That's assault."

"You can't do this!" Albie said. "Because of what Carmen said about the, uh, legal stuff."

"I can do whatever I want to thieves," Ethel said.

"We're not thieves," Carmen said, holding out her hands, eyes glued to the crossbow. "You must be confused."

But before I could jump in with another lie, Ethel ripped open the zipper on my backpack and the pile of clothes we'd chosen for the festival tumbled to the floor.

CHAPTER 20

ON THE BRIGHT SIDE, WHEN ETHEL HANDCUFFED ME TO A TABLE IN the back room, the chain was long enough for me to move my arm around. On the downside, the rusted metal handcuff chafed against my wrist. Also, she'd handcuffed me to a table.

And look, I'm well aware that trying to shoplift from a small business owner slash sketchy person wasn't my smartest or most ethical move. Let's move on.

Carmen watched me struggle. "It's a handcuff, Hattie. You can't wiggle out of it."

Albie jiggled the doorknob to the back room with one hand and cradled Scooter under his arm like a football in the other. His cheeks were tinged a dark red color. "Scooter is having trouble breathing. He thinks he might pass out, and so do I. Did I mention that already? Is this the MTP? What does a parasite feel like?"

"You're sunburned," Carmen said.

Albie patted his face in disbelief. "I'm sunburned? Am I going to get skin cancer now, too?"

I rattled the chain against the table. "We have bigger problems."

Carmen paused her pacing long enough to shoot me a withering stare. "I can't believe I trusted a compulsive liar. I should have known better."

The clothes were supposed to be a gift. A shiny thing to take the place of our drab DBD gear and bleak-looking lives and make up for our lack of Dream Fest tickets.

If first-class Ethel wasn't a first-class jerk, everything would have been fine. The woman looked older than time itself, but she moved faster than the American P.E. system had prepared me for.

After revealing the almost-stolen contents of my backpack, Ethel had holstered her crossbow (because yes, it was a legitimate crossbow) and slapped a cuff on my wrist in one smooth motion. I was too embarrassed to fight as she dragged me through the dusty store, behind the checkout counter, and down a narrow hallway lined with gleaming game pieces, until we got to a larger storage closet.

The worst part wasn't the cuff cutting into my circulation or the army of animals and playing pieces staring at us from the shelves. The worst part was that Albie and Carmen had followed me. If I'd been in their place, I would have run the moment Ethel's back was turned. They made staying look so easy.

The walls of the storage closet were lined with teetering metal shelves. Each shelf sagged with the weight of scattered *Land of Invaders* accessories—expansion packs, limited edition doll-size figures of some of the most famous playing pieces like the Reaper and the Chemist.

The center of the room was occupied by the squat, hexagonal table Ethel had handcuffed me to. The orange felt covering the table brushed my wrists with every movement.

I could practically hear the dice thudding across the fabric tabletop, the cards shuffling together. The smell of cigarettes and the slap of hands against the table. Playing *Land of Invaders* was one of two things my dad had taught me. *Play the players, not the board.*

The heels of Ethel's boots clicked down the hall. Albie set Scooter on the ground. "Run, Scooter! Run!"

Scooter tilted his head up at Albie and didn't move an inch.

Carmen stepped in front of the table. "Let me handle this."

The lock on the door unclicked and Ethel swung it open. Her white hair looked electrocuted, and a pin with a bow and three animal heads was clipped to her shirt pocket.

"You kids ready to make a deal? I've got a tournament starting tomorrow, and I don't want to have to call the cops before the Invaders arrive."

Carmen leaned back against the table. Someone who didn't know her might have thought she was relaxed, but I could tell by the stiffness of her shoulders and the tapping of her foot that she was nervous. "There's no need to call anyone. I'm sure we law-abiding citizens can work this out without bureaucratic intervention."

"Your big words don't intimidate me," Ethel said. "You thought you could come in here and just steal clothes, but Invaders always face consequences."

Albie spoke up. "No one had left the store yet so technically no crime was committed." Carmen and I stared at him. "What? My mom's a lawyer."

Ethel crossed her arms. "I'm the law here."

Carmen tried a new negotiating tactic. "I have an emergency credit card I can use to pay for the items."

"I don't want your money." Ethel jerked her head in Albie's direction. "I want him."

Albie stumbled back into one of the storage units. The shelf wobbled back and forth before stabilizing. "She wants to traffic me. Carmen, *do something*."

Carmen kept her cool. "You can't have Albie."

"I don't want the boy! What would I do with him?" Ethel scoffed. "I want what he possesses."

Albie's forehead wrinkled in thought. "Asthma?"

"A sunburn?" Carmen asked.

"Scooter," I said. Ethel's devious grin confirmed my suspicions. "Her player avatar is the Poacher, a character who gains power from animals. She wants to add Scooter to her collection."

"I think the MTP is getting to you," Albie said. "Nothing you're saying is making sense."

"It's from *Land of Invaders*."

"You Invade?" Ethel asked me, crooking her eyebrow.

"No." *Not anymore.*

Albie blocked Scooter with his body. "You can't have him."

"I'll give you three a moment to discuss your options while I check in with my weekend players. Either she," Ethel pointed at me, "goes to jail. Or the turtle stays with me."

My life was transforming into a bad Western. Next she was going to say this town wasn't big enough for the two of us.

Ethel unclipped a cartoonishly huge ring of keys from her belt and swaggered out of the storage room, locking the door behind her.

In her absence, the room was quiet enough to hear the distant drumbeat from Dream Fest. Jordan Banner would take the stage soon.

I cleared my throat. "I wasn't going to shoplift." Lie. "I was just coming to ask you guys a question." Another lie. "This lady is nuts." True.

Carmen whirled around, fingers and shoulders clenched with the restraint of her fury. "You got us kidnapped!"

"I didn't ask you to follow me."

"What was the question?" Albie asked. "That you came to ask us?"

My mind spun, grasping for a lie that would make this go away. All I saw was the Dimensional Door, spinning and spinning and spinning and never going anywhere.

"Was it the toxoplasma?" he asked hopefully. "Is that why you lied to us?"

The itch inside of me was a burning sensation. "Maybe."

Carmen resumed her pacing. "We have to give her the turtle. It's the only leverage we have."

Albie gasped. "How could you?"

"We don't have any choice!" Carmen said. "Where is Scooter, anyway?"

I scanned the floor and didn't see him. Scooter was smarter than I'd thought if he'd disappeared.

Albie made a face. "Like I would tell you! You want to add him to Ethel's Build-A-Bear Shop of Horrors."

"I'm not the reason we're here!" Carmen said.

I longed for the sting of a sour apple sucker, but the pinch of the handcuff against my skin was good, too. "You liked that I was getting things done until the things I was doing became inconvenient for you."

"You're a liar and a thief," Carmen snarled.

"Yeah, I am. But you think you're better than everyone because you've avoided doing anything interesting in your life and he"—I jerked my free thumb back at Albie—"is too scared to be anybody. And guess what? All three of us are going to be dead in thirty to sixy days, so none of that will matter. It won't matter that I lied about the clothes or that Albie was too scared to face his life or that you were too cowardly to do whatever it is you broke out of the hospital to do." I sat back, exhausted. "None of it matters."

Carmen's face was red with anger. "You. Stole. From. A. Small. Business!"

"What about the money Nana left you? Did you spend it all on the Dream Fest tickets?" Albie asked hopefully.

I chewed my lip and avoided looking at him. The truth always came out eventually, and eventually was always sooner than I wanted it to be.

"Oh no. Hattie. You didn't."

"I didn't think you'd actually fall for it," I said. *I lied because I wanted you to stay.*

"Why would you steal the clothes if you knew we weren't going to the concert anyway?"

"I was bored. It was something to do." *I wanted to do something nice for once.*

The lack of logic was too much for Carmen, and she collapsed into the chair next to me. Her big brown eyes filled with tears.

"I'm not going to see Jordan Banner," she said slowly and precisely, letting the information sink in. "I should be home with my sister. I shouldn't have left my parents and abuela. I thought I was doing the right thing, but I'm letting them down."

I wanted to tell her I felt the same. That every move I made was the wrong one, and I was always hurting the people I cared about the most, but I couldn't squeeze the words past the lump in my throat.

"I'll turn myself in," I said. "She'll let the two of you go. It'll be fine."

Carmen shook her head. "We're not leaving you here."

"Really?"

"It would be unethical to leave you with Ethel. We couldn't do that."

Once again, they were a we, and I was alone.

"Maybe it's the parasite, but I actually have a really good feeling about how this is going to work out," Albie said.

"That's definitely the MTP," Carmen said. "Delusions of grandeur is one of the symptoms."

The thump of Ethel's boots echoed down the hall. The handcuff was warming up to the temperature of my skin. I could say something terrible enough to make them leave me. Give up and let Ethel put me into a cell until my mom came to bail me out. She'd be so hurt, and I'd have nothing to salve her wound.

I hadn't come this far to go back with nothing.

I still had my phone and my videos and my nerve and $23,000 waiting for me. I tested the length of the chain.

"When I give you the signal," I told Carmen, "run."

Carmen cocked her head. "What are you going to do?"

Albie asked, "What's the signal?"

"You'll know it when you see it."

Ethel swung the key ring around her finger as she walked through the door. "You three ready to negotiate?"

"Turtle rights are human rights," Albie said.

Ethel gestured around the room. "I'll give him a good home."

"All of the other animals in this room are dead!" Albie shrieked.

Carmen raised her hand. "I'm curious, how exactly does one stuff a turtle?"

Ethel scoffed. "I'm not going to stuff him. I'm going to use his shell as a serving bowl."

Albie said, "You'll never find him."

Scooter chose that exact moment to waddle out from underneath the storage shelf.

Albie's eyes widened in horror. "Scooter! Run!"

I rattled the chain of the handcuff against the wooden table leg. Carmen and Albie inched together on the other side of the table. Ethel hooked her key ring to her belt loop and waited.

"Poacher." I clasped my hands together in my lap and plastered on the face I knew people most wanted to see on young women: bashful, ashamed, contrite. "You're clearly a hardworking American. And if you're hosting a tournament, you must be what, an orange-tier invader?"

Ethel smiled. "Three tournaments away from black tier."

"My dad used to play. He was good, too." I couldn't look at them when I said it, so I stared at a smudge on the floor instead. "When I was twelve, my dad left. He took everything with him—the car, the bank accounts, everything. I'd always been a daddy's girl and without him, I was no one. My mom had to give up the job she loved for a soul-crushing position to make ends meet and pay off his debts. We moved across the country, but it wasn't far enough. He's still got his hooks in me. I'd always wanted to be like him—even now I probably still do a bit. So I lied. I stole. We're all here because we were exposed to a rare . . . disease."

Carmen and Albie shuffled together. Carmen raised an eyebrow and I shook my head. Not yet.

"That's what brought the three of us together," I pressed on. "We never would have spoken otherwise. Life is survival of the fittest, and we aren't the fittest. The doctors are doing everything they can, but they tell us we only have a month to live. Maybe two. That's it. We're not adults yet. We can't vote. I've never driven a car, Carmen had never been in a boat, Albie has never been anywhere. And this might be our last chance." My voice broke. It felt true in a way I wanted it to feel false.

"I don't see what any of this has to do with my turtle," Ethel interjected.

"The point is"—I took a deep breath—"I was lost, but because of your integrity as a woman, a Poacher, and as a gameplayer, I've found myself again. You're right: You deserve this turtle. And I deserve full legal consequences for my actions. But first, I think we should recite the Vow of the Invader."

Ethel arched an eyebrow. I took a knee and clasped my hands together. Ethel sighed and knelt down in front of me. She was an orange-tier Poacher—she knew the kind of bad luck that came from not saying the vow.

"I am an Invader," I started. Ethel mumbled along with me. "I am a world builder and a taker."

I could feel Albie and Carmen's confusion. When you lie enough, sometimes people forget that you have a truth.

"This is the signal," I said calmly.

"The what?" Ethel asked.

"Now?" Carmen asked.

"Oh god," Albie said.

"Signal!" I yelled.

I curled my free hand into a fist and punched Ethel in the groin as hard as I could.

CHAPTER 21

CONTRARY TO POPULAR BELIEF, GROIN KICKS ARE EFFECTIVE ON people of all genders, races, and religions. Some might say a groin punch is even better. I was doing the best I could with what I had, OK?

Ethel wobbled on her one knee and keeled forward, falling into me. I hooked my arms around her neck, keeping my cuffed hand close to the table and making a V between the fist and elbow of my free arm to limit her range of movement.

Carmen stood frozen as a popsicle in front of me. "What the—"

"The keys!" I yelled and shook Ethel from side to side, jingling the key ring at her hip.

Carmen snapped out of her haze and scrambled to unclip the key ring. I moved my cuffed hand as close to her as I could. The chain held strong, cutting into the tender skin of my wrist. "Uncuff me!"

I pressed Ethel's nose into my shoulder and cinched my elbow tight around her neck.

But Ethel refused to go down without a fight. Her head was contained, but her arms were free. She slapped and clawed at my neck.

"Lazy, entitled, selfie-taking youths," she gasped in between big breaths.

I locked my hands together and squeezed through my elbow. Ethel was used to hunting things; I was one prey she wouldn't catch.

Carmen jammed a key into the opening on my wrist and twisted. It didn't work.

"Hurry!" I yelled.

"I *am* hurrying! You could have told me you were going to attack her."

Ethel let out a gargled moan and threw her head forward to headbutt me. She caught my right cheekbone with her forehead.

I closed my eyes against the ache blooming near my cheek. "I'm not attacking her. I'm doing a rear naked choke hold to control her range of movement."

"What?"

Ethel threw herself side to side, careening us toward the table, the shelves, the wall.

"My dad taught me two things before he left: how to play *Land of Invaders* and how to fight MMA-style. A rear naked choke is a blood choke that can render an opponent unconscious in ten seconds."

Ethel dug her nails into my arm and dragged them down. I gritted my teeth and held on as I explained, "It's not as effective from a forward-facing position, which is why she's still conscious."

Carmen stared at me blankly.

"So I can only hold her for a few more seconds. The key?"

"Right." Carmen shuttled through the keys. Something clamped onto my shoulder.

"Do you want me to record this?" Albie asked timidly from somewhere behind me. "For the documentary?"

"I'm not in it," I spit out between gritted teeth.

"Really? Why not?"

"Because no one likes me. She's biting me now!" I tried to keep my voice calm, but I was freaking out.

My wrist felt like it was going to snap in half in the choke hold. Ethel clamped down harder on my shoulder.

"She's chewing!" I pressed my arms deeper into her neck, imagining her wrinkled skin was the purple blob of the parasite. I squeezed and choked, tried to kill the thing crawling underneath my skin.

"She's crying." Carmen screamed as she tried another key. "ALBIE! Do something!"

"But my sunburn!"

"Seriously? Come on!" Carmen yelled.

"Something. Yes. Uh." I heard Albie's footsteps shuffling behind me. "Excuse me? Uh. Miss Ethel? I'm ready to talk about the turtle now."

Ethel unclenched her teeth, and I screamed in relief.

"Psych!" Albie leaped into my line of vision. He held up a small bottle and sprayed Ethel in the face.

I hid my face in Ethel's brittle hair while she choked and gagged.

"It burns! It burns!"

"Did you just pepper spray an old woman?" Carmen asked as she inserted a key into the handcuff.

"Don't be ridiculous." Albie stared at the small cannister in awe. "It's a throat spray. I use it sometimes after my inhaler because it gives me dry mouth—"

"No one cares about your allergies!" Ethel screeched.

I jerked her closer to me, away from Albie. "He's a cancer survivor. Show some damn respect."

"Got it!" Carmen's fingers were shaking as she unlocked the cuff clasped around my wrist.

My chafed arm felt naked without the metal kissing it. I used my newly free hand to grab Ethel's wrist and drag it toward the table.

Ethel flailed against me.

"Cuff her," I said.

Carmen cinched the cuff around Ethel's wrist and then jumped back like she'd touched a snake. "What now?"

"Run!" I shoved Ethel toward the table and struggled to my feet. Carmen sprinted to the hallway. Albie stopped to scoop up Scooter. I was steps from the door when a cold hand grasped my ankle and tugged, sending me sprawling to the floor.

"You think you're an Invader?" Ethel screamed. "You're just a kid with a costume."

I kicked out at her. Used my arms to try to crawl forward. But her grip was strong, and I was tired of always needing to fight. I'd gotten Albie and Carmen out. That was what really mattered. I went limp.

Albie charged back into the room and dangled Scooter over Ethel's head. "Let go!"

"Never!"

"Now, Scooter," Albie said calmly. For once, Scooter did what Albie said and pooped directly onto Ethel.

She uncurled her fingers from around my ankle and swiped at her face. Albie hooked an arm around me and tugged me to my feet.

I leaned against him as we shuffled out of the storage room and into the hall. Carmen slammed the door shut behind us.

We hurried through the back hallway and back into the store. An older man and woman browsing the jewelry section jumped at the sight of us.

"Excuse me." The man stepped forward and held up a clunky necklace. "How much is this?"

Carmen propelled us forward. "It's free. The owner is doing a huge sale because she's an asshole."

"Is that a turtle?" The woman asked.

"Uh... no?" Albie said.

Carmen took my hand and pulled me through the racks of colorful clothes and faded, frozen animals.

"Terrible customer service," the woman muttered.

Finally, we reached the front door and burst into the cool evening sunlight.

"Oh my stars!" Carmen said because sometimes she talked like a 1930s movie star.

"—dead!"

"Cannot believe."

"Wait." Carmen stopped and spun around. "Where's Albie?"

"Coming!" He burst out the doors with Scooter strapped to him in one of the baby carriers he'd been admiring earlier. My backpack was dangling from his arm. "Go, go, go!"

We sprinted through the parade of traffic waiting to get on the highway and cut into a wall of bushes lining the beach path we'd been wandering earlier. Albie leaned against a bush, chest heaving for air.

Carmen reached for his bag. "Do you need your inhaler?"

He shook his head. "Just give me a minute."

Carmen and I stood in silence, watching as Albie breathed. My throat was raw, and I could feel bruises blossoming on my arms and neck. Over the tops of the bushes, I could see a rainbow of lights flashing from the stages farther down the beach. It was hard for me to believe that Jordan Banner would go on at sunset, and we wouldn't be there to see him perform.

"We should go back to the boat," Carmen said to me. "I've got extra inhalers in my bag."

"OK," I said.

Carmen did a double take. "You're not going to argue with me? Tell some lie that will make us stay?"

I watched Albie's chest rise and fall. "It's Albie."

"It is." She reached for his arm. "Come on. Let's get you home."

Albie yanked his arm free and stumbled away. "I'm not going."

"Albs—"

Albie held out both hands to keep us away.

"On Monday I'll be good again," he said in a quieter voice, breathing deep and slow in between his words. "I've always been good. I went to the doctor's appointments, did the chemo, smiled at the five-year remission party like I'd won something. I stayed home and didn't eat dairy or sugar or date or do anything else that would have brought a single spark of joy to my life."

"You're a survivor," Carmen said.

"I didn't want to be a survivor!" Albie shrunk back. He took a deep breath before going on. "I didn't want to be the protagonist of some sick lit melodrama. I would have traded anything—my eyes, my hand, my poetry—*anything*, to not have cancer."

I wanted to film him. I wanted a sucker. But he wasn't done yet, so I stayed still and listened.

"I never played the cancer card. I never asked for anything. On Monday, I'll go home. Back to the hospital and the doctors. I'll get the test results and do whatever they say." He squared his shoulders and looked at me. "You said to play the dice roll we've got, right? I still don't really understand what that means, but I think this is my roll. I'm playing the cancer card. I'm going to this festival, and I want you to come with me."

The world had shrunk down to just the two of us until Carmen spoke again. "We don't have tickets."

Albie's eyes broke away from mine, and my lungs burned. I realized I hadn't been breathing and had to remind myself how to do it. In and out. In and out.

"We only have twenty-seven to fifty-seven days," he said. "But so what?"

Carmen looked at me as if I could talk some sense into him. *In and out.* I shrugged. "Can't argue with the cancer card."

Albie's reddened cheeks split into a smile. He winced and touched them gingerly. "Ow."

"I'm still mad at you, you know," Carmen said to me.

"I just rescued us from Ethel," I replied. "You should be thanking me."

"We were only there because of *you*!"

"Details."

"You're sorry, right?" Albie's eyes were on me again. "And you're not lying about anything else?"

I thought of the video inside Albie's house. The Catch a Dream donations on my phone. Carmen and Albie smiling up at the stars. I couldn't lose them.

"Nope." I turned to Carmen and raised my right hand in the air. "In the future, I will refrain from getting us locked up by creepy turtle enthusiasts."

"You're infuriating," she said.

"Thank you," I said.

She turned in the direction of the cascading lights and towering speakers. "How are we going to get into a festival we don't have tickets for?"

Albie cracked his knuckles. "Leave that to me."

CHAPTER 22

LEAVING IT TO ALBIE MEANT WE CHANGED IN THE BUSHES. CARMEN and I both protested but then Albie gave us a stern look and we relented. *It's Albie.*

"You look. Wow."

I was wrestling my cutoff T-shirt over my head when I heard Albie stumbling over his words. I smoothed the shirt over my stomach and noticed him staring at me like he'd just found me again after a long time apart. When he looked at me like that, it felt like no one had ever seen me before.

I grabbed a handful of suckers from my bag and used them to fasten my hair into two buns on either side of my head.

"I mean. You look, uh, you know, great," Albie said at last.

I used my phone's camera as a mirror so I could slather some dark purple lipstick across my mouth. With the dark color covering my lips I felt more like myself. "Obviously."

His fingers brushed the skin near my shoulder. "Is that—"

The place where his fingers touched me sparked. "Teeth marks from Ethel's dentures, yeah. I'm hoping it starts a hot new trend."

He dropped his hand. I grabbed my phone and put it between us, taking a video of Albie's new look. He was wearing mom jeans and a loose muscle tee that showed off his arms and the curve of his ribs. He had a bandanna looped around his neck, a bucket hat plopped on his head, and massive mirrored sunglasses hiding his eyes.

"I think the sunburn adds a nice touch," he said.

I tried to find the words. "You look—"

"Like that try-hard poet." I recorded Carmen breezing out of the bushes and doing a twirl. She looked effortlessly flawless in her glittery rainbow outfit.

Albie fist pumped the air. "Elliot Why! Yes!"

"But only because no one knows what he actually really looks like," Carmen finished. "It just seems like you raided his closet."

"I accept your compliment," Albie said.

"It wasn't a compliment." Carmen peered longingly down the beach to the cloud of lights and sound. "Jordan Banner went on at sunset."

Translation: We were missing the show.

"What's the plan, Oh Great Poet?" I asked Albie. Carmen and I were the ones with plans; we'd plotted our escape from the hospital, stealing the boat, breaking free from No Class Ethel. Albie was full of heart, not scheming. But he'd wanted to lead the charge here.

"Right," Albie said. "The plan. I, uh, have one."

"We can talk about it while we walk to the festival," Carmen said.

Twenty minutes later, we were no closer to entry to the festival and much closer to FOMO. We wandered along the perimeter of the festival. I kept my camera on to film everything. A black fence about twice our height separated the neat beach path from Dream Fest's neon lights and pumping speakers. Jordan Banner was on the main stage, closest to the ocean. I could barely hear the smooth sound of his beats over an EDM set closer to the fence.

"Almost there," Albie muttered to himself.

Carmen saw me recording the fence on my phone. "Think Albie could make the climb?"

"No way," I said. The fence was smooth, with no handholds, and too tall to jump.

I swiped up to check my Catch a Dream page again. I'd sliced together a short clip of Carmen and Albie revealing their festival outfits and posted it with the caption **Real talk: the Snack got a glow up.** The video of them trying on outfits in the store had racked up 15,000 views while Ethel was holding us captive, but I still had only $2,150 in pledges in my fundraising account.

"You are so addicted to that thing," Carmen said, staring at my phone with open disdain.

I pocketed it before she could see the screen. "As usual, your judgment and attitude are much appreciated."

She rolled her eyes. "I just feel bad for you, you know? Albie and I are having this holistic experience and being fully present with our processing process, and you're still drowning in screen time."

"Processing process," I repeated.

Carmen rolled her eyes. "Albie knows what I mean."

"No, I totally wish I had my phone," Albie said. "My siblings would love to see this."

We followed the curve of the fence as it branched away from the main entrance area and into a silent pocket near the back of the festival grounds. My feet were blistering inside the cheap cowboy boots I'd picked out at the store.

"This was a good idea, Albie," I started, "But—"

Albie stopped so suddenly that I ran straight into his back. "There he is."

He pointed to a guy perched on the hood of a massive gleaming truck. He had olive skin, shaggy blond hair, and a cigarette dangling from his lips.

"Not my type," I said.

"He's our guy." Albie hopped off the curb and walked over to him, pulling the bandanna up to his nose as he went.

Carmen surged after him. "That guy's bad news. I can tell."

I tugged on her arm and pulled her back. "We have to let him try."

Carmen sighed. "Fine. But if anything happens—"

"It's all my fault, you're turning me in, I'll never finish the grief processing process. I get it!"

We watched as Albie leaned against the hood of the truck and started chatting. The guy nodded and offered Albie a puff from his cigarette. To my surprise, Albie took it.

"Ohmygod." Carmen was rigid beside me. "It's *drugs.* What if it's laced with something? What if the MTP feeds on marijuana?"

"We'll be lucky if the worst thing the parasite does is make Albie a stoner for the last two months of his life."

Albie gestured with his hands, pointing at the fence, to us, and to Scooter strapped to his chest. Then they shook hands and the guy on the truck hopped off the hood of the truck and ambled to the driver's side.

"OK, he's coming back," Carmen whispered while fidgeting with her hair. "Be cool."

"I am cool. You're the one acting weird."

Albie hustled over to us and pulled down the bandanna. He was beaming.

"We're in," he said.

"How?" Carmen hissed. "Did you sell your body to get tickets? Albie, it's not worth it!"

"I recited some poetry to him," Albie said. "Appealed to his highest self. And now he's going to give us a lift."

It was mostly dark on the other side of the fence. The only light came from a few scattered load-in trucks. In the distance, I could see the three stages spread out like nesting dolls. The lights and smoke made everything hazy, and the electrifying sound of the music from each stage braided together. I picked out the melody of one of Jordan's first hits, "Generation Huh?" We were so close.

"Give us a lift how?" I asked. It wasn't like he'd be able to drive through the fence.

The truck headlights snapped on, flooding us in spotlight. It reversed out of the parking lot and sped onto the curbed sidewalk. Albie, Carmen, and I scrambled to get out of the way as it pulled up parallel to the fence.

Albie clambered into the truck bed and then up onto the roof. From that position, he was slightly taller than the fence.

I waited for Carmen to jump in with her uptight Virgo energy. When she stayed silent, I gave her a nudge. "It looks like Albie wants to use the roof of the truck as a launch pad to hop the fence," I said, waiting for the explosion of anger.

Carmen tilted her head. "It's not a bad idea."

"Exactly. It's danger—wait what?"

"I said it's not a bad idea," Carmen said over the rumbling truck engine. She climbed into the truck bed. I just stared at her. When had Perfect Carmen turned into an agent of chaos?

"That's the MTP speaking," I yelled. "It lowers inhibitions, remember? You're Carmen. You care about safety and rules and the law and all that nonsense!" Carmen took Albie's hand and he pulled her up onto the roof. "Think about Jillian!"

Carmen looked down at me, her gauzy skirt whipping around her legs. "It's statistically unlikely I've been infected with MTP. And I'm thinking about myself."

Carmen backed up into Albie, took two leaping steps, and hurtled herself over the fence. I hurried around the truck, expecting to see her body splattered on the grass.

She popped up laughing on the other side, picking shreds of grass out of her hair. "That wasn't so bad. Hurry before someone notices."

"Take Scooter." Albie detached the baby carrier from his front and dangled it over the fence, Carmen reached up and caught the bundle when Albie dropped it. Albie stepped back and gestured to the space in front of him. "All you, Hattie."

I peered through the car windows. The driver was listening to heavy rock and drumming on the steering wheel. "You're aware that you're currently aiding and abetting criminal activity?"

"I'm Ayden!" he yelled. "My parents retired here, and now I, like, live with them. But it's cool because we're, like, best friends, you know? They don't make me pay rent as long as I take care of their boat, which blows. But I'm a free spirit, so mostly it's cool, you know?"

"I do not know. That literally has nothing to do with what I just said re: criminal activity."

I turned away from the window. Albie had slid off the roof and opened the truck bed to make it easier for me to climb in.

He reached out his hand. "It's OK. I've got you."

No one had ever gotten me before. I took his hand and hoisted myself into the truck bed. He pressed his palms onto the roof of the truck and pushed himself back up.

"When did you get so acrobatic?" I asked.

"Your story about the circus inspired me. Come on."

He squatted down, and I didn't want to look afraid, so I took his hands again and let him pull me up onto the roof. We stood face-to-face, hands intertwined, and for a second it felt like the festival was a spotlight just for us.

"We don't have time for this main character moment!" Carmen yelled. She was holding Scooter's baby carrier at arm's length from her chest.

Albie untangled our fingers and turned me around to face the fence. I felt the heat of him against my back.

"You've got this," he whispered. "I'm with you."

A kaleidoscope of color and sound waited on the other side. Music, people, food, laughter. I wanted to cross over, but I couldn't find the strength to move.

"What are you waiting for?" Albie asked. It was hard to hear him over the roar of the truck engine and my heart thudding up to my ears.

"I'm scared." It came out in a voice so small I had to repeat it again. "I'm scared."

"I won't let anything happen to you." His body was warm and close, a solid presence trying to melt my panic.

My mom used to say those words to me when I was scared there was a monster in my closet. Even then, as a small kid, I had known they weren't true. She couldn't protect me from the monster living in our house the same way Albie couldn't protect me from anything on either side of the fence.

"What if I fall?"

Albie rested his hands loosely on my waist. "I'm not going to lie, it would hurt. You might twist an ankle. But you'd survive."

"What's taking so long?" Carmen yelled. Easy for her to say; she'd probably never been scared in her whole life.

"I know you love Jordan Banner," Albie said, trying a different tactic. "If we jump now, we can still see him."

Ayden popped his head out of the truck. "That's beautiful, dude."

Albie shook his head. "Not now."

"How do you know that?" I asked him.

"Because I know you."

I shrugged off Albie's warm hands and backed up. He hopped down into the truck bed to give me room.

I didn't want to miss Jordan Banner. I didn't want to be left in the dark while Albie and Carmen sailed to the other side. I didn't want to fall or be eaten alive by a parasite. I wanted to grow up. I wanted to live.

I took two leaping steps and then threw myself into the air.

CHAPTER 23

I WAS WINDMILLING THROUGH THE AIR FOR A SMOOTH TWO SECONDS before the toe of my boot nicked the top of the fence, and I tumbled toward the ground, landing on my stomach with a loud *oomph*. I wiggled my toes and fingers against the trampled grass. Everything moved. My body was still mine. I was alive.

Albie landed in a crouch next to me a few moments later. He smiled at me and picked some dirt out of my hair.

"Not bad," he said. "Your head OK?"

"No." Because what my head was thinking was something along the lines of: *I'm maybe a little bit in love with Albie.* I was a terrible person, and we were dying, but somehow, that was the realization that sucker punched me the hardest.

Carmen grabbed Albie's arm and pulled him to his feet. "Stop staring and move! We're missing literally everything."

The opening hook of one of my favorite Jordan Banner songs, "Dead Bet," reverberated across the field. Albie helped me up. My chest pressed against his for one second before he pulled away to hook Scooter back into place.

Carmen ran through the corridor of trailers and food trucks and into the massive hive of people buzzing across the festival grounds, waving at us to follow. I skipped after her, stomach flip-flopping with every hop. *In love. With Albie.*

We walked under an arch of rainbow-lit speakers shaking with sound so powerful it vibrated in my sternum. The main stage loomed on the other side of the arch, bigger than a cruise ship and surrounded by waves of smoke. The crowd was an ocean around it, bouncing balloons back and forth and shooting water guns into the air.

"There he is!" Carmen screamed and took off, throwing herself into the crowd with reckless abandon.

"This is. I didn't know. I can't believe." Albie's eyes glistened as he took it all in.

The feelings inside me puffed me up until I thought I might float off.

"I know." I threaded my fingers through his and dragged him through the crowd, stunned at the way our hands fit together, how my insides flipped in recognition of him. His pulse beat against my palm as we jogged to catch up with Carmen.

Jordan Banner emerged from the smoke wearing black jeans, a white T-shirt, and a flower crown. His black skin was coated in glitter and his hair was a new color—bleached blond with an orange stripe down the sides.

"I've got one more song for you, Miami," he said. "Are you ready?"

The crowd thrashed and roared, crashing toward the stage. Albie, Carmen, and I were carried with them.

It was like being inside a teenage unicorn's rave fantasy. Glitter and skin, a blaze of neon and sparkles and bodies wrapped together.

Jordan strutted over to the keyboard and plucked out the five-note melody of his most popular song, "If I Don't Make a Sound, I'm Not Here."

Carmen grabbed my hand and pulled me forward. "This is my song!" she screamed. I screamed back. It was my song, too.

Carmen elbowed us into the swarm of people, plowing closer and closer to the stage. The crowd broke around her like water. She was the type of girl people made space for.

She didn't stop until we were only a few rows of people from the front, close enough to see the stairs on the side of the stage guarded by a beefy security guard and the line where the glitter faded and the cords and stacks of black boxes began. More importantly, we were close enough to see the JB necklace Jordan was wearing and what looked like a fresh shark tattoo on his arm.

JB played the melody and whispered the words: *"What's the point of all this beauty if no one knows I'm here I'm here I'm here."* The beat dropped, the lights strobed, the crowd became a wild, surging wave.

Carmen picked up the muddy ends of her skirt and twirled. Albie lifted Scooter to the sky, and we danced.

"I'm here I'm here I'm here!" Jordan screamed into the microphone.

"I'm here!" Albie roared.

"I'm here!" I howled at the sky.

The three of us clasped hands, dancing in and out of flashing lights, grinning at each other and yelling at the sky. Albie's palm was warm and thudding against mine. We were jumping, spinning, stomping closer to tomorrow. And Albie was looking at me like I was transparent, and he could see exactly what was going on inside me.

There was no MTP. No Catch a Dream or lollipops or lies. Just us, living a story better than any lie I could've made up.

Albie tugged me closer and spun me until I was dizzy enough to fall into his chest. We laughed at the sky, entwined for one perfect moment before Albie spun me away and I stumbled into the crowd. The writhing tangle of bodies pushed me up and I danced back to our patch of ground. I tried to take Albie's hands again but they were balled into fists.

I followed his gaze to see Carmen tangled up with a girl wearing a neon crown tilted on her head. When I looked back at Albie, his eyes were teary. It didn't matter that Carmen would never want him back. He still had feelings for her. And I wasn't enough.

"I'm going to find a bathroom!" I yelled because I'd rather be alone and Jordan Banner–less than watch him look at her like that.

Albie nodded, barely glancing at me.

I fought my way to the edge of the crowd. The temperature dropped and the music quieted as I stomped away. I pulled out my phone. Twenty-seven missed calls from Mom. *Why the hell not.* I opened my voicemail and pressed play.

"You need to come home. Please, Hattie. I've been rerunning the samples on the MTP test products and—"

I pressed delete before I could hear anymore. Next.

"I was thinking about what you said about your dad—"

Delete.

"All I want—"

Delete. Delete. Delete.

The throbbing tangle of the crowd loosened as Jordan's song slowed and neared the end. I put my elbows up and fought back through the crowd of bodies to the front near the staircase, even though I would have rather popped a squat and emo'd out until the MTP took me. Once the crowd started to disperse, there was no way I'd be able to find Albie and Carmen again.

"I'm not moving!" someone yelled and elbowed me back when I was close enough to see Carmen's rainbow skirt.

I looked up to see blond hair. Sparkling eyes. A doughy face that even non-compulsive-lying students would want to deceive. "Mrs. Howard?"

"Hattie?" She jumped away from me, hands flying up to cover the Jordan Banner Baby tattoo crawling across her collarbone. "I can explain!"

"No, thank you!" I turned and burrowed into the crowd, keeping my head down until I snagged the end of Carmen's skirt.

"Hattie! There you are." Carmen squealed and pulled me into a hug that indicated she'd either taken some drugs from a stranger or the MTP was getting to her. I wasn't sure which would be worse.

"You won't believe who I just saw," I said.

Strobe lights flared on the stage. Jordan Banner yelled, "Thank you, Miami!" The crowd convulsed in the lights.

"Who?" Carmen screamed.

"Wait, where's Albie? He needs to hear this," I said, trying to mask the hunger in my voice with humor.

"I thought he was with you," Carmen said. "He followed you when you wandered off."

I spun around, looking for the muscle tee, the bucket hat, the smile. Every person was a bruised shadow with hints of neon glittering on their skin.

"Albie?" Carmen screamed. No one was listening.

"Albie?" I called.

An endless swell of people behind me. In front of us was the stage where Jordan had just been. To the right of the stage was a tented area with scaffolded stairs. A huge WWE-size man was pounding up them, holding a smaller, skinnier boy by the shoulder.

"Albie!" I grabbed Carmen and pointed.

Security had Albie. They must have figured out that he didn't have a ticket.

Carmen and I hurtled ourselves into the crowd without hesitation. I'd thought Carmen had crowd-parting abilities before. Now she pummeled through, using her elbows to break open a path before us, shoving anyone who got in our way. Without the music, the hum of the crowd sounded hollow.

Finally, we made it to the barrier at the side of the stage. Another WWE-size man stood at the foot of the stairs.

Carmen put a hand on the barricade to vault herself over.

"VIPs only," the man said and gently pushed her off.

"You don't understand—"

"Our friend—"

"VIPs only. I won't tell you again."

A pair of mirrored sunglasses popped up at the top of the stairs. Albie's bandanna was pulled up so high, I couldn't see his face. What if he had an asthma attack? His inhaler was in Carmen's bag.

"They're with me," he said.

The security opened the gate and waved us through.

Carmen clomped up the stairs. "Albie! Are you OK?"

Albie shook his head frantically and held a finger over his mouth. He turned and led us around a curtain through which we could see the stage, the DJ setup, and the crowd beyond, looking vast and endless.

We popped out on the other side of the stage and there he was. Distinguished jaw, blazing eyes, and bleached hair. Just standing there like a normal human being. Like he wasn't a pop god.

Carmen and I froze. Jordan Banner raised his arms wide and walked toward us with a smile.

"This can't be real," Carmen said. "Pinch me."

I pinched her.

"Ow!" She smacked my hand away. "What was that for?"

"You literally said 'pinch me.' "

"It was *literally* a figure of speech."

Albie widened his eyes and shook his head slightly as he got closer to us.

"These are the friends I was telling you about," he said shyly

"What's up, fam! Any friend of Why's is a friend of mine."

Jordan wrapped Carmen and me in a side hug. His hand touched my shoulder. His lungs were breathing air that was only a few feet from the air that my lungs were breathing.

My mind was short-circuiting, but one thing was abundantly clear: Jordan Banner thought Albie was Elliot Why.

CHAPTER 24

"HOW'S THE NEW SONG COMING?" JORDAN ASKED. "THE STUFF ON your socials is killing it."

Jordan Banner (Jordan. Banner. Still not over it.) grabbed Albie's hand and slung him into one of those half-hugs that guys do to display intimacy in a restrained way. Backstage was a dark cave compared to the spectacle exploding on the main stage. The four of us stood wedged between scaffolding and equipment, squinting to see each other in the flashlights of stage assistants hurrying by.

I could not believe that sweet, dumb Jordan Banner had mistaken sweet, dumb Albie for that mysterious online dude who wrote poems about being the sad and lonely misunderstood voice of his generation.

Albie sputtered. His bandanna was pulled up to his nose, floppy bucket hat hiding most of his hair, eyes hidden behind giant mirrored sunglasses. He didn't look like himself, but he was still Albert Chang, and he would definitely mess this up.

I stepped forward, hand extended, ready to smooth the situation over. I wasn't special or talented or good at pretty much anything, but this was something I could handle. Carmen and Albie were the ones with friends and family and the mysterious ability to make people like them. Getting us out of this would be my contribution to the team.

But my mind flatlined when Jordan Banner turned toward me. He smelled exactly like I'd imagined: sparkles and dreams. "He. I. You. Capiche?"

Albie stepped in front of me, shaking his head subtly. He cleared his throat and said in a deep, gravelly voice, "The songs will be birthed when they're ready. We're all on this journey through our communal subconscious together."

Jordan bent his head toward Albie's and whispered something in his ear.

Carmen stepped closer to me and hissed, "He spoke in complete sentences. It's getting to him the fastest."

She meant the parasite.

Jordan's eyes widened at whatever Albie whispered back to him.

Whispered. In Jordan Banner's. Ear. How was Albie pulling this off?

I bounced on the balls of my feet, ready to run. We could dart around the scaffolding and jump off the stage, disappearing into the crowd in seconds. Surely the greatest artist of our generation would see right through Albie's rich-kid-pretending-to-be-a-different-rich-kid-who-is-also-a-tortured-artist act.

Instead, Jordan snapped like he was at a slam poetry reading.

"We have to get him out of here," Carmen whispered, keeping a bright smile plastered across her face.

"I think Jordan . . . likes him?"

Carmen's eyes narrowed. She wasn't used to being the second-most competent person in the room.

"What's with the turtle?" Jordan gestured to Scooter, who was still dangling from Albie's chest.

"In the end, we're all just turtles being carried around by Mother Nature," Albie/Elliot responded smoothly.

"Albie's a hero," I whispered. He was pulling off a lie that even I wouldn't have been able to sell.

"This isn't him. It's the parasite."

I shook my head. No way I was letting her ruin this for Albie, even if she was the unrequited love of his life. "No, I think it's all him. We don't know how the parasite works." I thought of my mom's frantic voicemail. She was still finding out how bad it was. "Besides, you're the one who keeps insisting that we might not even have it."

"Wow, that's deep." Jordan shook his head, looking like he was upset he hadn't thought of the turtle thing first. He turned and gestured to us. "So who are your experiential partners?"

"Is that a sex thing?" Carmen asked. I pinched her arm to shut her up. These weren't exactly ideal circumstances, but I was about to meet my idol. I'd been dreaming of this day for years.

"This is Hattie," Albie/Elliot said, cutting me off before I could introduce myself. "Up-and-coming actress. She was on that show with the hot teenagers. Very promising future. And this is Carmen. Professional F1 boat racer."

"Big fan," I said. Jordan's perfect white teeth were practically glowing in the dark. "My character is. On the show."

"Pull it together," Carmen muttered out of the side of her mouth. To Jordan she said, "I've heard of you. Congratulations on the show."

I wondered why she was being so cold to him. Earlier, she'd sounded like a total stan.

"Tight." Jordan turned away, taking the spotlight beam of his smile with him. "We good, Why? Gotta be honest, when you didn't respond to my last message, I thought you were ghosting me."

I took out my phone and hid it with my body as I recorded the scaffolding and black road cases scattered around the backstage area, slowly panning the camera over to show Jordan Banner's back as Albie animatedly explained the power of poetry to him. The Snack Attack fans were going to *freak*, and Bannerheads would be clamoring all over the comment section to figure out what Elliot Why and Jordan were working on.

I wondered how long it would take before I could call him JB in person.

Jordan asked, "Y'all want a picture?"

"Absolutely!" I managed to say as I handed him my phone.

We huddled together in the shadow of the Dream City stage: Albie's face was hidden by his disguise, Carmen let her Virgo energy fly, and I didn't have enough lollipops to hide how happy I was. Jordan waited until the lights onstage flashed to snap the pic and then handed me my phone.

"You on the set list?" Jordan asked.

"Not performing." Albie/Elliot clasped his hands together as if in prayer. "Just here to ingest the raw meat of experience."

My mouth hung open. Was this how people normally felt around me? Like I was a broken toilet that could spout shit at any moment?

"I respect that," Jordan said, leaning away as a guy with a sleek ponytail and tight black jumpsuit came up and whispered in his ear. "Sorry, my mic's about to go hot again. But I'll hit you up after the finale about the after-party tomorrow. Location's not going out until right before to keep paparazzi away, but I'll add you to Glen's list."

"I'll check my cal," Albie/Elliot said.

"We will definitely be there," I said at the same time.

"And hey," Jordan said as he gave each of us a hug, "stick around for the second finale. Best view is from right here. Glen, would you get Why's new number so we can get in touch about the collab?"

Albie lifted his glasses for a second when Jordan's back was turned and winked at me. Glen—the mere mortal who'd managed to secure the best job on Earth—put Albie's cellphone number into his massive tablet. There was a slight hiccup when Albie had to check the settings of his phone to find the number and explain to the assistant that he didn't have it memorized because of his anti-imperialist views. Whatever that meant.

"Where's the party again?" Carmen popped her head in to ask. "Ballpark?"

She could play it cool around Jordan Banner but couldn't keep her mouth shut when an opportunity to coordinate calendars popped up.

"Jordy will be in touch." Glen propped the clipboard against his chest and slid out of our corner.

We lasted approximately .05 seconds before losing our functioning brains.

My mouth hung open as I turned to face Albie. "Who are you and what have you done with Albie Chang?"

"Can you believe it?"

"You were amazing!"

"After-party, baby!"

The lights dimmed and Jordan's name echoed across the beach. "One more time, Joooordan Bannnner!"

Fire cannons shot into the sky and the stage exploded in lights and sound and confetti as Jordan strutted onto the stage to perform a surprise finale and burst into the chorus of one of his oldest hits, "Boomer Crooner."

We danced until my lungs felt like they were about to explode. The fog stung my nostrils and the confetti stuck to my sweat-soaked skin. Albie rested his head on my shoulder and the blood in my veins ran electric.

"Hey!" Carmen tugged on my sleeve.

I shrugged her off, balancing Albie's head on the knob of my shoulder. "Not now!"

She stepped in front of us, blocking our view of Jordan's dance sequence.

"I don't want to be overdramatic," I said, "but if you don't move in two seconds, I will probably murder you."

"*Look!*" She pointed to the crowd.

"What? He's a pop star," Albie sighed. "People love him."

"Not there." Carmen grabbed our shirt sleeves and angled us to the side. "There!"

We were looking at the side of the stage we'd been standing closest to. I followed the line of the barricade fencing to the bottom of the stairs where the WWE security guard was talking to someone with white hair and—

Bad news.

It was Ethel. And two men in DBD jackets were standing right behind her.

CHAPTER 25

JORDAN BANNER LAUNCHED HIMSELF INTO A BACKFLIP FROM THE drummer's kit, and the crowd erupted. They rushed toward the stage, creating a churning tsunami as they catapulted crowdsurfers toward security and clambered onto each other's shoulders, doubling the height of the wave.

"This is everything," Albie whispered.

I squinted to make out the two DBD officers. A short, muscular guy and a tall, blonde woman. My mom wasn't there. I couldn't tell if my heart was clenching from relief or disappointment.

"We have to get out of here," Carmen said.

Albie was too mesmerized by Jordan's performance to respond.

Carmen jerked his shoulders and spun him toward Ethel and the DBD officers.

Albie rubbed his eyes. "I think the MTP is getting to me."

"You're not seeing things," Carmen said. "DBD found us."

Albie rested his hands on Scooter's shell and rocked back and forth. "You don't know that. We could be having a shared hallucination."

Carmen snapped her fingers in front of his face. *Pop pop pop.* "Wake up! If the DBD agents catch us, they'll take us back to the ward before we can go to Jordan's after-party. And if Ethel catches us—"

"She'll take Scooter," Albie said, covering the place on Scooter's head where his ears would be if he weren't, you know, a *turtle*.

"I was going to say she'll turn Hattie in, but sure. Let's go with the Scooter thing."

Carmen spun in a slow circle, taking in our surroundings. The park and festival were in front of us. Behind the stage was a tangle of stairs and scaffolding leading out into a city of tents and RVs that dead-ended at the ocean. She pursed her lips and turned to me. "What do you think we should do?"

She was asking me because I had cast myself as the con. The one brave enough to get into trouble and smart enough to get out of it. It had felt liberating, on the roof of the truck, to tell Albie something true. But now I saw that I was no different from the dumb girls in horror movies who opened the door to the basement; only instead of finding a serial killer in the darkness, I found the shadowy parts of myself—and now making it out before they hacked me to pieces felt impossible.

"Should we hide backstage?" Carmen asked. "They can't get up here without passes. Or make a run for it? Get lost in the crowd? Hattie?"

The spinning Dimensional Door. The voicemails on my phone. Parasite. Twenty-seven days. *I need help, and I don't know how to ask for it.*

"We can't leave," Albie scoffed. "Jordan Banner personally invited me to the top-secret festival after-party tomorrow."

"Us. He invited us," Carmen corrected him. She peeked her head around the curtain. "I don't think they can see us from this angle."

The stairs jutted out to the side and front of the stage. It was far enough away that the DBD officers' navy jackets blended into the crowd if I wasn't focusing on them and Ethel looked too short to be intimidating. Maybe they hadn't seen us yet, but they clearly knew we were around here somewhere.

"Uh." I still couldn't get the words out.

"Hattie?" Carmen's voice was frantic.

"I—I can't," I finally managed to say.

"Right." Carmen nodded once, then rolled her shoulders back. "OK then. Plan B: Run."

She grabbed Albie's arm and dragged him away from Jordan Banner's closing notes.

He dug in his heels. "But the party," he whined.

In one sharp motion, Carmen turned, grabbed the bucket hat off his head, and crumpled it in her hand. "The parasite is making you think none of this matters, but I know Hattie and Scooter matter to you!"

Albie patted his head in shock. "You took my hat."

"Hattie's having an existential crisis, and you have asthma. I'm a track star and natural leader. I can get us out of this, but you have to do exactly as I say. OK? We're going to make a run for the boat. We'll sail out a bit and then come back when the coast is clear."

Albie snorted. "Coast. Clear. It's a literal coast. Get it?"

Carmen slapped Albie's shoulder with the crumpled bucket hat.

He rubbed his arm. "I needed that."

Carmen looked back at me. "For Scooter?"

I knew what she was really saying was *For Albie*. I nodded. "For Scooter."

Albie put his hand on his heart. "And for the after-party."

Carmen and I exchanged a look. Either the MTP was getting to him sooner than us, or whatever Ayden had been smoking was stronger than we'd thought.

"Stay close," Carmen said.

We sandwiched Albie between us and jogged into the maze of equipment backstage. I looked back once to see Jordan taking a third bow while cannons shot balls of confetti into the sky. I could no longer see Ethel or the security guard at the foot of the stairs, but a flashlight beam cut through the darkness where we'd been standing.

"They're coming," I said.

Carmen broke into a run.

We raced through the black-clad stagehands and down a set of rickety metal stairs at the back side of the stage. The spotty grass field before us was littered with white mess tents and trailers. The moon replaced the rainbow of lights pouring from the front of the stage, bathing everything in silver.

I followed the shimmering trail of Carmen's skirt as she dashed around tents and RVs, running alongside the ocean. There was a small security checkpoint blocking the exit of what I now realized was the staff and talent section. I looked back and saw flashlights bobbing through the dark behind us.

"That's them!" a voice cried.

"Albie, do your Elliot Why thing," Carmen commanded. To me she said, "Be cool."

"As if I could be anything else," I huffed.

We followed her lead and slowed to a walk. It was hard to breathe past the thudding of my heart. *MMA. A parasite in my bloodstream. My mom's crackling voicemail.* I focused on the back of Carmen's head instead.

We walked through the security checkpoint. They were trying to keep people out, not in, so they barely gave us a second look. Albie really sold it though.

"Elliot Why." He clasped his hands in front of his chest and nodded at them. "Thank you for your service. Elliot Why."

We'd barely stepped past the fence when I heard Ethel's voice shout, "Stop them! Stop those kids!"

"Stay calm," Carmen directed. Albie and I walked with our heads stiffly forward, not daring to look back.

"Halt!" Ethel screeched. She sounded closer than before.

"Serious question: Do you think she brought the crossbow?" Albie asked.

"Let's hope not," I said. The crossbow looked like a prop for her *Land of Invaders* cosplay, but given her level of dedication to the game, I suspected it might be fully functional.

"Albie, as soon as it's safe, we'll take an inhaler break," Carmen said. "Until then, try to keep up."

Carmen plunged into the mass exodus of people leaving Jordan Banner's set and broke into a run. Her posture was perfect. Shoulders back, legs kicking with ease. I definitely didn't look that good while running, but the panic in my chest loosened with every step. We were being chased and there was a parasite eating my insides, but all of that was harder to think about when I was so bad at cardio.

I followed Carmen's billowing skirt and Albie's neon muscle tee into the thickest part of the crowd, past the smaller stage and the food trucks and endless beer gardens, until we popped out of an exit on the far side. Carmen jogged down the path running parallel to the beach.

The air in my lungs felt glass-sharp. I stumble-jogged after Carmen, leaving a trail of confetti floating behind me like feathers. I kept my eyes on her back and tried to listen to the sound of my feet pounding the pavement instead of the new chorus of voices in my head telling me I'd never be able to keep up.

Carmen cut through a patch of bushes and plants, and the maze of docks where we'd parked *Seas the Day* that morning finally came into view.

The festival was a distant roar. It was just us and the moonlight, sandwiched between silent Miami skyscrapers and the lapping ocean.

Carmen slowed to a stop behind a palm tree. I bent over, hands on my knees, guzzling air.

"Shh!" Carmen peered around the tree. "Look."

Flashlights bobbed on the dock. The orange streetlamps illuminated people in DBD jackets moving down the aisles, shining their lights into each boat they passed.

Carmen pressed her back flat against the palm tree. "So *Seas the Day* is out. We'll have to find somewhere else to hide. Any ideas, Albs?"

I looked behind us. The beach path was deserted save for a few cyclists whizzing past. No sign of Albie.

"He was right behind me," I said.

"You *lost* Albie?" Carmen sputtered.

"You said to keep up!"

Carmen and I turned and crashed back through the bushes, slapping each other with the prickling branches as we retraced our steps.

"If something happens to him, I swear—" Carmen started.

"I know."

"I see him!" Carmen plunged ahead. I followed but collided with her back when she stopped short in a small clearing off the side of the path. Albie and Ethel were circling each other. Ethel had her hands up in a fighting stance. Albie was wheezing.

"Stay back!" Ethel said when she saw us.

"He needs his inhaler!" Carmen said.

The running had cleared my brain enough to know that I could not stand still and let this happen. I lunged, but Carmen stopped me with a straight arm. "We don't know if she has a weapon. Wait for the opening."

"She didn't bring the crossbow," I said.

"*Wait*."

"Take off those glasses and fight me like a man!" Ethel yelled.

"That's an incredibly patriarchal interpretation of what it means"—Albie gasped for air—"to be a man." He paused to take a few deep breaths. "I am going to take them off, though. Because they are sunglasses, and it's dark, and I can't see you very well with them on."

Albie yanked the glasses off and tossed them to the ground.

"I'm going to wear that turtle's eyes as a necklace," Ethel said and moved into a fighting stance.

"Hurt people hurt turtles," Albie whispered.

There was no lie I could tell to get us out of this situation, but I was sick of just standing still. I shoved past Carmen and dove into the circle.

"Rear naked choke!" I yelled. Ethel whirled on me—she was surprisingly fast for someone her age—and grabbed something from her pocket.

"Weapon!" Carmen screamed from behind me.

My life didn't flash before my eyes. I didn't see a scrolling montage of lollipops and lies. I thought, *Not yet.*

And then my entire face was burning, and I couldn't see anything. I fell to my knees in the sand. My eyes stung and my face was somehow both on fire and numb at the same time.

I heard grunting and screaming. A slap. A slice. A moan.

"You pepper sprayed me!" That was Albie.

"You did it first."

"That was throat spray!" His words were cut off by a coughing fit.

Not yet. Not yet. Not yet.

I heard a short burst of maniacal laughter followed by retreating footsteps.

I wasn't sure if it was minutes or hours later when I was finally able to peel my eyes open. Carmen was kneeling over Albie. His eyes were red and swollen. She was doing compressions on his chest.

"I told you she might have a weapon!" Carmen yelled at me.

Albie shoved her away. "I'm fine." He sat up and continued hacking. Carmen handed him his inhaler and he took a few puffs from it.

Even when his breathing began to even out, something still felt wrong. The moon was dangling lopsided from the sky and the air was cold and dry. It took a few minutes for my vision to clear and for me to realize what had happened.

The baby carrier was empty.

Scooter was gone.

CHAPTER 26

ALBIE WAS INCONSOLABLE. THE STRAPS OF THE BABY CARRIER dangled loosely from his chest. His tears pooled in the bandanna around his neck. The swagger of his Elliot Why persona had completely evaporated.

"Do you want to turn ourselves in?" Carmen asked Albie. "We can find the DBD officers and go home."

Albie had to pause to take a few deep breaths before saying, "I'm not leaving."

"Because of the after-party tomorrow," Carmen said and held out his inhaler.

Albie swatted the inhaler away. "Because of Scooter!"

My eyes were puffed up so much I could barely keep them open to see the raw-red-meat color of his face. Based on the burning feeling inside my nostrils and throat, I was guessing my face looked the same. Tears were streaming out of my eyes, but I wasn't crying, and mucus dripped in globs from my nose.

Carmen ticked off our problems on her fingers. "We have no place to sleep, no way to get home, and no money. No water or medical kit to get this pepper spray out of your eyes. But we do have an invitation to a party tomorrow, so there's that."

"I'm not going anywhere without Scooter," Albie said.

"It's. Jordan. Banner," Carmen said slowly.

"It's. My. Endangered. Turtle," Albie said.

"I have some. Money, that is." I was barely able to squeeze the words out of my burning throat. I patted around inside my backpack until I found a small black wallet. "I lifted this off of Ethel."

Look, I'm not a street orphan in the 1840s. I'd never pickpocketed before. I hadn't been able to see anything because of the pepper spray and while scrabbling around to find a weapon happened to latch onto Ethel's wallet.

"I'm not going anywhere without Scooter," Albie said again. He spoke slowly, each breath labored. "That includes the party."

"Me neither," I said. Only instead of Scooter, I meant I wasn't going anywhere without Albie. Because I was pathetic and didn't care that he was in love with Carmen, and because he was my ticket to the $23,000 I needed to earn my mother's respect.

"You know how I feel about Jordan," Carmen said.

"You didn't even talk to him," I said.

"You were too ashamed to tell us you were a fan," Carmen spat back.

"You're supposed to be the responsible one! It's Albie. You're not even listening to him."

Carmen glanced over at the ocean. Through my puffy, pepper-sprayed eyes, I watched the emotions roll over her face for a moment before she smoothed her expression into one of absolute confidence. "Right. OK. Let's find a place to sleep."

Albie held on to my wrist and I held on to Carmen's, and together, we followed her past the hazy outline of boats bobbing in the bay and into the hazy outline of buildings in the city. There were bruises on my shoulder and neck and confetti stuck to my legs and it still felt like my entire face was swelling shut, and I'd never see Jordan Banner again. I was too exhausted to focus on anything but the warmth of Albie's hand clasped around my wrist.

It felt like we'd walked all the way back to Marsh Rock by the time Carmen paused under a buzzing neon light advertising the Sands Motel. The L-shaped building behind it was flamingo-pink. Anywhere was better than going home.

"Wait here," Carmen said and went inside to get us a room.

It was quiet save for the cars zooming past on the road and the buzzing glow of the sign. Albie kept his hand wrapped around my wrist, his fingers tapping at the nest of veins leading to my palm.

"I can't believe I lost him."

I couldn't believe a lot of things, mostly that we were talking about a turtle when we'd just met Jordan Banner.

"We're going to get him back," I said. "We'll get un-pepper sprayed. Get some sleep. And tomorrow we'll find him."

Carmen emerged from the lobby with two room cards and a bottle of hand sanitizer. She squirted some into her hand and rubbed it in from her shoulders to her fingertips.

"Disgusting," she murmured.

She led us around the back of the motel to room 106. The room had trampled pink carpet and two beds with thin, itchy-looking comforters. The white-blue light of the pool glowed through the windows.

Albie slid down to the floor and put his head in his hands. "Why would she turtlenap Scooter? She doesn't even know his napping schedule."

Carmen knelt down next to him. "People are terrible."

I went to the bathroom, lathered up my hands with soap, and washed my face, rinsing over and over and over, until the burning subsided and there was only a slight red ring around my eyes and nose.

I checked my phone. The video of Albie and Carmen dancing at Dream Fest was my biggest yet. The last clip was a brief glimpse of the two of them backstage, Albie facing Jordan Banner, Carmen staring down at the floor. The comments section was a flurry. Everyone was trying to figure out who and where we were.

I think he goes to my school.

That's def Jordan Banner's music playing in the background.

I blocked anyone who mentioned St. Croix High or Dream Fest, but internet sleuths were relentless. I'd once spent two days online tracking down what happened to a beanie Jordan Banner left behind at an awards show. I knew we didn't have long before the internet put the pieces together and uncovered our true identities.

On the bright side, my Catch a Dream account had $5,000 in pledges. Only $18,000 to go!

I reapplied my dark purple lipstick, kicked the bathroom door open, and went straight for the minifridge. Small, glittering bottles of alcohol were lined up inside of it like soldiers. A sticker on the front of the fridge advertised how much each bottle cost.

"We can't pay for that," Carmen said.

"I'm not going to pay for anything," I replied. This was Exit Ethics, after all. "Who's up for a swim?"

••••

Albie floated across the pool in a hot pink donut-shaped floatie. Either he'd forgotten he couldn't swim or the bravado of being Elliot Why had made him not care about the mass of water beneath him. Carmen and I sat on the deck, toes dangling in the water, watching him spin back and forth across the pool.

"You're acting stranger than usual," she said.

I took a swig of brown liquid from one of the minibar bottles. It tasted like the fire that had been inside of me all along, smoothed the lump in my throat enough for some true words to fall out. "I've decided something."

Carmen swirled the water with her toe. "Yeah?"

"I don't want to die."

Carmen laughed, then stopped herself when she saw the look on my face. "Oh, sorry. I thought that was a given."

"Nope. I just decided."

She resumed her toe swirling. "I guess I was wrong then. We do have something in common."

Albie spun his pool donut in slow circles with his hand. His eyes were rimmed pink from the pepper spray, his face tinged red with sunburn. "I'm tired of not wanting to die. It's exhausting."

"Cheers to that." I unscrewed the cap of a bottle filled with clear liquid and took a sip, trying to hide my gag of disgust. I'd never drank before. It's off brand, I know. Hot tip: If you give off the vibe of someone who drinks and parties, you get all of the reputational benefits with none of the hangovers or unsafe situations. But my dad had given me a sip of his beer at one of his *Land of Invader* games once. All his friends had laughed when I spit it out.

"I think the parasite is getting to me," I said, taking another drink and savoring how it burned all the way down my throat. "I feel all fuzzy."

"Pretty sure that's the alcohol," Carmen said.

"If I can have Scooter, I'll be OK with everything else," Albie whispered to himself.

"That's bargaining," Carmen said. "You're making really good progress through the stages of grief, Albs."

"I'm not a stage. How many times do I have to tell you?"

"Jeez," Carmen said under her breath.

The tension between the two of them felt thicker than the Florida humidity. Was Albie still jealous of Carmen dancing with the girl at the festival?

"I don't understand how they found us," I said, pushing the thought of Albie and Carmen out of my head and focusing on the warmth in my stomach. I'd made sure not to show the name of the boat we'd stolen in my videos. They probably didn't even realize I *was* shooting videos; no one knew about my burner account. Could Mrs. Howard have reported us? But she probably hadn't been told about DBD.

"Uh, well . . ." Carmen said.

"What did you do?"

She took a swig from one of the bottles. "I told my parents we were in Miami when I called this morning."

"Arghh," Albie and I groaned in unison.

"They were freaking out! I panicked and told them we were in Miami so they wouldn't lose it. They must have told DBD."

At least it hadn't been my fault. For once.

"I mean, I guess I can't really complain; I did get us locked in a storage closet," I said. *Also there's the minor detail of how I'm posting videos of you and Albie online to make money.* "We've all made mistakes."

"Cheers to that." Carmen and I clinked our bottles.

Albie looked like he was starting to doze off in the deep end.

I hadn't eaten since lunch. I could feel the alcohol slide all the way down my throat and hit my stomach, making everything far-off and flickering.

"At least your family cares," I said. "You have so many people waiting for you at home. Plus you're a lesbian icon, so that's cool."

Carmen scoffed. "I'm not an icon. I'm the only gay person most of the people in Marsh Rock have ever met. Do you know how much pressure that is?"

"I can't imagine," I said honestly. "But at least you have Jillian."

Carmen spun her toe in the water more aggressively until she'd created a small cyclone. "Yeah."

"And maybe a parasite!" I said, trying to cheer her up. "How many teenagers can say *that*?"

"Can you feel it? The parasite?" Carmen asked. "I don't feel any different."

She was being serious, so I closed my eyes and paid attention to what was going on under my skin. Tingling. Tension. Pain.

"I think I can feel it, but then I'm not sure." I opened my eyes. "I've always known something was wrong with me, so I honestly don't know if this is how it feels to be eaten from the inside out or this is just how it feels to be alive."

Carmen stared at me. "That was really beautiful. You should talk like that more often."

I scoffed and took another swig of the clear liquid. "No thanks."

"I mean it." Her voice was forceful enough to draw my gaze back to hers. "You like to joke, but when you say something serious, it's like . . . I don't know. You really let us see you."

"OK, save the sappy stuff for Jillian." Fireworks exploded above the beach—not the butterfly, romantic feeling kind of firework, an actual literal firework—popping and sparkling into dust against the inky black sky. The crackling sound jolted Carmen back to reality.

"Jillian." Carmen said the name like she'd forgotten it.

I'd known she was running from something. Why else would perfect Carmen have architected a hospital escape? I didn't think it could have been her girlfriend, but it was all starting to click into place: not going back home, not calling her, dancing with that other girl at the concert . . .

"I'm hungry," Albie moaned from the corner of the pool. "Aren't you guys starving?"

Carmen scrambled to her feet and went to the deep end, rolling her shoulders and positioning herself to dive in. I pulled out my phone and pressed record as she put her arms up and fell flat into the water in what had to be the worst belly flop I'd ever seen.

Albie laughed. Carmen swam to him in a few graceful strokes and spun his floatie in circles, towing him around the pool easily.

"Hattie, put the phone down and get in here!" Carmen said.

"I can't get my hair wet," I lied. "Because of the dye."

They fell back into an easy rhythm with each other, giggling and talking and looking at the stars. Whatever tension existed earlier had totally melted away. Carmen even coaxed Albie out of the floatie and gave him a swimming lesson in the shallow end of the pool.

And I watched it all from behind a screen.

The way Albie's sunburned neck and arms glowed in the red-and-gold light of the fireworks. How at ease Carmen was around him, moving his arms and lifting his legs to help him do a front stroke. The way his eyes trailed her every move.

When the last of the fireworks were sputtering out in the sky, Carmen pulled herself out of the pool and looked down at Albie.

"You're OK," she said, sounding like she was saying it to herself rather than asking him.

"I still can't swim," he said. "Hattie, back me up here."

"At least you didn't drown," I said.

"Yet," he snorted.

Carmen glanced between the two of us. "Well, I'm going to bed," she announced. "See you in the morning."

Albie climbed out of the pool and sat down beside me. His wet tank top clung to the lean muscles of his stomach. I looked up at the moon instead of the water dripping down his skin.

"What a day," he said, shaking out his hair in my direction.

I laughed and shielded my face from the droplets of water his hair flung all over me. "Thirty-to-sixty-days Albie is a hell of a guy."

"So is thirty-to-sixty-days Hattie," he said. "Though I'm not sure the timeline has much to do with it."

"What can I say? Some people are just born with the *it* factor," I joked.

He smiled to himself. And then he looked at me. *Really* looked at me. I wanted to kiss him the way I'd wanted to jump off the roof of that truck and into the lights.

But Albie was the one who leaned forward, eyes on my lips. He paused when he was a few inches away.

"Exit Ethics?" he asked.

I think I really like you. "Yeah."

He cupped his hand around my throat and pulled me to him, fingerprints splayed across the back of my neck. His pulse was pounding. We were breathing the same air.

I opened my mouth and dragged him closer to me. Knotted my hands in his hair and crawled over him so our legs were intertwined. He kissed me until my lips were chapped and aching and my clothes were soaked through.

I was shaking when he pulled away, skimming his thumb from my waist to my hips.

"How do you feel?" he asked, watching his other hand as it twisted in my hair.

A simple question with so many possible answers. A joke. A deflection. A lie.

Elated because he chose me and not Carmen. Confused that someone so thoroughly good thought I was worth kissing. Relieved because, for the first time since learning about the MTP, I was going to sleep without nightmares.

I couldn't stop the smile taking over my face. "Happy."

For once, I was telling the truth.

CHAPTER 27

I WOKE UP IN THE EARLY MORNING LIGHT, SPRAWLED ACROSS ONE of the white pool chairs, the bungee-like bands cutting into my back and hips. Someone in a Sands Motel polo and a vintage dad mustache was staring down at me.

"You can't sleep out here," he said.

I rubbed my eyes. "I'm not sleeping. Anymore."

Albie was curled up next to me, mouth hanging open, hands wrapped around my waist.

It was coming back to me. Jordan Banner. Albie and I in the cool blue light of the pool and the stars.

"The pool is for motel guests," the manager guy said. "You need to leave. *Immediately*."

"We're guests, aren't we?" I asked, not entirely sure. *Carmen did get us a room, right?*

My head was thudding harder and faster than I'd been pounding shots of liquor the night before—a feat I hadn't thought was possible. I pushed myself up and saw the remnants of our revelry. Strips of confetti were plastered to the pool deck. Carmen's gauzy rainbow skirt floated in the pool. Albie's bandanna and hat were in a heap at the foot of his chair. Some tiny kids in goggles and floaties were playing with the liquor bottles that had rolled into the water.

The manager pointed at us. "Out. Now!"

I gave him a salute and he stomped off.

I looked at Albie again. Because he was asleep, and I didn't have to make myself look away. His lips were tinged purple from my lipstick and his shirt was hiked up around his stomach. His eyes fluttered open under my gaze, wincing in the sun until they focused on me.

He squeezed my waist. "G'morning."

"You know who doesn't think it's a good morning?" I jerked a thumb to where the motel manager's eyes were burning into us from the lobby. "Mr. Kill Your Vibe is kicking us out of this motel."

"Typical," Albie said. He unwrapped himself from me and stood up, swaying slightly. I grabbed his hand and pulled myself up. We tiptoed around the slimy edge of the pool and exited through the gate.

"This headache," Albie said, "do you think it's the parasite or a hangover?"

He took a wrong turn and righted himself when he saw the direction I was walking.

"You didn't drink anything last night," I said. *Had he forgotten what happened?*

"Oh. Huh." He dug his palms into his eyes. "About last night—"

"Don't worry about it," I said. "It can stay between us."

I meant for it to come out differently. Like: It stays between us because last night we created a precious thing, and I didn't want to share him or it with anyone else. But from the way Albie's eyes twitched at my words, I knew I'd said the wrong thing. Again.

There was a long pause and then Albie said, "Oh."

We stopped in front of room 106.

I put a hand on his arm. "I didn't mean—"

The door flew open.

"What the hell is this?" Carmen opened the door wide enough for me to see the TV buzzing in the middle of the room.

An anchor wearing a stiff suit and very obvious toupee said, "New updates this morning in the case of three missing teens from Marsh Rock. Police say they've connected the teens to an account on the website Catch a Dream."

My stomach slid down to my toes.

The TV cut to the videos I'd posted of Carmen and Albie dancing in the spinning lights at Dream Fest. Carmen and Albie playing in the pool. The video of Albie stealing a book from a hospital gift store. The shots of Albie's photos on his family's refrigerator.

"Is that my house?" Albie asked, shouldering past me to get a better look.

I reached for one of the lollipops I'd stuck through my buns and popped it into my mouth.

"The teens appear to be in Miami. It's unclear if they're being held against their will. The creator of the videos hasn't shown their face, but experts say this mysterious figure could be a kidnapper. Here with us now, Miami small business owner, Ethel Montgomery."

The camera cut to a shot of Ethel standing in front of the creepy display case of her shop. "Three kids tried to rob my store yesterday. What's happening to our country?"

"Now we go back to Meredith Williams, who is live in Marsh Rock with the parents of two of the children," the anchor said.

Carmen and Albie shrunk away from the TV. Their parents huddled together in front of the hospital; my mom wasn't with them.

Albie's dad jumped in before the reporter even asked a question. "Our son is a cancer survivor with a weakened immune system. He needs medical care. If you see him, please—"

It cut back to the news anchor with the toupee. "And now to a representative from DBD, who will explain why the teens may have run away—"

Albie lunged for the remote and pressed the power button. The television snapped to black, leaving the room in silence.

Carmen turned on me. "Care to explain?"

"I'm with Albie," I said. "Not interested in hearing anything else from DBD."

"You were in my house?" Albie said, his voice soft and broken.

I squared my shoulders. Cocked a hip. Swirled the lollipop around my mouth. When disappointing people, it's always best to fully commit. "Surprise."

"Why?" Albie said, slowly lowering himself to sit on the bed.

"For the documentary. I've been breaking into people's houses and filming personal mementos. Capturing what really matters to people. You left the back door unlocked, so I just slipped in."

Albie's fists sunk into the squeaky mattress. "But it's . . . why my pictures?"

I'd asked myself the same question a hundred times. I'd broken into houses with diamonds in drawers and credit cards on the counter. I never took any of it. Only memories. As if I was collecting pieces of other people in the faint hope that someday I'd be able to assemble them and make myself into an actual human being.

"I don't know, I just . . . The contrast of your cancer photos with the photo of you with the books was a good image for one of the montages. And then your dad came home and I had to hide, but you were on the dock . . ."

Understanding crept across Albie's features. "That's why you were in the lake. The splash. You're the reason I fell in."

I focused on the sour taste of the lollipop hitting my tongue. "Yeah."

He ran both hands through his hair. A spark of anger hardened in his eyes. The familiar comfort of disappointment.

"Are you lying?" he asked quietly.

I bit my lollipop so hard it cracked. "Always."

"But this isn't for some stupid documentary," Carmen jumped in. "You posted everything. You made it look like Albie and I were *in love*."

"That doesn't make any sense." Albie's leg jittered enough to make the whole floor look like it was moving.

"Jillian's going to be heartbroken," Carmen said. "And you used us. Did you even care?"

"I was only thinking of myself," I said. The truth, again. Heavy and cold.

Carmen stepped up so we were nose to nose, chest to chest. "According to Hattie's Catch a Dream, the price for our identities, for Albie's health, our privacy, everything you took with that *thing* was $23,000, Albie. Do you think it was worth it?"

"Why do you need $23,000?" Albie asked, trying, as always, to make sense of my mess.

Every good liar agrees on at least one essential fact: The truth always comes out. My dad once told me the difference between a good liar and a great one was knowing when to hold a bluff and when to fold.

I took the lollipop stick out of my mouth and said, "I'm trying to pay off my mom's credit card debt before I die. It's my fault she has it, and I don't want to leave it with her when I go."

The words hung silently in the air for a moment.

"That's the best you can do? Seriously?" Albie asked. "I was expecting a better story."

"It's the truth," I said. The problem with being a compulsive liar who acts like she doesn't care is that when you *do* care about something, it's impossible to make someone believe you.

The upside is that when everyone expects nothing from you, it's easy to deliver.

So, I did what cowards always do. I ran.

CHAPTER 28

IMMERSING MYSELF INTO THE SUFFOCATING BLANKET OF FLORIDIAN humidity felt like justice. I ran around the gated pool, past the neon sign. Pounding my feet on the pavement, I didn't stop until my toes reached the hot sand and there was nothing but the ocean stretching out in front of me.

I sunk down to my knees, relishing the burn of the sand against my skin. The ocean was dotted with spots that I imagined looked like the MTP crawling across my nervous system. My fingers fumbled for my phone, dialing the only number I knew by heart.

"Hattie? Hattie!" My mom picked up halfway through the first ring. "Oh, thank god. Where are you? Are you OK? Whatever it is, I'll come get you."

All I could offer in response was a choking sob.

Mom's voice pressed closer to the speaker. "I'm here, honey. I'm here."

"I ruined everything," I gasped.

"Breathe with me, Hattie. One. Two. Three. Four."

It had been years since her voice felt like a balm instead of a burn. I inhaled and exhaled in time with her count, and gradually, the fist clenching inside my chest began to loosen.

"I'm here. Everything's going to be OK." She breathed in sync with me through the crackling phone. "I've been in the lab for days. Running and rerunning the tests. Re-creating the MTP and the scenario where you were exposed. And you know what? It's not working. The parasite never attaches. It's possible, probable even, that—"

"Stop." My voice was hoarse and bruised-sounding. "Stop lying. It won't make me want to come home."

"I wouldn't lie to you," she said, and I could hear the accusation in her words. Only a liar assumes that everyone else is lying, too.

"Right." I cleared my throat. My mother's muted disappointment was the kind of comfort that could untangle the panic in my chest.

"But I do want you home. So badly. Please, honey—"

"I'm not coming back," I said, surprised at the evenness of my voice. "Not until I pay you back. I said it was your fault, but it's not. It's mine."

"Oh, honey, no. Is that what you think? None of this is your fault."

A family walked past on the beach. The dad had a kid in one arm and a cooler in the other. He stumbled, and the mom, who was pushing a stroller slowly across the sand, said something that made him tilt his head back and laugh.

"Please don't see the best in me," I said, focusing on the black spots on the horizon to keep my voice cold. "There's nothing there. It's hollow, Mom. Just a void that destroys everything."

She listened to my shallow breaths for a few moments before she said, "I remember when I held you for the first time. I was alone in a hospital room, and you had been screaming for hours and I couldn't figure out how to make you stop, and your dad was nowhere to be found. I wasn't worried, though. You know why?"

I bit my lip. Scrunched up my nose. Breathed through my mouth. I was tired and a parasite was literally eating me alive, and the humidity was thick enough to make me feel like I was drowning.

"Because I took one look at you and loved you so much there was no room for fear. I loved you bigger than the fear was wide," she said. She must have realized that talking about science and the parasite wasn't going to get to me. Stories had always been the best way to capture my attention. "I wasn't scared when you fell off the roof and broke your arm."

"I didn't fall," I mumbled. "I jumped."

"I wasn't scared when you ran away or came home with a pierced lip or told people you were an acrobatic orphan." Her voice cracked. "It was only when that drone crashed that I really got scared. I'm terrified of a world without you. But let me tell you something. That love I felt when I held you for the first time? It's only gotten bigger. And it's not going away. I'm not lying about the tests with the MTP, Hattie."

"You've always been a terrible liar."

"True." She laughed, then cleared her throat. "The results are in from the lab."

It felt like the waves lapped in slow motion against the shore.

"I have them. I need you, Carmen, and Albie to come home."

I unfolded my cramped legs and stood up, brushing the sand away.

"Hattie?"

"I heard you," I said. "We'll come back. There's just something I need to do first."

"Good." Her voice was hesitant. I'd lied to her so many times before.

I tried to harden myself into feeling nothing, but the words still slipped out. "I'm sorry for everything else."

"Don't be sorry. Be here."

"I love you big," I said. The words she had whispered in my ear every night when I was still small enough to need to be tucked into bed.

"I love you bigger," she replied.

I checked my Catch a Dream account. $5,400 in donations. Then I put my phone away and started hiking across the crowded beach. The burn in my legs as they sunk into the sand propelled me forward, across the street and down the road until I was standing in the flickering neon shadow of the Sands Motel.

My mom had definitive evidence of the thing we'd been told was taking up residence in our bodies. Carmen had said she wanted to be home before the results came in. Albie would follow her because she was his best friend. Our story would be over, and I wouldn't have $23,000 or anything else to show for my trouble.

I'd meant what I told my mom. We would come home. Just not yet.

••••

"I'm sorry, OK?" I flipped my shirt up to wipe the sweat off my face. It was almost midday and being outside without being in the water was inhumanly cruel.

In a move I really hadn't seen coming, Albie and Carmen didn't open the motel door when I returned. I knocked and pounded and even kicked the doorknob. Nothing.

Luckily, I had the deadbeat Dad experience, so I slid to the ground and started talking. A monologue delivered through a door can be a powerful tool.

"I know sorry isn't enough," I tried again. "Sorry doesn't change things. If I had the power to change things, you know I would. I'd go back and lock Albie in his room so he wouldn't fall in the water. I'd stay out of other people's houses and stories and quarantine wards."

I heard hissed whispering beyond the door. They were still inside, and they were debating. Good.

"I know I can't understand what either of you is going through. I don't know what it's like for you growing up as the Cancer Kid or one of the only openly lesbian girls at school." I rested my head against the door. "All I know is how it feels to be living on a deadline. And I know I did the wrong thing and it's impossible to forgive. But it was also supposed to be impossible for parasites to turn us into zombies, and here we are. So I guess I'm asking for the impossible."

The door I was leaning on opened abruptly, sprawling me across the carpet. I looked up at Carmen's annoyingly perfect face.

"Were you lying? About the reason you were raising money?"

I shook my head, grateful she'd asked me a question I could answer truthfully.

She reached out a hand and pulled me up to a sitting position. "You made my dad cry on local TV news. I can never forgive you for that."

"Understood."

"But I get how it feels to never feel like enough," she said. "To feel like you owe your parents something you'll never be able to pay back. And I look really good in all of those videos, so it's whatever."

"Are you kidding me?"

Carmen and I both jumped at the sound of Albie's raised voice. I'd never heard him raise his voice above a mumble. But when I looked at him, he didn't look like Albie anymore. His hair was tousled, his muscle tee was revealing the real, actual muscles of his arms, and his voice was strong.

"We can't let this go," he pleaded with Carmen.

"I'm not letting anything go," she said. "I'm choosing to move on."

He sat down on the bed. "I've never had a choice about anything, and this is one I don't want to make."

Carmen sat next to him on the bed. She patted his knee and said, "That's good, Albie. You're getting to acceptance."

Albie jumped to his feet. "I'm not a stage! You can't just put my emotions into neat little phases. This is my life! First it was the cancer and now it's a parasite and all of it means that I'm not fit to survive. And that's fine. I can deal with that. But I'm not going home without Scooter, I'm not going home without hitting up this party on Jordan Banner's private island. And I'm not going home with the person who ruined my life."

"What?" I asked.

"You ruined my life!" he sputtered.

"No, I heard that part." I waved him off. "The part about Jordan Banner's private island?"

"Jordan invited us to Faye Island," Albie said.

"*The* Faye Island? The island where he wrote 'Stan By Me'?"

"Uh . . . sure," Albie said.

"We have to go," Carmen said. "All of us."

"What about the videos? Aren't you even a little bit mad about that?" Albie asked. "She's been using us to make money."

"So? I've been using her as an excuse to avoid going home. And you've been using her as an excuse to do all the reckless things you were too scared to do on your own. Hattie is one of us."

"We can't trust her," he said.

Carmen shrugged. "Probably not."

"She'll lie again," he said.

"That's likely."

"How can you be OK with this?"

"Because life is short, and Hattie is a member of the Color Guard, and I want to go to this party!" Carmen turned to me. "Besides, we'll be back by the time the test results are in. Right, Hattie?"

My phone was a dead weight in my pocket. "Yeah, of course."

"And you won't film us without our consent?" she asked.

"Sure."

Carmen shrugged. "That's good enough for me. Exit Ethics, Albie. I'm done expecting people to be someone they're not."

Albie was silent for several heavy seconds before he said, "I still don't forgive you."

I crossed my arms so he wouldn't see the weight his hurt dropped on my shoulders. "Noted."

Carmen pointed to a greasy-looking sandwich on the nightstand. "I got you a breakfast sandwich."

My stomach growled as I reached for it. "Thanks."

Albie turned slightly toward me. Progress. "I think I know how we can get to the island. We just need to figure out a way to get Scooter back."

The test results were in. I knew it, and I wasn't telling them. Like any good liar, I knew Albie and Carmen would find out the truth eventually, and when they did, they'd hate me. Saving Scooter was the least I could do.

"I have an idea," I said.

CHAPTER 29

THE BEADY EYES OF A STUFFED FOX STARED DOWN AT ME. I PUT A sucker in my mouth and stared back.

"What are you doing?" Carmen asked.

"Warming up."

My purple hair was tucked under a baseball cap and I was wearing an oversize MIAMI sweatshirt I'd found in the motel gift shop. Carmen was wearing her DBD polo, her brown hair pulled back into a no-nonsense ponytail. An analog clock in the display case flashed the time: 1:43 P.M.

The plan was simple: Ethel had said she was hosting a *Land of Invaders* tournament today. I'd enter and convince her to wager Scooter, then win Scooter and probably also a bunch of money. Albie would be so happy he would have to forgive me and go back to kissing me, and we'd all live happily ever after on Faye Island. Or something like that.

Carmen and I stood side by side, necks craned back to take in the Ethel's First Class Secondhand Shop sign.

"How'd you get so good at *Land of Invaders* again?" Carmen asked. She was not as skeptical of the plan as I'd expected.

"My dad was a gambling addict. *Land of Invaders* was one of his highest-paying games. He taught me how to play before he left."

I was surprised by how easy it was to say out loud.

"Huh," Carmen said. She jerked her chin at my mouth. "Can I get one of those?"

I handed her a sucker. She popped it in her mouth and screwed up her face. "These taste terrible."

"That's kind of the idea."

"You're not as mysterious as you think you are, you know. Hard exterior, cinnamon roll interior, dad issues, Jordan Banner fan."

"Focus!" I snapped in her face. "We're doing this to get back to Jordan Banner."

"He was different than I thought," she said. "I didn't expect him to be such . . . a person."

"There's nothing I love more than a Banner deep dive, but we don't have time. Have you heard from Albie?"

"He's at the docks. Securing transportation."

I swallowed. He hadn't said a word to me as we packed up the motel room.

"Don't worry. He'll come around," Carmen said.

"He shouldn't. I did something unforgivable."

"You made a mistake, but I don't think it was unforgivable."

Her words stung like alcohol splashed on a cut. I had no desire to stay in that pain. I pulled the door open and motioned Carmen inside. "Stick to the plan."

"Right. The plan. I know what that is."

I couldn't tell if the MTP was affecting her judgment or if we'd reached a new understanding after the events of the last few days. Whatever the case, I needed to get this over with before she snapped out of her haze and remembered she'd never been chill about anything in her life.

A few vacationers flicked through the racks of clothes lining the shop floor. A girl about our age was slouched behind the register, scrolling idly through her phone.

"You can't go back there," she said when I walked around the counter's edge.

"I'm here to play," I said and walked past her into the hallway.

"We have a plan," Carmen informed the girl. I grabbed her arm and towed her away before she could draw more attention to us.

A sliver of light shot from underneath the closed storage room door. I could hear muffled voices and clattering dice from within.

"How do we know if they're playing yet?" Carmen asked.

"I can hear the Dimensional Door," I said, listening to the creaking wheel spin. I shook my head when I heard the player announce their move and said to myself, "If your player hasn't purchased a shield wall, your Reapers are definitely going to a Witch Trial."

Carmen spat out the lollipop I'd given her. "Wait. Are you . . . serious about this game?"

"Irrelevant."

"You *are*."

The rap of my knuckles silenced the spinning wheel and murmuring voices. I knocked with the rhythm of the die-caster—a pattern all Invaders would know. *Tap. Taptap. Tap. Taptap.*

Ethel flung open the door. She was wearing a floor-length cape.

"You," she snarled.

"Me," I said.

"What are you doing here? I beat you last night. Fair and square."

"If by fair and square you mean pepper spraying two kids, then sure." Over Ethel's shoulder I could see three other players gathered around the table.

"Kids these days. Can't even handle a little pepper spray."

"You couldn't handle a decongestant spray," Carmen butted in.

"My friends at DBD will be very curious to learn your whereabouts," Ethel said.

"Go ahead. Tell them. But first, I want to play."

Ethel grinned. "Did you hear that? She wants to play!" The players around the table chuckled.

I checked the board. The Poacher, Augur, and Reaper were already in play. I'd have to get my player to the fortress within three moves to have any chance of winning before they could combine their powers and diminish my blood magic.

"You're running a tournament. The cost of entry is two thousand armor coins," I said, reciting information from a flyer I'd found on a local tabletop gaming site.

"It's a high buy in," Ethel smirked. "Only players—"

"In the international orange or national purple tier would have the coins," I said. I reached into my backpack, pulled out a drawstring pouch, and tossed it to Ethel.

Her eyebrows shot up to her hairline. She opened the pouch and saw the pile of armor coins inside. "Where did you get these?"

“I earned them,” I said, which wasn't exactly true. Those were the coins my dad had left behind. It was pathetic, but I always carried them with me.

“But that would mean—”

“That I'm a purple-tier Invader,” I finished for her. “And according to the rules of the land, you have to let me play.”

“I don't have to do anything,” Ethel said. “I'm an American.”

I raised my voice. “What will the other Invaders think when they learn the tier system hasn't been honored? They might question the integrity of the entire tournament.”

A middle-aged bald man with brown skin shuffled his asset cards and said, “She's right. The code of the Invaders states that an Invader cannot be denied invading rights unless a defending army overpowers them.”

“I don't see a defense tower,” I said. Thankfully. If they'd had one, I would have had to duel for the right to enter and that could've gotten messy fast.

“We've already begun,” Ethel said.

“Good. You'll need the head start.”

Ethel and I stared each other down. Good thing I'd gotten plenty of practice with the fox out front and didn't flinch.

Ethel's nostrils flared. “Fine. The Invader is bid to pass.”

She moved out of the way. I bowed my head and stepped into the room. “The Invader enters.”

The room had been transformed since Ethel had handcuffed me to the table the day before. Dark velvet curtains blacked out the windows. The rickety shelves were covered with black sheets.

Except for one. A massive terrarium rested on the shelf behind Ethel's head chair. Scooter was inside, chewing on a carrot.

"What the hell is going on?" Carmen muttered to herself as she entered the room. "What language are you speaking?"

"We play in Caltec," Ethel said. "Though we retain some of the inflections of the Genop style of play."

"There are made-up *languages* in this game?" Carmen asked.

"No Pokwin?" I asked as I took a seat in the plague corner of the table. Pokwin was the most complicated gameplaying language in the *Land of Invaders* multiverse. It was also the language I knew best. My dad hadn't believed in making things easy.

"Only if the wormhole is activated," Ethel said. She dealt my asset cards and die chart.

"How are we playing copper?" I asked, examining the chart.

"Steampunk rules," the bald man from earlier said.

"This is Jim." Ethel pointed at him, then to a dumb-looking twenty-something boy with freckled white skin next to him and an older woman at the end of the table with the kind of leathery tan skin only found in Florida. "Bo and Jessica. Jessica doesn't talk during gameplay."

"A Silent Strategist," I said. "Acknowledged."

Carmen slapped her cheek lightly. "It's the MTP. It's making me hallucinate Hattie as a person who likes board games."

"Sit down," Ethel said. "Peasants are not allowed speaking privileges during gameplay."

I pulled Carmen down into a chair behind me, nodding my head to the shelf behind Ethel. "She'll adhere."

Carmen's jaw dropped when she saw Scooter smooshed into the terrarium. She looked to me. I shook my head and dragged my gaze to the board. To get Scooter, we needed to focus.

"The game is *Land of Invaders*," Ethel said as she rattled a handful of colored dice. "The play is Invader Ups. Winners take all and losers be damned. Here?"

"Here," we all said in unison.

Ethel scattered her dice across the table and the game began.

Ethel had a strong attacking position with her Poacher piece and two harbors. Jim was close behind with his Augur and a monopoly on the southern mining territory.

"Player character?" Ethel asked me when it was my turn.

I cleared my throat. "Necromancer."

The other players paused. The Necromancer was a rarely used piece. It was too volatile, its power too limited to specific states of play and the ability of the player to maneuver the Necromancer to the Central Cemetery so it could amass an army.

"The Priest would be a safer choice," Jim said.

"I know."

If the Dimensional Doors worked in real life the way they did in the game, I'd spin it back to last Sunday morning and ride my bike straight into the marsh instead of to the Changs' house. I'd keep Albie from falling in the water and Carmen from entering the gates of Cul du Lac. But I had no wheel to spin or lies to play. The only thing I could do for them was win, and the Priest wasn't a winning piece.

"Necromancer it is," Ethel said and handed me the black-cloaked figure. She was incapable of disguising the glee in her voice. She thought she had me.

Playing resumed. Bo eliminated Jessica's army with a Trojan Horse. She left the table in tears without breaking her vow of silence. I moved my Necromancer to the fortress to break up Jim's and Ethel's armies, eliminating Bo's Reaper in the process. He kicked over a chair on his way out.

At the beginning of each round, we bought in with our armor coins. Jim hedged his bets while he tried to get his Augur in position with the Dimensional Door. But at the last minute, Ethel's Poacher blocked his path with a snare trap.

Sweat dripped down my back as I read over my asset cards again and again. A clock ticked mercilessly over the door.

Carmen mimed pointing to her watch. Jordan's party started at nine. I shook my head. Read the asset cards again. There was no time. There were only Invaders.

Jim surrendered on the seventh round of gameplay after Ethel took out a huge chunk of his army and I attacked him from behind.

"Well met," he said and pushed back his chair, shoulders slumped in defeat.

Then it was only Ethel and me. Her Poacher was in a good position in the Westward Forest, and I suspected she was hiding a stockpile of weapons in her asset cards.

I knew I could tie her in three moves. A tie would move me into the red tier, the level my dad had been at when he left.

"Hattie?" Carmen whispered. Her knees were bouncing erratically. She didn't understand the gameplay, but she knew we were close.

I wasn't there to advance tiers. I was there to get Scooter and bring him home.

I spilled the rest of my armor coins onto the table. "No return," I said.

"You know my coin is spent," Ethel said.

"What does no return mean?" Carmen asked.

"All in," Jim explained. I locked eyes with Ethel. "Either you win or lose everything. It's the essence of Invaders. If your coin is spent, you wager real world."

Ethel narrowed her eyes. "You can have an outfit from the shop."

I dragged my palms down my legs under the table. They were soaked in sweat. "I want the turtle."

Ethel examined her cards. "You're nowhere near the cemetery. It's a certain death mission. I have all the weapons and you have nothing to wager in return."

I pulled her fat wallet from my backpack and slapped it onto the table. "If you win, you can have your wallet back."

Her eyes widened and she reached forward. "You stole from me! Again!"

I slid the wallet out of her grasp. "You pepper sprayed me."

"You'll never win."

"Then play," I said.

My hands were trembling so fiercely they jiggled the table. Ethel noticed and grinned. Good.

"Buy in accepted," Ethel said. "No return."

"For Scooter," I said.

"For the glory of defeating you in battle," she said. "And for my Froyo membership card. I'm three purchases away from a free scoop."

Ethel rolled exploding dice and used them to buff her army. She moved her Poacher over one quadrant, which meant she was close enough to use her flying powers to challenge me on the next round.

"Game over," she said. "My army is blocking the cemetery."

My whole body was shaking with anticipation. I rolled the dice and didn't bother checking how many moves I'd received. I only needed one. I moved my Necromancer into the abandoned quadrant where Jim's Augur piece lay fallen.

"I play my summoning card to resurrect the Augur and meld our powers," I said. Ethel sat forward. "With these powers I will blow up the Barter Bridge and ghost walk to the cemetery where my army awaits."

The board was a scattered mess of coins, armies, and assets. Ethel kicked her chair back and stood over it, examining my position.

"What does that even mean?" Carmen asked.

"You cheated!" Ethel cried.

"Powerful move," Jim said and offered me his hand to shake.

"The Necromancer can only raise active players," Ethel said.

"According to the Constitution, the Necromancer can raise any piece on the board unless a bylaw is passed before the start of play," I said. "There was no vote."

"She has you there," Jim said.

"Cheater!" Ethel yelled.

"Will someone please tell me what's going on?" Carmen pleaded.

I pressed my shaking hand to the table. Now that it was over, I could barely believe I pulled it off. "I won."

CHAPTER 30

"AND THEN HATTIE SPUN THIS FANCY DOOR THING AND THREW ALL these coins in, which seemed like a pretty dumb move at the time, *but* it set her up to raise Dead Jim's army from the dead, which, for reasons I don't totally understand, meant she won," Carmen said, her words slurring together in excitement.

Albie stared at Carmen blankly. "The only word I understood in that sentence was 'dumb.'"

"Ethel refused to give up Scooter, so I pointed her to a little thing called Chapter 849," Carmen continued.

"Is that from the Bible?" Albie asked.

"It's state law," I said quietly. "It says it's illegal to run an unregistered, high stakes gambling game. She handed Scooter over pretty quickly after that."

"You should have been there," Carmen sighed dreamily. "You have to see Hattie play. She's a literal wizard at this game."

Albie looked down at the crate he was carrying. One of Scooter's paws (hooves? limbs? I wasn't totally sure how turtles worked) was poking through a hole. We'd all agreed it was best for him to keep a low profile until we got out of Miami.

"Thank you," he said, the first words he'd spoken to me since that morning.

I put a lollipop in my mouth and swallowed as much of the sourness as I could in one breath. "Anything for Scooter."

The three of us were standing at the edge of a tangle of docks on the opposite end of the beach from where we'd docked *Seas the Day*. A locked wrought-iron gate blocked us from entering. I would have found it obnoxious before, but now that I understood how easy it was to steal a boat, the lock seemed smart.

The boats were nicer than the ones in Marsh Rock. Their hulls were barrel-chested and the insides were big enough for rooms with glittering chandeliers and full kitchens. People in white attire scuttled around, looking like natural extensions of the boats. We looked out of place in our used clothes, the sandwiches and chips Carmen and I had grabbed at a convenience store tucked under our arms.

Carmen snapped out of her momentary obsession with my *Land of Invaders* skills. "Our driver is late."

Albie rocked back and forth on his heels. "He'll be here."

I checked my phone.

The video of Carmen giving Albie a swim lesson had nearly 100,000 views and my Catch a Dream account had nearly $10,000 in pledges. Commenters were begging for another video. Some had seen the news story about us and were putting together who we were and what we were doing. It was more money than I could fathom, but not nearly enough, and without Carmen and Albie, I had nothing left to film.

"Yo! My poet who didn't know it. Except you do. Because you read me some."

Carmen and I turned to see Ayden, the stoner kid who'd helped us sneak into Dream Fest, swaggering down the dock.

Carmen shook her head. "Please tell me that's not—"

"O captain, my captain!" Albie clapped Ayden on the back. "This is his parents' boat."

Ayden fumbled with the lock on the gate and led us down a row of massive boats, stopping in front of a small, speedy-looking yellow one with *#YeahBuoy* painted in red on the side.

Albie smiled at the yellow monstrosity. "He manages the boat for the family, so he knows how to drive it and stuff. Right, Ayden?"

"Nah, my license is suspended." Ayden scratched his armpit. "Oh, you mean the boat! Bet."

"If your license was suspended, why were you in your truck last night?" Carmen asked.

"I know, right," Ayden nodded.

"Wonderful," Carmen said.

Albie slid on his mirrored Elliot Why sunglasses. "Do we need to have a fight where you insist you won't come because of safety and I have to play the cancer card and Hattie films everything so she can make money off of our tragedy? Or can we just skip to the part where we get on the boat?"

I put my phone away. I'd brainstorm filming ideas later. "I'm good with skipping the drama."

Carmen made a face. "Can you drop us off in Marsh Rock on Monday? I need to oversee a homecoming committee meeting. Also, the test results are supposed to arrive first thing in the morning."

The mention of the test results deflated every good feeling in my stomach and chest.

"Sounds possible," Ayden said.

"But can you do it?"

"That's what I just said!"

"Our education system failed you." Carmen sighed. "Whatever. Let's get this over with."

Albie leaned on the metal frame and yelled, "Faye Island, here we come!"

•●●•

"Truth or dare?" Albie asked to no one in particular.

"Truth," I said. "Definitely truth."

Albie jumped a little, as if he had forgotten I was there. We were in the bow of *#YeahBuoy*, sitting as far away from each other as possible. Ayden had sped away from Miami for forty-five minutes before idling the boat while checking his navigations. Carmen sat behind us in the spinning chair next to the driver's seat.

"We cannot be desperate enough to play Truth or Dare," she said. "Ayden, I think that map's upside down. And Hattie, you cannot be desperate enough to choose truth."

She had no idea. "Yes we can, and yes I am."

The ocean stretched out from us in all directions, shades of blue patched together with white caps and curling waves. I'd learned from my dad that words weren't enough to bring a person back to you, but I still wanted to try.

"OK," Albie said. Scooter was sitting in a nest of papers on the deck. Albie was stroking his shell with one hand and dangling his other hand over the side of the boat, flicking his finger through the water. Carmen had asked him why he wasn't freaking out about the water, given that he couldn't swim, and he'd said that Elliot Why could swim. He'd looked it up, and he needed to be fully immersed in his character.

Albie clenched his jaw. "Where's your dad?"

If he'd asked yesterday, it might have been thoughtful. But it wasn't yesterday, and he'd decided not to forgive me. Asking about my dad was the simplest, cruelest thing he could think of.

I wrapped my fingers around one of the lollipops in my pocket. I had only three left, and I didn't want to waste them. "That's really what you want to know?"

"Yup."

Then again, there was no time like the present. I unwrapped the lollipop and slid it into my mouth. "I don't know."

"That's all? I thought you would have a better story than that," Albie taunted.

I focused on the sourness coating my taste buds, the rhythmic slapping of the water against the boat.

"The last time I saw him I was thirteen," I said slowly. "Mom had kicked him out and changed the locks, so I had to let him in. I thought he was coming back to hang out with me, that all the questions he was asking were because he missed me. I showed him where she kept her credit cards. I didn't notice when he slipped them into his bag. Within days, he'd reached the limits on all of them—gambling addiction—and because they were still legally married, there was nothing my mom could do about it except move us to Florida, sell her soul to DBD, and hope that one day she'd be able to pay it back. Credit card limits, prenups—these are the kinds of useful things they should be teaching in schools."

Albie just stared at the horizon.

"But, uh, last I heard, Dad got kicked off the *Land of Invaders* tour and was living in Atlantic City. I stopped looking after a while."

The boat quieted and I was left with only the thoughts in my head, the roar of them as persistent and deep as the ocean.

I sparkled my fingers. "Ta da. It's not as good as the rumors at school. Just some cliché daddy issues like everyone else."

They still weren't saying anything, and I'd been filling the silence inside my own head for so long that I couldn't stop. When you've been hiding, being seen is more painful than fading away. "Or maybe he's still with the circus? Or waiting for me at home? I could be lying."

"I'm just . . ." Albie curled his hand into a fist against Scooter's shell. I braced myself for the blow of his words. "I'm sorry. That sucks."

Kindness was worse than anger. It extinguished some of the fire in me, and I needed that fire to survive.

"It's fine. Whatever." I sat up. "Carmen, truth or dare?"

She looked up from Ayden's map. "I'm not playing."

"It's not a game," Albie said abruptly. "After this party, it's over. We go home. We sit in the hospital. We wait. This is our last chance—our only chance—to live at all. This is our chance to be honest. To do the things we want to do before it's too late."

Ayden pounded on his chest with his fist. "Told you he's a poet."

"Fine. Dare." Albie really could make Carmen do anything. "I dare myself—"

"That's not how it works," Albie said.

"You have to specify the bylaws," Carmen said. She looked at me. "Invader rules."

"Proceed," I said.

Carmen swallowed four times before she worked up the nerve to say it out loud. "I dare myself to break up with Jillian. I don't love her anymore. I haven't in a long time."

I watched Albie's face open up at Carmen's revelation.

"Why haven't you done it before now?" he asked.

"We're the only queer couple at our school. Do you know how much pressure that is?" She rolled her shoulders as if her back was aching under the invisible weight. "I feel like if we break up, I'm letting my community down and giving the town an excuse to be total bigots. Everything I do is under a microscope. I can't just be Carmen—I have to perfectly reflect all the values of queer folk and Mexican folk and I just—I can't."

Perfect Carmen. That's what I'd been calling her in my head since I met her.

"You shouldn't have to feel that way" I said. "That blows."

"I didn't know," Albie said. "Why didn't you tell me?"

"You survived cancer," Carmen said. "I didn't want you to have to deal with anything else."

"We're supposed to be friends," Albie said.

"That's deep," Ayden said. "I figured out the coordinates. We're going that way."

He turned the engine back on and the boat shot off into the choppy water. Albie curled into himself.

Carmen held her dumb phone over her head. "As soon as we have service, I'm going to call her."

I took out my phone and leaned over the side, recording the boat bouncing over the choppy waves.

"You can film me."

I fell back into my seat at the sound of Albie's voice. "What?"

"I looked at your page. I didn't know I had such strong demographic appeal with the youths, but the Snack Attack is your moneymaker. So film me."

I wanted to politely refuse, but who was I kidding? The desire to capture him was stronger.

"Uh. Thanks." I framed his face in shot and captured the hair curling around his ears, the sharp line of his jaw, his finger tap-tap-tapping on the gunwale.

"If you need a video for your fundraiser, I can do something more interesting," Carmen said.

I clicked my phone screen to black. "No. That was just for me. For memories I mean."

The sharp, salty breeze cut through my clothes and made me shiver. Albie didn't notice.

"I'm going to perform my poetry tonight," he declared.

"Yeah!" Ayden fist pumped the air.

"I didn't know you actually wrote poetry," I said. "I thought that was just something you told Ayden to manipulate him into committing a crime."

"Hey," Ayden drawled. "I don't need to be *manipulated* to commit a crime. Don't insult me."

Albie tore through his backpack and wrestled on his Elliot Why costume. Bucket hat. Bandanna. Sun-bleached muscle tee. He pressed a piece of paper to Scooter's shell and started scribbling. "I haven't yet. I'm sure I'll have something good by tonight."

Crush is the most accurate descriptor in the English language. I wrapped my arms around my knees and watched Albie write. It was ecstasy, to be close enough to watch his eyelashes flutter against his cheeks, to see him chewing his lip as he wrote. It was excruciating, his coldness toward me, knowing I could never have him. Crushing.

Carmen and Ayden wouldn't be able to hear us over the motor and the wind.

"Albie," I started quietly. I didn't know how I was going to finish, but I knew I'd gotten a taste for the truth and now I was hungry for more.

His head snapped up. Maybe he was more interested in me than I'd realized.

"I'm still mad at you," he said, but his voice had that ooey-gooey cinnamon-roll quality.

"Albie, I—" I started again. I knew the ending this time.

"Hold that thought." Albie stood up and pointed over my shoulder. I turned and saw something emerging on the horizon

Faye Island.

CHAPTER 31

IF A FAIRY AND THE OCEAN HAD A BABY AND THAT BABY WAS AN island, it would be Faye Island. The sprout of land appeared before us, a mirage-like speck in the middle of the bright blue sea.

Ayden slowed down as we approached. "Y'all sure this is it? Once I was fishing with my buddies and we saw a dolphin, so we ditched the nav chart and followed it for a few hours, but it turned out it was a trash bag."

"I have so many follow-up questions," Carmen said.

"There's no time." Albie tugged his bucket hat down over his ears. His bandanna was knotted around his neck, the mirrored sunglasses dropping down his nose. The shirt drooping low enough to expose his ribs completed the look. I still didn't think he looked like Elliot Why—people saw what they wanted to see—but he also didn't look like himself. "Let me do the talking, OK? And Hattie, remember you're supposed to be an actor. Should be easy for you."

His anger spiked and softened from one moment to the next. I didn't want to give him the satisfaction of knowing how much it hurt.

Ayden cut the engine to a crawl as we drifted closer to the island. One side was blanketed by a white sand beach. A thick grouping of trees lined the perimeter. From the distance, I could see brightly colored paths cutting into the trees and winding across the rest of the island. A building that looked like a castle squatted in the middle, turrets and towers spinning out above the jungle.

Ayden pulled in parallel to a dock where each plank of wood was painted a different color of the rainbow. Carmen hopped out to tie the rope to a cleat. She'd donned her neon pink shorts from Dream Fest, blending in with the explosion of color coating the island. I was still wearing my pale pink MIAMI sweatshirt and black shorts.

"As soon as I can get service, I'm calling Jillian," Carmen said as she flipped the thick rope into a knot. Her chaotic energy from the *Land of Invaders* game had funneled into a singular focus. "She needs to know before the results come in, don't you think?"

The lack of signal on the ocean was a relief. I could no longer see the video views and dollar signs ticking up or the red numbers of my mom's voicemails, calls, and texts, her worry growing the longer she went without hearing an update on my promise to come home. As long as we were on Faye Island, the test results didn't have to exist.

"Definitely," I said.

That was when things started getting weird.

Exhibit A: Albie was convinced Scooter was sick. Also, he was being a jerk.

"Just look at him," Albie said. "He's depressed."

"I'm sure he's just nervous about being on a boat," I said.

Albie turned his back on me. "If he hadn't been turtle-napped, he'd be fine. Kemp's ridleys are very sensitive."

My stomach turned with guilt. "Maybe."

"Or maybe I gave my MTP to Scooter."

"It's not contagious," Carmen said. "To be contagious, a virus has to—"

"I know how viruses work! I literally had cancer."

As Ayden and Carmen tied up the boat, Albie strapped Scooter to his chest in the bougie baby carrier.

"You sure you want to bring the wildlife?" I asked. So far, bringing Scooter to public occasions hadn't worked out particularly well for us.

"I can't just leave him! He's going through a difficult time right now," Albie said. "The separation anxiety wouldn't be good for his mental state."

"You know Scooter is a turtle, right?" I asked.

"That's like saying *Land of Invaders* is just a game," he snapped.

I could see my reflection in his glasses. Buns piled high above my ears, my once-dark purple locks bleached lilac by the sun. Half of my body was lobster red from falling asleep on my side by the pool. The other half was a slightly darker shade of pale.

I didn't recognize myself until I unwrapped a lollipop and popped it in my mouth. The sour taste reminded me I was not the kind of girl who allowed words to wound me.

"You ready?" Carmen asked. "Got your inhaler and everything?"

Albie rested his hands on Scooter, who was strapped to his belly. "I'm a method actor. The inhaler is staying on the boat."

"But—"

"I was born for this," he said, shaking out his shoulders. Carmen gave me a look and helped him step down onto the dock.

I rustled through his backpack until I found his inhaler and stuffed it in my own bag. Just because we weren't friends anymore didn't mean I wanted him to die.

"He really likes you, you know," Carmen said, as she helped me off the boat.

The bad thing about Carmen was she was smart. She noticed everything. The good thing was she was easier to read than fan fiction.

"Don't you have a girlfriend to break up with?"

Exhibit B: Carmen didn't bite back, which was somehow worse. "Yeah."

"One more day," I told her. "Then we can all go home."

She tilted her head back to catch the sun. "Make your peace with it, Larken. I have. It's never going to be enough."

As we stood on the deck, waiting for a teen celebrity to pick us up from a rich stoner kid's boat, I convinced myself our one last day would be. Enough, that is. It had to be. It was all we had left together.

A figure strode down the dock to meet us. As he got closer, I saw it was Glen, with his tablet firmly in place against his hip and his hair gelled back.

Ayden fiddled with the radio while we waited. "Looks like there's a storm blowing in."

"Not now, Ayden!" Albie snapped.

Ayden dropped his hand from the radio and took out a joint.

"Hello, travelers," Glen said. "My name is Glen, and I'll be your metaphysical guide for the duration of your Faye experience."

"I thought you were JB's assistant," I said.

"That was on the mainland," Glen replied. "And only his fans call him JB."

"Caught me," I said, cheeks blushing under my sun-weary skin. I still hadn't admitted the depths of my Jordan Banner fandom to anyone. The number of truths I had left to tell exhausted me.

We followed Glen down a yellow walkway lined with tiki torches and painted rocks. A few face-painted revelers wandered the beach or splashed in the water.

"Some ground rules for your visit," Glen said as he led us down the winding path. "No pictures of Jordy. No posting on social media unless preapproved by me or another member of Jordy's team. No illegal activity. Besides the drugs."

"Obviously," Carmen mumbled, eyeing a couple leaning against a tree, looking completely blissed out.

"Break any of these rules and you will be arrested and punished under maritime law," Glen continued.

"*What?*" Carmen asked.

"I'm kidding," Glen said. "The real punishment is much worse: Mr. Banner will remove you from his good vibes meditation list. For life."

"Anything but that." My lips twitched.

Albie lowered his sunglasses to glare at me. Apparently, he hated me *and* no longer found my jokes amusing.

The path came to a crossroads in front of us. The yellow path led straight ahead, to the castle rising from the trees. The left path was painted purple and looked like it led to a dance party, and to our right was a red path that dead-ended in front of a large circular tent pulled to a point at the top. A few people in leotards and clown noses milled outside it.

Albie and Carmen were so shocked by the sight of the tent they froze.

"The Cirque de la Vie is completing a month-long residency at the island where they've been asking the question: Are we the audience? Or are we the circus?" Glen said.

"Isn't that the circus you lied and said your dad was in?" Carmen asked.

"My mom took me to a show there once," I said. "It was a good day."

"Sweet." Carmen raised her hand. "Metaphysical Guide slash Personal Assistant Glen, where's the best cell service on the island? I need to call my girlfriend and break up with her before I lose my nerve. It's a whole coming of age, owning your truth thing."

Glen pointed to the purple path. "Good luck with your journey. We will continue to Jordy's tower."

Carmen was already stepping away. "I'll catch up with you later."

"Wait, we should stay together," I said, stomach flipping at the thought of being alone with Albie.

Albie ignored me. "Good luck with the break up," he said, sticking close to Glen.

Carmen gave me a wave and then jogged down the purple path. We had only one more day left, and we weren't going to spend it together.

I tore my gaze from Carmen's retreating figure and followed Albie. I didn't have anywhere else to go. "Hey, wait up."

The path widened until I could walk side by side with Albie and Glen. Each step revealed more of the mansion. It looked like a medieval castle, except every turret was a different color and the exterior walls were splattered and fingerprinted with paint.

"How are you going to convince Jordy to let you perform?" I asked.

"I'm Elliot Why. I was born for the stage," he said, and he sounded serious in a way that made my stomach churn.

Glen led us around the perimeter of the house. Through the windows I caught glimpses of beanbags and old arcade games. We walked past a pool with a waterfall flowing out to the ocean and a slide that spiraled from the second floor into the water.

On the opposite edge of the house was a tall, skinny building. A crooked sign was nailed to the ground in front: RAP-UNZEL'S TOWER.

"Oh, it's a *literal* tower," I said, tilting my head back to see the top. "I thought that was just an overdramatic figure of speech."

Glen shook his head in disappointment. "Jordan Arthur Banner, Grammy, MTV, and Nickelodeon's Teen Choice Award winner, is never overdramatic."

The tower was as tall as some of the skinny palm trees snaking up from the ground around us. The top was pointed like a hat, the level beneath it lined with circular windows.

The door swung open, and Jordan stepped out in joggers and a sun hat. His torso was covered in neon painted swirls. "Elliot! My man!"

Despite myself, my heart lurched at the sight of him. We'd met briefly backstage, but now was my chance to really talk to him, find out how he'd gone from beauty vlogger to the international pop sensation my generation deserved.

"Greetings," Albie/Elliot said in a cold voice.

"I think I finally get the turtle," Jordan said, leaning forward to tickle Scooter. "He's a metaphor for the ways we try to protect ourselves from the world but inevitably have to venture out into society—the ocean—in order to live. Even though joining the world risks our death, we do it because it's also the only way to ensure our survival. The turtle is a living illustration of the impossibility of the human condition."

"Exactly."

Jordan cocked a hip against the doorframe. "I'm glad you're here. It's good to have a friend amongst all these strangers."

"Strangers?" I asked. Jordan looked over in surprise, as if just now seeing me. "There's people everywhere who know you."

"They know me," Jordan said. "But they don't know. You know?"

"Bet," Albie/Elliot said.

I tilted my head. Jordan looked younger in person. His skin was smooth and unwrinkled, but an invisible sadness hung around him like a cloak. Red lines streaked his eyes, circles dug deep underneath, and his shoulders slumped forward slightly. So different from how he'd been onstage yesterday.

"It doesn't stick," Jordan said. "Everything is hollow because no one knows who I really am."

Hollow. That was the word.

"Anyways." Jordan shook himself out of his leaning position as if waking up. I got the feeling his deep words were his form of currency, the only way he knew how to buy people's attention. "Come on up, Elliot. Glen can take your friend to the club while we chat. I've got a cheese plate."

Glen stepped aside, leaving the path open for me to walk away.

Albie shrugged in my direction and headed toward the tower, not even looking back to check that I was OK with this plan.

"You can't eat cheese," I said.

"I'm not me anymore," he replied. "I can do whatever I want."

"You're right. I don't recognize you."

He turned back then. A wave of concern rippled across Albie's face. He opened his mouth to say something.

"Get up here, man!" Jordan called from inside the tower. "We've got worlds to build."

Albie clamped his mouth shut, turned, and disappeared up the winding stairs. No *Goodbye* or *See you later* or *Remember when we kissed and it felt like cracking open a star?*

I should have known better. I'd broken the first rule of compulsive lying: If a con seems too good to be true, it usually is.

CHAPTER 32

After being kicked out of Albie and Jordan's jam sesh, I followed the brick path to the club and sat at a table by myself, wallowing in my own misery. I raced through the buffet line, grabbing only a sad-looking salad and some oranges before someone tried to talk to me about the weather and I had to retreat.

So I sat by myself with my sad salad and let the misery pool in my stomach until the sun set over the trees and a spotlight snapped on. Albie walked in the center of the stage with his arm out to block the glare. I stood just outside the box of light the dance floor carved out of the jungle, cloaked in the shadow of a palm tree. The lights were so bright that he probably couldn't see anyone in the crowded club, and I knew he wasn't looking for me. The darkness comforted me just the same.

"People of Faye Island!" Jordan Banner stood beside Albie, now wearing his signature glittered makeup and an outfit that included a black leather jacket and fairy wings. "It's my pleasure to introduce the headlining act of this evening's entertainment. He's a lover, a poet, and an animal rights activist. More than that, though, he's my friend."

I wondered what Albie had said to Jordan Banner to convince him that he was a friend and if it was the same thing he'd said to me.

"What the hell's happening?"

I jumped at the sound of a voice so close to me in the shadows. Carmen stood on the edge of the dance floor. Her neon shorts glowed against her skin and her normally sleek hair was piled into a messy bun.

The club was backlit in sherbet-colored light, shadows of peach and pale pink roaming over the faces gathered below. People gathered around tall tables on both levels of the tiki-covered bar. Torches spaced between them made it look like the whole place was slightly on fire. I could see Ayden on the second level, holding a joint in one hand and a tiki torch in the other, the same stupefied look on his face as always.

"Albie's performing his poetry," I said.

Jordan was still giving an impassioned speech about turtles and art. The people in the crowd mmed and aahed, cheered and clapped, an echo chamber of affirmation.

"Jeez, I didn't think he'd actually go through with that," Carmen said.

"Mhm. How'd the breakup go?" I asked.

Carmen chewed her lip. "Jillian didn't take it well. My parents told her about the MTP and she thinks the parasite is impacting my critical thinking."

"Is it?"

Carmen crossed her arms and stared down at her perfectly white sneakers. Jordan Banner, my favorite singer, was improvising slam poetry onstage, and I was so focused on Carmen, I couldn't comprehend a single word.

"Maybe," Carmen said at last. "But I wrote a break-up letter to Jillian six months ago. And I've been keeping all the gifts and notes she's given me in a box because I'm planning on throwing them out. I don't feel impulsive. I feel like I checked something off my to-do list."

"That's your answer, then."

"Car?" A tall girl with light brown skin and tightly spiraled hair touched Carmen's hand.

"Coming." Carmen squeezed her hand and dropped it.

"Car?" I mimicked.

Carmen tucked a few stray strands of hair behind her ears. "I went to the circus tent for better reception, and then my phone died so I had to borrow Angela's. And I promised her we'd dance."

"Don't you need to stand still so you can focus on taking notes on the greatest pop star in our generation?"

Angela tugged on Carmen's hand again.

"He's just a person," Carmen said. "I'll catch you later."

The two of them melted into the crowd with their arms tangled around each other.

Jordan Banner's words zoomed back into focus. "Still got it," he said, waving down the applause. "Now, let's give it up for my friend, Elliott Why!"

I wondered what Albie's poetry would be like—kind and deep, or hurt and prickly. I had only one sucker left, and I didn't want to use it until I absolutely had to. I took my phone out and started recording. Not for the Catch a Dream account. For Albie. This was his moment, and I wanted him to be able to live in it forever if he wanted to.

Albie rested his hands on Scooter's shell and began.

"Earth. Rock. Gas. Hole. Fill. Turtle. Hurt. Hurting."

The background music dimmed to a quiet, insistent thumping. I could see Angela lean close to whisper in Carmen's ear, Carmen laughing in return.

And Albie, with a spotlight-cast halo circling him, cutting his body off from his shadow. The light made the bandanna translucent and revealed the sunglasses for the cheap plastic they were. He was reading the lyrics off a piece of paper. I could see his hands shaking.

"The girl I want. I know she's here." The bandanna muffled the words. "You have . . . shiny hair. Other parts of you are round."

The last line was accentuated by a fart so loud, at first, I thought it was a sound effect.

Someone laughed. The crowd was getting restless, shuffling on their feet, people downing shots and cracking their necks like they might burst into choreographed dance moves at any moment.

"Parts of me get—excited!" Albie hurried through the words. Each one was punctuated by a juicy, loud fart. "When you come around."

The whole crowd was chuckling now. Jordan stood to the side of the stage, a puzzled expression worrying his face.

"Is the farting part of the performance art?" someone jeered.

Ayden leaned over the railing on the second level and declared, "I gave that kid a ride." Everyone laughed, but I don't know if they realized it wasn't supposed to be a joke.

Albie crumpled his bucket hat and chucked it into the crowd. His hair was plastered to his head with sweat. He ripped off the bandanna, crunched the sunglasses in half.

"Is this what I get for telling the truth?" he yelled. "She's not even here."

The words might have been poignant if they hadn't been accompanied by a rumbling fart.

"It was the cheese!" Albie said finally, his voice getting frantic. "I'm lactose intolerant."

The crowd was bent over laughing, gasping for breath. I lowered my phone and deleted the video. I didn't want to see any more.

"I think I'm going to be sick," Albie whispered into the mic.

Then he wrapped his arms around Scooter, clomped down the stairs in front of the stage, and took off running into the jungle.

••••

There are moments that make you reconsider your life choices. Leaving behind Jordan Banner's private concert to chase Albie through the jungle was most definitely one of those moments.

"Albie!"

A branch slapped me in the face and stole the words from my mouth. I shoved the branch away and pressed on, chasing the sound of crashing foliage somewhere ahead of me.

"Albie!" I yelled. "Stop!"

He didn't stop, though, and I'd lost sight of him. I slowed to a walk. It wasn't until I'd looped around the entire island that I realized maybe he didn't want to be found at all.

But I kept walking, marching through the trees and under the stars like I had a purpose. The main compound was the one marker of civilized life on the whole island. Outside of its colorful lights and thumping music was just trees and shadows, the kind of quiet that made the spiraling thoughts in my head fester and bloom.

I'd barely been alone since the hospital. I'd been on boats, busy streets, fighting Carmen, flirting with Albie, and throwing videos onto the internet in hopes they'd have the magic of a shooting star.

I walked right up to the edge of the rainbow-painted dock and stared at the row of boats bobbing alongside it.

#YeahBuoy was right there. Carmen and Albie had chosen their own paths. I could choose mine. Leave. Disappear. Ditch the phone and the videos and the attempt to tell the truth. The MTP was going to end me soon anyway and all of this would go away.

All of this would go away.

Once, the thought might have filled me with relief. Now it filled me with sadness, right up to my throat. So much grief lodged inside me I could barely breathe around it.

I kept walking until my feet blistered in my boots. The island wouldn't give, and neither would I. I wasn't like my dad; I was the kind of person who stayed.

I sat down, hugged my knees to my chest, dug my fingers into the cool sand, and looked at the stars draped across the sky. My mom told me that a star is a fiery ball of chemicals formed from gravitational collapse. It twinkled from the distance; it was burning up close. I'd only learned how to burn from a distance.

Under the spark of a thousand burning stars, I sat in the eye of the hurricane of my own emotional spiral and waited. Thirty to sixty days. Carmen was right. It was never going to be enough.

CHAPTER 33

THE JUNGLE WAS A WILD TAPESTRY OF SOUND. BARKING BIRDS. Thumping music from the club. Trees whispering to each other. Someone gasping for air.

Wait.

Someone was gasping for air.

"Albie?" I uncurled and stood up, scanning the dark tree line until I made out the lumpy shadow of a limping form. "Albie!"

I ran to him, fumbling in my cluttered backpack for his inhaler. When I reached him, I dropped to my knees, dumped the entire bag out, and sifted through the mess of *Land of Invader* coins, dirty clothes, and lollipop wrappers until I found it.

"Take this." I thrust the inhaler into his hands. His skin was pale and sweaty in the moonlight, each breath a wheeze.

"I don't—want—an—inhaler."

"You need it." Agonizing. To be so close to him and not be able to touch or comfort him.

He grabbed the inhaler from me and took a few puffs. "I wish—I was different."

"I don't."

Finally, he took a deep breath.

I dusted the dirt from my hands and slowly gathered my belongings.

"I ate all this dairy you told me not to eat, and I got really sick and I couldn't breathe." Albie inhaled deeply. "And you weren't even there."

"I was," I said. It hadn't occurred to me that I was the girl in the poem. "I was there, and I left to come find you when you ran off."

"You left Jordan Banner and his super cool party to come find me? After everything we did to get here?" Albie sounded skeptical.

"You're my friend." I said, standing up. "Jordan Banner is probably the number-one love of my life. But he's not my friend."

Albie leaned against a palm tree, tilted his head back to look up at the sky. "You know, you really hurt me. You *used* me. I thought you liked me—"

"I do like you!"

"Just listen!"

The moon cast the two of us in silver shadow. I wanted my phone, to watch this on a screen instead of with all the pain and immediacy of real actual life. I wanted my jokes, my lollipop, my lies, all the pieces of armor I made from people's assumptions about me.

But I curled my itching fingers into a fist and didn't reach for anything, kept my eyes on Albie.

"I thought you saw me for being something more than the cancer kid. I thought you trusted me enough to tell the truth! I should have known better than to think that someone like you was really interested."

"Someone like me?"

The wind was picking up, ripping at our clothes and hair and bending the trees.

"You're like . . . this whimsical creature from another world. You don't care what anyone thinks and you're not afraid of anything."

"That's not true."

He smelled like sour milk, and the sunburn was flaking across his forehead and cheekbones. He was angry with me, but he was still there.

"I'm afraid of losing you." I pressed on, uncurling my fists. "I'm sorry for what I did, and I'm sorry that I hurt you. There's no excuse or reason, and I know I can't make it up to you or expect you to trust me." I took a deep breath and closed my eyes as the rest of the words tumbled out, "But I like you so much it's like a physical ache. You're kind and generous and the only person who understands how funny I am. I'm more than interested in you. I think I'm maybe a little bit in love with you."

When he didn't respond right away, I opened my eyes. We watched each other breathe the same air, listened to our hearts beat in sync, and, for once, I didn't want a phone between the two of us or to be anyone other than myself.

"Just a little bit?" he asked, a smile creeping onto his face.

"Don't ruin it."

I tilted my chin up and locked my eyes on his. His gaze flickered from my forehead to my lips. I closed the space between us and brushed my lips softly against his cheek.

Albie didn't hesitate. He grabbed my chin and brought my mouth to his. A weird, low noise came from the back of my throat and that was it. He spun us around so my back was pressed against the palm tree and my hands were in his hair and his hands were . . . everywhere. And I couldn't believe I wasted so much time believing the stories I'd told myself about him when we could have been doing *this* the whole time.

His lips moved to my neck, hands on my hips. I tugged his hair to bring him closer and . . .

My phone buzzed. Once. Twice. Three times.

"I thought there wasn't supposed to be cell service," Albie growled against my throat.

I laughed. "Don't blame me!"

"I will break that phone if it tries to keep me from you." He slid his hand into the pocket of my shorts and pulled out my phone, wrist poised to chuck it over his shoulder into the brush.

"It's your mom," he said.

"Oh." I was so distracted by his hands that it took a moment to set in. *Oh.*

"She wants you to come home." Albie swallowed, hard and continued reading. "Because the test results are in."

The rest of the truth fountained from my lips. "I just found out this morning. You were already mad at me, and I didn't want the trip to end. But I was going to tell you tomorrow, I promise. And I should have told you just now, but I forgot. Honest. Albie, I swear I'm not lying. Your hands and your hair, and you couldn't breathe and then I couldn't breathe and I should have told you everything then, but I'd forgotten about anything else completely by that point and—I—"

He was scrolling back through the texts with my mom. "She texted you about it this afternoon."

"She told me on the phone this morning," I confessed.

The itching in my gut had turned into a wildfire.

Albie's breathing became shallower as his anger grew. "I want to be with you, but the lies—"

"Abort!" Carmen burst through the tree line and sprinted toward one of the paths cutting through the jungle.

"Abort what?" Albie yelled back.

"Everything!" Carmen spun and revealed that her face was covered in clown makeup for reasons I didn't quite understand but I assumed had to do with Angela. "We need to leave. Now. Jordan knows Albie isn't Elliot Why."

CHAPTER 34

I DIDN'T QUESTION IT. WE'D BEEN THROUGH ENOUGH OVER THE past few days for me to know that running was often the best and only option. I sprinted after Carmen.

"Why are you dressed like you're in the circus?" Albie yelled. He was behind us, fumbling to scoop up Scooter from the jungle floor.

"Why do you smell like a dairy farm?" Carmen called back. "Things happen!"

We sprinted up the beach and down the yellow path into the trees, following the silver spotlight of the moon. I swung my arms and kicked my legs, guzzled air in through my nose and out through my mouth. I always ruined things. It was silly to think Albie would have been an exception.

We ran past the club. In the late evening hours, it looked like an abandoned Western town, bottles and cans rolling past like tumbleweed. Carmen stared at it as we flew by, her face full of longing.

We trampled up dust behind us as we broke free of the jungle on the opposite side.

"Hat—Hat—"

I turned around, squinting to make out the shadowy path. "Albie!" I heard only wheezing in return. "Carmen! Albie needs his inhaler."

Carmen didn't slow down. "I'll get Ayden ready for takeoff. Meet us there."

"But—" The only thing left of Carmen was the sand she kicked up in my face as she ran.

I retraced our path through the trees until I found Albie leaning against a tree, clutching Scooter to his chest, and heaving for air.

"Where's your inhaler?" I asked. We'd just had it before he kissed me. Albie shook his head. It was gone.

"Shit, OK." I pried Scooter loose from Albie's grip and almost toppled over when I got the full weight of him in my hands.

"What are you—No." Albie stepped away from the tree and reached for Scooter. I held the giant turtle away from my body. I didn't care if he was an endangered species. He smelled weird and was basically a dinosaur.

"Come on. We've got to keep going. Do it for Scooter," I said and walked backward through the jungle, holding Scooter out toward Albie. He followed, wheezing for breath. "Deep breaths, Albie. I'm here. We're almost there. There's another inhaler on the boat."

My arms ached from Scooter's weight. Albie's wheezing was a ticking clock as we bumbled out of the trees and across the sand. At the end of the rainbow-colored dock, I saw shadows moving around a boat.

"We're almost there," I called over my shoulder. "Don't give up."

"Albert Chang?" someone yelled behind us.

Albie took a deep breath and yelled back "What?"

"It's him!"

I turned around to see Glen charging down the beach, his tablet producing an unnatural glow. Jordan Banner walked behind him, wearing a neon robe. With the makeup melting off his face, he looked as young and lost as we did.

I realized Albie's mistake before he did. It was Elliot Why who'd charmed his way onto a private island and performed the worst poetry. Not Albert Chang. Albie had responded to his real name.

Jordan planted his feet in the sand a few paces in front of us, blocking us from the dock.

"Elliot Why was photographed visiting a bar in Ashville last night," Jordan said. "Which is strange seeing how he was performing here. Care to explain?"

Albie put his hands on his knees and breathed.

"Body double?" I tried. But I was all out of lies.

Jordan's face fell. "I thought you were my friend."

Albie was still wheezing. "I—am."

Glen charged ahead. "Delinquents!"

I stepped between him and Albie and held Scooter out like a shield. "I've been a Jordan Banner stan for as long as I can remember. Please don't make me hurt you."

"You're despicable," Glen spat.

"Yeah. But I also know MMA."

"That's true," Albie heaved. "I've—seen it."

I looked at Jordan. "He wanted to be someone else. Just for one night. You of all people should understand that."

Jordan wrapped his robe tighter around himself. "Identity theft is a serious crime. I can't let this go."

I footballed Scooter under one arm, looking between Jordan and the dock. Albie would never make it.

"Argh!" Albie charged forward with fist raised and punched Glen in the groin.

Glen crumpled to the ground. Jordan gallantly dove to catch him but missed completely and twisted his ankle.

"What the hell was that?" I asked, staring dumbfounded at Glen writhing around in the sand.

"Groin punch," Albie huffed. He squeezed past Jordan and limped down the dock. "Sorry, Glen!"

I gingerly stepped over Jordan and said, "I'm so sorry about this. I'm your biggest fan. 'Don't Go Gently' changed my life. I mean it."

"Not the time," Albie coughed over his shoulder.

"Albie!" Jordan yelled. "That was the worst poem I've ever heard."

Albie hung his head. I hooked my hand around his arm and dragged him forward. We'd already been given a terminal diagnosis. An insult from a pop icon was nothing.

The two of us staggered down the dock, stumbling toward *#YeahBuoy*.

"Hurry!" Carmen yelled. She was standing behind the helm.

"Where's Ayden?" I asked. Sure, Carmen had proven she could drive a small dinghy, but *#YeahBuoy* was a speed racer.

Carmen pointed behind her. Ayden was sprawled across the deck of the boat.

"Tequila, you've betrayed me for the last time," he moaned.

Carmen turned the engine on. "Get in!"

I waited for Albie to board, then handed him Scooter and climbed on myself.

"I punched Glen . . . you know. Down there," Albie said between breaths. "To slow him down."

"Punched?" Carmen asked.

"That's what Hattie did!" My mind flashed back to the cramped storage room, punching Ethel because it was the only way I could help Albie. "I thought it was MMA."

I didn't have the heart to tell him that the groin punch was a Hattie original.

Carmen nudged the throttle forward and the boat lurched away from the dock, tumbling me into Albie.

"I've got it," Carmen said and tried again, plowing us into the waves with choppy movements. We motored away from Faye Island. I could see Glen tapping frantically on his glowing tablet, Jordan on his knees on the sand beside him. In the murky evening light, the colorful island looked like a goopy clown mask, a sloppy attempt to hide the sadness underneath.

I pawed through Albie's backpack and handed him his backup inhaler. My heartbeat didn't slow until his breathing began to even out.

"Was the poem really that bad?" Albie asked when his breathing was back to normal. "Please don't lie."

I would've traded my pinky finger for a sucker in that moment. "Yeah."

Albie nodded to himself. "Awesome. So I'm a terrible poet. Also. Carmen, the test results are in. Hattie's known since this morning."

"Are you kidding me?" Carmen wailed. If she hadn't been steering the boat, I was pretty sure she would have throttled me.

"I was going to tell you," I whimpered.

"I backed you!" Carmen yelled over the chopping wind. "Albie wanted to leave you behind, and I had your back. But you knew. You *knew* how much the results meant to me."

I swallowed. What was there to say? Carmen had forgiven me before. And I'd broken her trust again.

I tried to talk, but the wind swallowed my words. I left Albie with Ayden's lolling figure and walked to the helm. The sky was a bruised purple, drooping close to the water. It was almost morning, the eyelid of the horizon about to open.

"I was going to tell you, I swear," I said.

Carmen flexed her fingers around the helm.

OK, that clearly wasn't going to work. Maybe I could distract her? "What happened with that girl from the circus? Is that where you—"

Before I could finish my question, Carmen cut the engine, pulled her elbow back, and snapped it into my boob.

"Did you just punch me in the *breast*?" I stumbled back into the first mate's seat.

"Carmen!" Albie set Scooter down and scrambled to his feet to get between us.

"We're dying, Hattie!" Carmen screamed. "How could you not tell us about the test results?"

I gripped the sides of the chair, steadying myself against the rocking boat. Everything was spinning. Carmen stepped forward. I didn't know what she was going to do, but I hoped she could punch me hard enough to black me out and make all of this go away.

Before she got the chance, a roll of thunder grumbled overhead, jerking all of our eyes to the sky. Then the sky broke open and rain barreled down.

The storm was here.

CHAPTER 35

THREE BOLTS OF LIGHTNING CRACKED ACROSS THE SKY IN UNISON, illuminating the black clouds with electric purple veins. The rain pounded against the thin canopy covering the stern and cockpit.

Carmen shoved past me and took the helm. The engine kicked on a second later and the boat plunged forward. The boat rocked and rolled against a wave, sending me sprawling to my knees. I cradled the phone to my chest. Without Carmen and Albie, it was all I had.

"The results. What did they say?" Carmen asked.

"We have to go back to Marsh Rock to read them," I screamed over the wind.

Carmen flexed her hands around the helm. "The only reason I agreed to this stupid escape attempt was because we said we'd come back before the test results. You promised."

I lied. It's the only thing I know how to do.

"You were running away," I reminded her.

Carmen looked down at me. "You used us to make money."

"Yeah! I did!" I pulled into the chair. "I was scared, and I lied, and now Albie hates me too so you might as well get in line."

"I don't hate you," Albie said. "I like you, but you keep lying to me. There's a difference."

"Well, maybe you should hate me," I said. "I'm the reason you fell in the lake!"

Albie hung his head. "I didn't fall in because of you. I was at the lake because of Carmen."

Carmen let her eyes drift away from the waves for one second. "Me? You know I train in the lake in the off-season. I was going to come over for breakfast after."

I peered over the side of the boat. The dark water looked alive and merciless. There was nowhere to run.

"I went out there to find you and tell you I didn't want your pity friendship anymore," Albie said.

Carmen was so surprised that she dropped her hands from the helm for a second before a wave slapped into the hull and she righted us again. When she spoke, her voice was low and cold. "What do you mean?"

"You were the only friend who kept visiting me in the hospital," Albie said. "The other kids dropped off after a few months, and you came three times a week every week."

"Because you were my best friend," Carmen said.

"I was a commitment," Albie said. "And you don't break your commitments. Look at how long you've stayed with Jillian."

"I broke up with her," Carmen countered.

"Good for you. Maybe you should break up with me, too."

"This is the MTP talking."

"You feel sorry for me!" Albie spit the words with such force that Carmen and I both flinched. "You act like my babysitter, not my friend. And I let you because I was used to doing what people told me to. I went to the lake that day to tell you I didn't need a hospital visitor anymore. I can carry my own inhaler."

"Except you literally refused to bring it with you on Faye Island," I said. The fear of watching him struggle to breathe was still a cold fist in my chest.

"I learned my lesson!" Albie said. "I won't make the same mistake again."

"I take care of you," Carmen said.

"That's not what friendship is," Albie said.

"This is Hattie getting in your head," Carmen insisted, staring resolutely at the wall of water ahead. "You've never had a girl show interest in you before, so you don't know how it feels and it's messing with you."

I slapped the gunwale with all the strength in my arms, but the rain drowned out the sound. "You think you're so much better than everyone else because you're good at pretending. You're a better liar than I am, and I have a clinical diagnosis."

"One doctor saying you might have a compulsive lying problem isn't a clinical diagnosis!" Carmen screamed.

I reared my hand back and punched her in the boob.

"Ow! What was that for?"

"You punched me first!" We stood apart, each of us cupping a hand across our chests. Albie took another puff of his inhaler.

"She's exactly who we thought she was," Carmen said.

I stepped away from her and dug my hands into my pockets. I turned them inside out on the deck and the only thing I found was lint and gum wrappers. No lollipops. No money. No denials.

#YeahBuoy cut across the choppy waves at a diagonal. The sun was fighting to break through the storm clouds as it crawled up the horizon. The wind ripped us back and forth, back and forth.

I marched to the bow of the boat, where there was no canopy to protect me from the rain. Scooter was asleep on the deck. Ayden was passed out on the opposite seat. I lay on my back and let the cold rain pound against me.

The secret to not caring about anything is to destroy things before you get the chance to develop feelings. My whole life I had crashed from catastrophe to catastrophe, vandalizing and lying and causing other people problems so I wouldn't have to face my own.

The smell of cheap alcohol and dirty money when my dad left.

The look on my mom's face when she got the first credit card bill and learned how much debt he'd taken on in her name.

The feeling of Albie's hand tangled in mine, warm and steady.

I'd dreamed of becoming an adult capable of earning my mother's forgiveness. I'd tried to become that person now, and all I had to show for it was a cracked phone screen and a sore boob.

Thunder rolled across the sky, and the wind kicked into a frenzy, whipping around us fast enough to sound like a voice. I took out my phone, knowing what I needed to do.

I stood in the center of the boat, blocking Albie and Carmen's view of the storm.

"Move!" Carmen yelled.

"Sit down!" Albie pleaded.

I held my phone up and turned the camera to face me. It was the first time I'd really looked at myself in weeks. The purple dye in my hair was fading to lilac, my cheeks had turned rosy from the sun, and there was no anger left in my eyes.

I started recording. Albie clutched the back of a chair. Carmen looked above me, eyes trained on the sea.

"Hello e-people." I closed my eyes and let out a deep breath. This was the last card I had to play. *Tell the truth.* When I opened my eyes, I trained them on Albie and Carmen behind the helm. "This is Hattie. I'm the creator of this channel, and the person who's been filming Albie and Carmen."

The camera angle was tight on my face, revealing how my lips were stained green from the lollipops.

"It's a long story, but last week, the three of us found out we probably only had thirty to sixty days to live. Carmen ignored it. Albie was devastated." Carmen scrunched up her nose in a way that made me think she was fighting back tears. Albie held my gaze. "I was pissed. I felt like my life so far hadn't been great, and I'd been counting on transforming into an adult to redeem my existence."

The rain slithered down my face and arms. I tried to burrow inside myself and find the place where the parasite was crawling through the marrow, but all I felt was me.

"I was no one special before last week. I was born in New Jersey. My dad left when I was twelve. I gave him my mom's credit cards because . . ." Because I was stupid. Because I was dumb enough to think someone could care about me. "Because I was a kid, and I wanted my dad to love me. He racked up a huge gambling debt in my mom's name, and she had to take a new job to pay it off. I ruined her life. That's what the Catch a Dream money is for. I wanted to pay off my mom's debt because . . ."

All the cruel excuses I'd told myself rose to the tip of my tongue. Because I didn't want to die owing her anything. Because she blamed me for the debt.

"Because I love her and I wanted to help," I said. Carmen flexed her hands around the steering wheel. "But all that's over now. The test results to confirm our diagnosis are waiting for us back home. I'm sorry for a lot of things—losing the turtle, conning Jordan Banner, committing some minor felonies—but the thing I'm most sorry for is disappointing the people I love. My mom." I looked at Carmen, then at Albie. "And Carmen and Albie. They deserve better, and so do I."

I was totally drenched. The rain really wasn't letting up. "This is the last video. I'm going to live the rest of my life—however long that is—in the real world."

I was fumbling for the button to stop recording when I realized there was one more truth I still had to tell.

"Oh, also my real name isn't Hattie," I said. "It's Henrietta. OK, that's all."

I set the video to upload and slid my phone under one of the seat cushions. I didn't need it anymore. Carmen and Albie were silent in the storm.

I rested my hand on Scooter's shell. It was slick with rain but still warm underneath. He was protected. "What do you think, buddy?"

Scooter's response was to swing both arms at the padded seat and start scratching like a maniac. His eyes were beady and alert, and there was a little foam at his mouth.

"Albie!" I called, my heart galloping into my chest. "There's something wrong with Scooter!"

CHAPTER 36

THE SKY WAS DUMPING RAIN BY THE BUCKETFUL. I PLACED MY PALM back on Scooter's shell and found it trembling.

"Scooter!" Albie staggered to the bow, fell to his knees, and scooped up Scooter into his arms. "I never should have left you." I watched as Albie set Scooter on his shell and pulled his legs in and out in a froggy motion. "Breathe, buddy!"

Ayden chose that moment to snap out of his drunken slumber and sit straight up. He looked back at Carmen captaining the boat, up at the sky chasing us with wind, and then at Albie giving Scooter CPR. "Bro. What's up with your wildlife?"

"He's not wildlife!" Albie screamed in frustration. "He's a Kemp's ridley! One of the rarest turtles in the world, and he's sick."

"Dude." Ayden flung himself back on the seat. "That's not a Kemp's ridley. That's a gopher tortoise."

"He's dying!" Albie said. "Wait. What?"

"You can tell by the scales on his legs. He's not endangered. He's wild and probably just needs to burrow," Ayden said, covering his face with his arm. "Can somebody turn the lights off? It's so bright."

"We're outside," I said.

"Ugh." Ayden twisted so he was lying facedown on the seat. Within seconds, he was snoring again.

"He's drunk," Albie said.

"Yeah. But he grew up on boats." I took off my sweatshirt and balled it on the ground. Scooter didn't curl up or fade in on himself. He crawled to the nest of fabric and dug in. "He does kind of look like a gopher."

"He's not in danger?" Albie said, breathless.

"No. He looks happy."

Albie's body was still, but I could see a puzzle rearranging behind his eyes. "I'm—"

"Help!" Carmen.

Albie and I were on our feet in an instant. We hurried to the back of the boat, bent in half against the wind, each step a battle. A gust hit the canopy covering the cockpit area and tore it off, leaving *#Yeah-Buoy* naked and exposed to the storm. In the distance, I could just make out a hazy blob through the gray sky and sleeting rain. Land.

Carmen's arms were wrapped around the helm, her forehead resting on top. She was breathing fast. "Get Ayden."

"He's passed out," Albie said.

"I can't." The wind snatched the words from Carmen's throat and carried them away. "I can't do it."

Carmen was the captain. She always knew what to do, where to go, how to be. When we'd wanted to escape from the hospital, she'd made a plan. When I'd frozen backstage at Dream Fest, she'd guided us out. The word *can't* sounded like a ghost coming out of her mouth.

I nudged her out of the way with my hip and wrapped my hands around the slippery metal. "I've got the wheel. It's OK."

Carmen slid down the side and put her head between her knees. "It's called a helm."

Even in the throes of a panic attack, she couldn't help correcting me on my nautical terms.

"Not the time," I said. "Albie, help her."

"Don't touch the throttle," Carmen murmured.

Albie was already on his knees, his hand on her shoulders. "Breathe with me. In for four. Out for eight."

"Put on your life jackets!" I barked.

"Can't. Believe. I. Didn't. Think. Of. That," Carmen said in between choppy breaths.

Albie dug around under the seats until he found four life jackets. He chucked one at Ayden before buckling on his own and then helping Carmen with hers.

I had no idea how boats were supposed to work, but I was pretty sure the waves weren't supposed to come over the sides. The familiar chorus piped up: *You have no idea what you're doing. You let everyone down.*

I planted my feet and screamed so loud even the wind couldn't swallow my cry. There was a speck of land on the horizon. I didn't look down at my hands or up at the raging sky. I looked ahead, focused on only what I could see.

I pulled hand over hand, inching the helm to turn us in to the bay. The waves crashing around us seemed taller than any of the trees we'd left behind on Faye Island. The rain fell in sheets so thick I could barely see.

"We're never going to make it!" Carmen gasped.

"I can do this." I lifted my hands a fraction of an inch and the wheel spun frantically toward the left. Oops. I planted my feet and caught the wheel with my hands, correcting our course.

#YeahBuoy inched toward the hazy piece of land. A bolt of lightning broke open across the sky, illuminating a neat row of docks. The path was impossibly narrow, I didn't think it was designed for speedboats our size, and I had no idea how to squeeze us into the bay.

I'd made it sound like I had everything under control to make Carmen feel better, but get real. My only extracurricular activity was being a massive disappointment. We were screwed.

The rain was beating against my skin, pouring so fast I had to blink rapidly to keep my eyes clear. I bent my legs and tweaked the wheel—erm, helm—to the right, then held steady to line *#YeahBuoy* up with the entrance to the bay.

The wheel—seriously, why do people call it a damn helm?—was slipping. My muscles ached. It would be so easy to let go.

My whole life didn't flash before my eyes. Just one scene: my mom, tucking me into bed on a night my dad didn't come home, believing the best of me when I only showed her the worst. *Be brave, Hattie. Be brave.*

The water was rising, the wind was strong.

I corrected to the right, gripping the wheel so tightly my fingers ached.

"Hattie." Albie was behind me.

"I can do this," I repeated through gritted teeth. I'd called myself a liar enough times for it to become true. I was hoping the same would happen if I said I was capable.

"I know." He wrapped a life jacket around me and cinched the straps. His breath was warm on my frozen skin, his hands steady and strong. "But just in case."

He wrapped one arm around my waist and pulled Carmen up with the other. She trembled as she placed a tentative hand on the helm next to mine.

"Exit Ethics?" I asked.

"Exit Ethics," they said.

I reached for the throttle—the one Carmen had explicitly told me not to touch—and pulled it back. Boats don't have brakes, and neither do I.

Albie buried his nose in the crook of my neck. Carmen winced. I spun left, right, center hold, squeezing *#YeahBuoy* down the waterway.

The facts: We were moving too quickly. We were going to hit the dock. The impact would capsize the boat. Albie couldn't swim.

I locked my hands around the wheel and yelled, "Brace for impact!"

THE THREE OF US HUDDLED TOGETHER. I LINED THE WHEEL UP AS best as I could and then yanked the keys out of the ignition. The purring engine went silent, and the wind surged the boat forward into the bay.

Carmen squeezed my hand. Her breathing was evening out. "This is it."

"You can't swim," I yelled to Albie.

"That's what the life jacket is for," he yelled back.

The boat lurched forward and headed straight for a sun-bleached dock.

I closed my eyes and waited for the crash. The wind and rain went silent against the backdrop of my own beating heart.

Bump.

A light, hollow sound drifted up from the hull. I waited for the water to rush in *Titanic*-style or the boat to tip toward the sky. When nothing happened, I opened my eyes.

There was no hidden iceberg or water gushing in. *#YeahBuoy* had nudged its way to the dock and come to a complete stop. We'd made contact with barely more than a tap.

Albie's eyes were still closed. He patted his head, then Carmen's.

"Are we dead?" he asked. "I thought the afterlife would have better weather."

The light impact had rolled Ayden onto the deck. He staggered to his feet and examined the damage. "Not cool, bro! My parents are going to kill me."

"You weren't conscious, so you don't get to complain," Carmen said. "Hattie? You OK?"

My hands were still clenched around the wheel, clothes hanging soppy and loose from my torso. Blue and red sirens spun through the curtain of rain coating the shore. The police were waiting for us.

Every vein in my body felt electrified.

"I'm . . . amazing," I said breathlessly. "It was a one in a million shot and I made it."

Albie covered my fingers with his. "Of course you did."

I grinned. "Perfect aim. Landed right at the dock. Sailed through the literal eye of a literal storm and got us home."

"I mean, technically speaking we're not home. We're in West Palm Beach, and you did low-key crash the boat," Carmen said. Albie raised an eyebrow. "But yeah. You did great."

I rested my head on Albie's shoulder, watching as the clouds scattered up ahead, fleeing from the emerging sun and taking the rain with them. Light beamed through, coating the once-gray world in gold and quieting the raging wind to a lilting breeze.

A policewoman strode down the dock, three guys in DBD windbreakers behind her.

"I wish I was as committed to anything as DBD is to those windbreakers," Albie said, and I wanted to kiss him because he was the only other person on the planet who probably thought about those windbreakers as much as I did.

"Whatever happens next," Carmen said, "we should stick together."

I nodded and settled into Albie's arms. This was a story I didn't want to exaggerate. For the first time in my life, I wanted to tell the truth.

••••

They took us to a beige stucco police station with an army of palm trees out front and deposited us in a small room with a huge mirror and no windows. Ayden stayed with the boat.

"The captain has to go down with the ship, dude," he said.

"Ayden. We've been through this," Carmen said. "I was the captain and then I transferred my duties to Hattie. At best, you were a drunken deckhand."

Ayden shook his head as the policewoman guided us away. "That doesn't sound like me."

The police said they'd notified his parents, who were driving down to Palm Beach to have a chat with their son about responsibility. I had a feeling the conversation would end with him still living at home without a job and he'd be just fine.

I sat between Carmen and Albie in the interrogation room, across from a Black policewoman with a shaved head and a very red-faced Jeff, who had hustled over from Marsh Rock. Scooter was asleep on top of the table. All of that fake burrowing really took it out of him.

"I'm Officer Johnson, and I'll be conducting the interview," the police officer said and set a tape recorder on the table between us. Excitement poked through her serious exterior. We were probably the most interesting crime to happen in this small town in years.

"We're not saying anything without a lawyer present," Carmen said and crossed her arms.

Albie chewed his lip. "The MTP will get us soon. It doesn't matter if we confess."

I waited for Carmen to fight back, to insist yet again that we probably hadn't even contracted the MTP in the first place.

But she dropped her arms. "You're probably right."

Albie's and my eyebrows shot up. "Carmen," he whispered. "Do you realize you just moved from denial to acceptance?"

She rolled her eyes. "I was never in denial."

Albie leaned back in his chair. "And she's back."

"Enough!" Jeff interjected. His eyes were bloodshot, his face a purple shade of rage. "Do you realize what you've done? How much trouble you've caused?"

Officer Johnson said, "You're in my department as a courtesy, Mr. Buttikiss."

"Your last name is Buttikiss?" I asked. The world was truly a magical place.

"Focus," Albie mumbled under his breath.

"And yes, I know exactly what we've done," I continued. "Stolen a boat, ditched that boat in Miami, shoplifted, put an older woman in a choke hold to escape, snuck into Dream Fest, impersonated a celebrity, played an incredible game of *Land of Invaders*, borrowed a nicer boat, and then lightly crashed it."

"I cannot emphasize this enough," Carmen said, "but the *Land of Invaders* game Hattie played was impeccable. I've never seen anything like it."

Officer Johnson and Jeff stared at us in dumbfounded silence.

"That's all you have to say for yourself?" Jeff asked.

"We also probably ruined your chances of getting with my mom, but to be fair, I'm pretty sure she'd already put you in the friend zone, so I really don't think that's on us."

"The tortoise was a gift," Albie said, gesturing to Scooter. "But there was the other shoplifting at the hospital gift store."

I snapped my fingers. "You're right. I forgot about that one." I looked at Officer Johnson. "In the past, I've had a tendency to lie compulsively, so you should maybe fact-check me."

She flipped through her notes. "The owners of the boat that was stolen from Marsh Rock are looking to press charges or recoup the damages."

I could see myself in the mirror over her shoulder. My wet hair was twisted into a knotty bun. There was mascara smeared under my eyes, and my cheeks were less sun-kissed and more sun-frenched. I didn't have a lollipop left or any good rolls of the dice, but it was the first time I'd been able to look myself in the eye in years.

"It was all me," I said. "And honestly, I'm not sure if I can even blame the MTP for my behavior."

"What's MTP?" Officer Johnson asked.

Carmen, Albie, and I looked to Jeff to provide an explanation.

"That's classified," he mumbled.

Officer Johnson leveled her gaze at the DBD insignia on his windbreaker.

"DBD is not liable for criminal actions undertaken by minors not in its care," Jeff said.

"For context, we were in his care until I convinced them to break out," I explained to Officer Johnson. "This is all my fault. Carmen and Albie had nothing to do with the crimes."

"She's a delinquent," Jeff said, narrowing his eyes at me. "We should have separated her from the others from the start."

Carmen shoved her chair back and stood up. "Hattie's lying. We all wanted to break out. I was the one who came up with the escape plan that worked. They never could have done it on their own. No offense."

Albie stood up beside her. "The celebrity impersonator thing was all me. Look at her. She doesn't even look like Elliot Why."

"Neither do you," I said.

"That's beside the point! And I snuck us into Dream Fest. Hattie didn't want to jump the fence."

"What we're trying to say," Carmen said, shrugging her shoulders back. "Is that we're a team. So if one of us is in trouble, we're all in trouble."

Officer Johnson looked up at her and said, "You're definitely all in trouble."

"Oh. Well. Good," Carmen said. She and Albie sank back into their seats.

"Now," Officer Johnson sat forward, finally in control of the room. "Tell me what happened. Start at the beginning."

So we did. Carmen told her about her girlfriend and family, the perfect image she was terrified to lose. Albie told her about surviving childhood leukemia and how unfair it was to be asked to survive again, why being Elliot Why was an answer to all his questions. I told her about my dad and *Land of Invaders*, my mom and the debt weighing down her life.

It all might have led to a very emotional and heartwarming learning moment if Mrs. Chang hadn't slammed through the door and started berating Officer Johnson about the constitution and Miranda rights.

"Your mom is so cool," I whispered to Albie as Mrs. Chang leaned over the table and gave the officer and Jeff a look so cold it made me shiver.

The rest of Albie's and Carmen's families weren't far behind. Mr. Chang and Albie's older brother and sister inched into a corner, keeping their distance until Mrs. Chang finished her speech about the right to an attorney.

Carmen's parents, abuela, and younger sister tumbled in after that.

"She's alive!" Carmen's mom gushed. "And look at her! She's more beautiful than ever!"

Her dad was wearing his PRESIDENT CARMEN shirt, her abuela was thumbing a rosary, and her mom and sister were carrying floppy cardboard signs that said BRING CARMEN HOME. Her abuela yanked Carmen's chair out and the four of them engulfed Carmen in a hug.

Albie's brother James squeezed in between the two of us and jabbed his finger near my eye. "This is all your fault."

"Mostly, yeah," I said, but the words felt false on my tongue.

"Actually," Albie said, tapping his brother's shoulder. "Escaping the hospital was my idea."

James blustered. "Get out."

Mrs. Chang paused her berating of Officer Johnson long enough to turn to us and say, "Don't underestimate your brother. Just because Albert's been sick before doesn't mean he's immune to stupidity."

Albie looked at her in shock. "Thanks, Mom."

Albie clambered out of his chair and huddled with his family in a corner, dragging his mom away from poor Officer Johnson and Jeff.

"Excuse me, but this is a police station, not a reality show!" Officer Johnson cried.

I was the only one who heard her though. That familiar itch clawed its way up my throat. The desire to burn, destroy, lie—anything to feel different.

"Hattie."

It was barely a whisper over the cacophony in the room, but I would have known her voice anywhere. Two steps and I was at the door, arms thrown around her neck. My mom stumbled back a step but steadied herself quickly, wrapping a protective arm around my head.

"You came back," she said, awe laced through her voice. Her hair was twisted into a lopsided bun, and there were deep purple circles punched under her eyes.

There were so many truths I needed to share with her, but I settled for: "I missed you."

She kissed my forehead. "Me too."

I squeezed her tighter and something rustled between us. I pulled far enough away to see the three large envelopes my mom was clutching in her other hand.

The test results.

CHAPTER 38

CARMEN NOTICED THE ENVELOPES A MOMENT AFTER I DID. SHE looked at me, the envelopes, my mom, the envelopes again.

"You have the results," she said. The word *results* silenced the noise in the room.

Officer Johnson let out a defeated sigh and kicked back from the metal table. "Y'all just take the room. I need to handle some paperwork anyways."

The families stayed clustered around Carmen and Albie. Albie's family in one corner. Carmen's family in another. Jeff flying solo at the table. Mom and I in the center.

Mom kissed me once more on the side of the head and then let me go. "I have to tell them. Stay with me?"

I nodded.

Mom stepped forward into the dingy lighting of the single overhead bulb suspended from the ceiling.

Jeff deflated a little bit when my mom avoided eye contact with him. The space felt smaller with the door closed and the walls boxing us together. Especially when the room erupted into chatter again.

"—miracle we got them back"

"Negligence and lack of transparency."

"The results—"

"—you had no right!"

My mom slapped the envelopes on the table one by one, and the room slowly hushed again as everyone took them in. Carmen Diaz. Albert Chang. Henrietta Larken.

"Did you really have to use my full name?" I whispered to my mom. "And at such a sensitive time?"

"Later," she said, a hint of amusement in her voice. Just because I was growing didn't mean I was a different person. She shook her head twice and the warm face of my mother was replaced with a *Trust Me, I'm a Scientist* façade.

"We have the test results," she said.

Albie and Carmen inched toward each other.

Carmen cleared her throat. "I don't think I'm going to open them just yet."

Jeff sputtered to life again. "DBD—"

My mom cut him off. "For liability purposes, DBD would prefer the three of you open the test results now, in the presence of DBD scientists and within earshot of law enforcement. But we cannot force you to view the results or take medical action based on them."

The adults erupted into another argument about what defined medical action and why the parents hadn't been sent the test results first.

Albie and Carmen leaned across the table, beckoning me toward them.

"I feel good for once," Carmen said. "Why ruin it?"

"You need to know if you have it," I said. "We all do."

"I'm tired of fighting," Albie sighed. "But I want to live. Those results are my best chance at figuring out how to do that."

"And we"—I gestured between Carmen and myself—"need to stop running. You hid from the truth with Jillian. Don't do it here."

Carmen narrowed her eyes. "That was a surprisingly logical argument. Are you sure it's not the MTP talking?"

I jerked my head toward the envelopes. "Only one way to find out."

Albie stepped forward for the group. "We're ready."

My mom spread her fingers across the envelopes. "First, let me go over what we've discovered in the lab. The MTP product was not as far along in the development process as we'd forecast when launching this round of testing. Initially, we believed you all had a fifty-three percent chance of infection. We've now downgraded that likelihood to twenty-five percent."

"How could you make such a grievous miscalculation?" Mrs. Chang asked. I could see the numbers calculating in her eyes. Twenty-five percent. Thirty to sixty days.

"Arrogance," my mom said. "Additionally, the strain of MTP itself is weaker than initially projected. Any trace remnants of the product are likely to have only minimal effects on someone of the subjects' age and health."

"So you're saying . . ." I started, my mind refusing to compute the words on its own.

"It's incredibly unlikely that the MTP will impact you at all." Her face was serious, but there was a smile in her voice when she said it.

"I told you I didn't have it!" Carmen said, shoving Albie in the shoulder with one hand and reaching across the table to flick my arm with the other. "You never should have doubted me about what I saw on Jeff's slideshow!"

"So much for your stages of grief," Albie muttered, rubbing his shoulder.

"How did this happen, Lauren?" Jeff flipped through the folder on the table, searching for answers. "After all the preliminary testing."

My mom drummed her fingers along the envelopes. "Maybe I'm not as good of a scientist as I thought. Or maybe my work was sloppy." The drumming stopped. "Or maybe I'm an incredible scientist who did an intentionally bad job creating something that never should have existed in the first place. Who's to say?"

"So we're probably not infected," Albie repeated.

"What I'm hearing is that we could have skipped the whole coming-of-age, near-death situation," I said slowly. The weight of her words took time to settle in. "None of this had to happen."

"I explained our infection probability tables to them," Jeff said with a shrug.

"I tried to tell them!" Carmen said, a smug smile tugging at her lips.

"I left you a dozen voicemails explaining it," Mom said.

But I'd only listened to the beginning of a few of them. She'd said something about rerunning the MTP samples and I'd deleted it because I didn't want to know how far gone we were.

"I told you on the phone that the MTP wasn't attaching," Mom said. "I thought you understood."

"I thought you were just trying to comfort me!" I sputtered.

"We even put out that local news story with a representative from the lab saying there were no conclusive results," Mom continued.

"We didn't make it past Dad explaining how immunocompromised I am," Albie said.

"I knew it!" Carmen pumped her fist in the air. She turned to Albie and me, shaking her head. "And you two thought I was in denial."

"You are!" Albie and I said at the same time.

"Not anymore I'm not!"

"OK, agree to disagree. But I'm not on board with the life lesson of this saga being 'listen to your parents,'" Albie said. "No offense Mom and Dad."

"This is why communication is so important," Carmen said, turning to my mom. "The fearmongering in your original presentation activated our amygdala in a way that made staying in that hospital impossible. Personally, I'm grateful for our little escapade because I had some growing to do and it was cheaper and safer than psychedelic drugs, but still. You might want to consider a different approach."

"You're literally a hundred years old," I muttered.

"Thanks for your feedback," my mom said. "I'll add 'get better at presentations' to my to-do list. Right under 'stop trying to make a zombie parasite.'"

"I like her more than you already," Carmen said to me.

"Wow, thanks," I said.

Carmen's and Albie's parents watched the volleying match between the three of us with quizzical looks.

Finally, Mrs. Chang cleared her throat. "I'd like to see the results now. We've been told to expect nothing before. The body can surprise you."

The dingy light swinging over the table cast the envelopes in and out of shadow. *I have it. I have it not.*

My mom nodded. Albie swiped his immediately. I inched mine toward me without picking it up. Carmen picked hers up with her fingertips and held it away from her as if it might have the MTP, too.

The envelope was thin and orange. The kind with the clasps on the back that can snap off if you fiddled with them too much.

"Whatever you find out," my mom continued, "I'm going to do everything I can to help."

Albie opened his first. His parents held hands as they peered over his shoulder.

"Negative," he breathed out in relief. His mom's face crumpled momentarily before she regained her composure.

"Should I email Dr. Wong for a conference just to be sure there aren't any side effects?" Mr. Chang asked.

"No," Albie said. No *uhs*. No questions. He'd left Elliot Why behind—thank all the pop gods in existence—but some of the confidence had stuck.

Carmen opened hers next, unfolding the clasps and the flap of the envelope with gentle care.

"I knew it," she said. "Negative!"

Her family wrapped their arms around each other until they became one big blob.

I stared down at the envelope and didn't even wish I had a lollipop. I just wished Mom and I were alone.

"I'm here," my mom whispered.

I ripped open the envelope and took out the thin sheet of paper. It was watermarked everywhere and there were a lot of big words I didn't know how to pronounce. One word in the middle was bolded in a larger font.

"Positive."

My mom's eyes flooded with tears. Albie and Carmen were at my back in an instant.

"It's OK. It'll be OK. The product was weak," my mom said, swiping at her eyes. "We'll get you the best treatment and monitor you until it's out of your system. At most, you'll experience a few adverse side effects, but most likely you won't feel a thing."

Not feeling a thing used to be the dream. I'd consumed enough lollipops to pepper my teeth with cavities in pursuit of it.

The voices came back in an instant, scratching at my insides, scrawling the fears I had lived inside of for so long.

You are poison. Something is wrong with you.

But I'd steered a boat (mostly) safely through a storm. I'd made two friends. I'd met Jordan Banner. Won possibly the greatest game of *Land of Invaders* ever played. Kissed a boy who liked me back. Been brave enough to stay and brave enough to come home.

"Well, this is unfair," I said. Carmen, Albie, and my mom laughed. The rest of the room inched away from me like I had an infection. Which, I guess, I did.

Three rapping knocks echoed on the door. Officer Johnson carefully swung it open a moment later, cramming all of us farther into the room.

"Sorry to interrupt, but we do need the room for less heartwarming criminal activities."

"Of course, Officer," Mrs. Chang said.

"Carmen is student body president," her dad said, pointing to his T-shirt.

"I don't care," Officer Johnson said, stepping out to hold open the door as we piled through and entered the bright, buzzing station. "Marsh Rock has jurisdiction anyway."

Carmen's and Albie's families chattered, their relief a palpable presence in the air. My mom stayed right by my side, her presence warm and steady as always.

Outside the station, the air was heavy and humid. As always. But also, fresh and new. The rain had swept out some of the suffocation, and the sun was timidly peering out from the thick blanket of clouds drooping across the sky.

Albie and Carmen were waiting at the top of the concrete stairs. Below was the real world and their futures, and, in a more literal sense, their parents bringing the cars around.

Carmen took me by the shoulders and stared into my eyes. "You will get through this. If for no other reason than you want me to stop visiting you in treatment every day. I've had a lot of practice at hospitals."

"I don't even know if I'll go to the hospital," I said.

"Even better! Home visits are also a specialty of mine," she said.

"You don't have to—"

"I'm your friend, Hattie. You couldn't keep me away." She gave Albie a quick hug and then skipped down the stairs, looking lighter and more balanced than the President Carmen I'd met in the school office. "I'll text you!"

I was pretty sure she didn't have my real number, but I was also pretty sure that wouldn't matter. Carmen could always find a way.

Albie's family surrounded him like a security task force as they herded him down the steps and away from the station.

"Hattie, I—" He called over his shoulder. I could hear Scooter rustling inside the carboard box.

"Bye, Albie," I said. I didn't want to be there when he had time to slow down and remember how many times I'd betrayed him.

Then it was just my mom and the humidity and me. I was wearing the same clothes I'd worn to Faye Island, but it felt like I'd outgrown them. My hand was locked around the crumpled test results.

Mom guided us into our clunker car and slid me into the passenger seat.

She turned on the AC then twisted to look at me. "Hear me, Hattie: Nothing is wrong with you. Nothing has ever been wrong with you." She pried the results out of my hand and scanned them. "There was only a trace presence in your system. That means there's almost no MTP."

"I'm glad it was me instead of them."

"I'm glad I was so horrified by that job that I subconsciously messed up making a mutated biological weapon," Mom said. "The human mind is a wonderful thing."

I laughed. "I won a *Land of Invaders* game. I'm red tier now. Like Dad was."

We hadn't talked about the game since he left. He took the board and the pieces and any magic I'd believed in with him.

"You were always such a good player." She paused to clear her throat. "Most of the time I feel like a terrible mother."

"You're not."

She shook her head. "I never planned on doing this alone. I tried to be strong when your dad left. I didn't cry. I got a good job and made enough money and kept him away from you." She brushed a piece of damp hair away from my face. "But I was so busy trying to be strong for you that I didn't see you. And maybe you didn't need to see my strength—you have plenty of that on your own. Maybe what you needed was to see me fall apart and then put myself back together."

"Mom—"

She held up her hand. "I took this stupid job and did things I knew weren't right because I wanted to be strong for you. But it chewed me up. Even if it hadn't been you in that water, it would have eaten me alive. You were right; it was a mistake to take this job. I'm going to quit, and I'm going to become the kind of mother you deserve."

It was the passionate sincerity in her voice that broke me wide open. "You're my mom. You don't have to do anything to deserve me."

Mom squeezed my hand.

"You're so brave, Hattie. You don't pretend to be OK when you're withering inside. I love you, and I'm here for you. I can't believe how lucky I am that you're my daughter. Do you hear me?"

I listened to the steady sound of her breathing. "Lies are so much easier than the truth."

"I know. But I don't think you want an easy life. I think you want a good one."

She held my hand until the tears fogging my vision had cleared and my fingers unclenched from the results page.

"About the parasite," my mom started. "It's not going to kill you. Not even close."

"I know."

It was the most terrifying truth of all.

I was going to live.

CHAPTER 39

Positive.

The word was printed in big capital letters sprawled across the page. When I held it over the murky swamp of water surrounding Marsh Rock's bay, the paper looked translucent and thin.

I'd spent the week since our crash return devoting myself to my new mission to Tell the Truth (Most of the Time). This included but was not limited to:

- Signing up for a film class at school. I didn't need to be an adult to pursue my dream of being an artist, and I didn't need a financial reason to make something beautiful.
- Trying to make an appointment with Dr. Ryan. She informed me she saw only patients attached to the hospital but gave me a list of recommended therapists in the area, who I was going to do some research on and reach out to soon.

- Refilling my locker at school and apologizing to Mrs. Howard for being a punk who used her compassion against her. We even bonded over our love of Jordan Banner.

- Writing an apology note to the Hendersons taking full responsibility for stealing their boat, *Seas the Day*. They'd decided not to press charges as long as we paid for the damages the boat had incurred from not being docked properly.

- I posted an apology note on my Catch a Dream account. Followers had donated $21,351 to the cause after my impassioned live. I gave them the option of receiving a full refund or donating the money to help pay for our restitution fees.

- I also emailed Ayden's parents telling them their son was a good kid and we used his kindness against him. They responded that he'd done something seriously wrong and they'd had enough and were putting their foot down. They'd kicked Ayden out of his room. Now he had to live in the guest house out back. Tough life.

- My last note was to Ethel, to remind her that I was a better *Land of Invaders* player than her. (What? It's the truth!)

I was at the edge of the town I was learning to think of as home, with one more truth to tell. A local newspaper was investigating what happened at DBD. Mom was staying at her job a little bit longer so she could go full whistleblower and tell them everything. I was supposed to drop off my test results with the reporter on the way back.

Positive.

The last truth I need to tell. To myself and to the world. I thought I was going to die, and so I lived differently, but now I knew I wasn't going to die and had to learn how to live all over again.

I twisted the lollipop stabbed through my bun. Lately, the taste of them had been painfully sour instead of soothing. I dropped my hand and breathed in the salty air. It was time to go.

"Hattie!"

My heart pounded at the sound of my name coming out of his mouth, and I suddenly realized that all of this—the apologies and amends, going to the marsh and talking to the reporter and trying to find a therapist and be better—it was for me, but it was for him, too.

"Albie?"

I turned around and there he was. The bucket hat and ridiculous glasses were gone. His hair flipped past his ears, his shirt was buttoned all the way to the collar, and he was hugging a giant terrarium to his chest. He looked so cute, it was physically painful.

"What are you doing here?" I asked.

He tapped the terrarium. "Letting Scooter go. Come with me?"

I folded my test results and slipped the paper into my pocket. "As long as we don't have to steal a boat."

"I've retired. Peaked too early."

"The best ones always do."

The two of us left the safety of the splintered docks and wandered parallel to the water, my feet sticking in the sand with every step. The pond was so big it appeared to go on forever, but I knew it bled into the ocean not far away. Like everything, it changed.

The two of us didn't exchange another word until Albie planted his feet in the sand and said, "Here."

He set the terrarium down and cradled Scooter to his chest. "You're home, buddy. I thought you couldn't survive in the outside world, but I was so wrong. You weren't sick because you were weak. You were sick because you are wild, and people were trying to keep you in captivity."

Scooter wriggled his legs. Albie waded forward a few steps and set him down. He waddled into the reeds faster than I'd ever seen him move and started digging into the sand.

Albie's hands looked devastatingly empty without Scooter. I fought through the sand and made my way to him.

"I hate goodbyes," Albie said.

"Me too."

The sounds of the pond drifted up to us in a chorus: croaking frogs, buzzing insects, waves crashing in the distance. Down below, it was all sand and dirt, the inevitable end of all existence. Up above, though, it was just me and him.

"Have you talked to Carmen?" I finally asked.

"Yeah."

"I'm excited she went to visit the girl from the circus. Didn't think she had it in her—"

Albie cut me off. "It's you. I don't want to say goodbye to you."

"We can hang out for a bit," I replied carefully. Telling the truth was one thing. Getting my hopes up was another.

"No, I mean, uh, ever." He shuffled so he was facing me. "I've . . . thought things about people before and didn't tell them and I want to tell you. I think you're amazing. You're smart and funny and adventurous, and you don't apologize for who you are." He finally met my eyes, smiling. "Honestly, I didn't understand what it means to go weak in the knees until I woke up next to you and was scared I wouldn't be able to walk again."

My cheeks darkened. For the first time since I could remember, I couldn't think of a single lie. "You're making me blush."

Albie brushed his thumb down my cheek. "Good. Because I plan to continue making you blush. Henrietta Larken, will you go on a date with me?"

I flicked his forehead. "Don't call me that!"

"Ow!" He ducked away from me. "You said that's your real name."

"That doesn't mean you should *use* it."

"Fine. *Hattie*." He dragged his thumb from my cheek to my neck. His other hand was threading through my fingers.

"Albie."

He tilted his face down. "I like you."

My heart thudded inside my chest. The itching sensation was back. I used to think feeling it meant I was in danger; now I knew it just meant I was alive. "I like you."

I thought we couldn't be any closer than we already were, but then he kissed me and I wondered how I'd lived so long without breathing the same air as him. My hands were in his hair and his hands were on my waist, and for once, I didn't want to be anyone else.

We kissed until my lips were swollen and Albie's hair looked electrocuted. Then we waded out of the marsh with our fingers intertwined.

"Are you going to monitor Scooter from afar?" I asked.

"Actually." He dropped my hand and jogged toward a minivan. He grabbed a backpack from the front seat and tossed it to me. "Remember how you said you would date me?"

I raised my eyebrows. "I didn't say that. Did you drive here?"

"I think it was implied. And yes. My parents are working on treating me less like their sick kid and more like their kid who happened to be sick that one time."

"Impressive."

"I know. I was thinking we should go on the first date now, seeing as how you have treatment tomorrow and everything."

"Sounds logical." I unzipped the backpack. Two wigs, a few pairs of large-framed glasses, and some obnoxiously bright jumpsuits were crammed inside.

"I thought we could go to the Elliot Why poetry reading in Palm Beach," Albie says. "Jordan Banner might be there, though, so obviously we can't go as ourselves."

"Also, we crashed a boat there"—I mimed checking a watch—"last week."

"Exactly."

I picked up a frizzy purple wig and plopped it on my head. "It's a date."

He picked me up and swung me around in a circle. Kissed me in the air and against the car and then finally pushed me away and helped me inside, muttering something about how I needed to "stop distracting him."

The future was uncertain as we drove out of the marsh and into town, chasing the sun across the sky. Maybe Elliot would recognize us from the news stories and kick us out of the poetry reading. Maybe I wouldn't do well in the film class. Maybe Albie's parents would rescind his driving privileges or the girl from the circus would break Carmen's heart or the MTP would cling to me more stubbornly than the doctors anticipated.

But as the minivan broke free of the marsh and raced toward the pink sunset, Albie threaded his fingers through mine again and one thing was clear: Right then, in that very moment, we were finally alive.

ACKNOWLEDGMENTS

Thank you to my agent, Christa, and her assistant, Daniele, for your hard work and advocacy over the years.

Thank you to Emily, who molded this book into the best version of itself with her spot-on edits and encouragement. Thank you also to the rest of the team at Amulet for your hard work to make a massive Word document into a real, actual book.

Thank you to Cam, for always asking about my writing, taking my words seriously, and bragging to other people on my behalf so I can pretend to be modest and humble. Every day is the farthest we've ever gone, and every day I am more deeply grateful to get to choose you over and over again. As long as I get to die first. I lub you.

Finally, I would like to give a big shout-out to myself for writing (and then rewriting again from scratch, LOL joke's on me) this book while working a demanding full-time job in the middle of a global pandemic. It wasn't easy, but it was . . . no wait, it was just incredibly difficult the entire time. I'm really proud of myself for doing it anyway.

ABOUT THE AUTHOR

Alikay Wood was once described by a wedding DJ as "five feet of fury." When she's not shredding up dance floors, she's writing books about friendship and "unlikeable" girls. She lives in California and is probably avoiding writing by rollerblading, crushing trivia competitions, or camping.